Barkerville Beginnings

Canadian Historical Brides

British Columbia ~ Book 4

By A.M. Westerling

Print ISBN 978-1-77299-764-4

Books We Love

A quality publisher of genre fiction.

Airdrie Alberta

Copyright 2017 by A.M. Westerling
Series Copyright 2017 by Books We Love Ltd.
Cover art by Michelle Lee

Library and Archives Canada Cataloguing
in Publication

Westerling, A. M., author
    Barkerville beginnings / by A.M.
Westerling.

    (Canadian historical brides ; book 4, British
Columbia)
Issued in print and electronic formats.
ISBN 978-1-77299-764-4 (softcover).--
ISBN978-1-77299-761-3 (EPUB).--
ISBN 978-1-77299-762-0 (Kindle).--ISBN 978-
1-77299-763-7 (PDF)

        I. Title.

    PS8645.E797B37 2017
C813'.6   C2017-901704-7

        C2017-901705-5

Dedication

Books We Love Ltd. dedicates the Canadian Historical Brides series to the immigrants, male and female, who left their homes and families, crossed oceans and endured unimaginable hardships in order to settle the Canadian wilderness and build new lives in a rough and untamed country.

Acknowledgement

A hearty thank you to Caroline Zinz, Librarian and Archivist, Barkerville Historic Town. I really enjoyed working with you! And thanks to my very dear critique buddies, Vicki, Moira and Toni. I couldn't do it without you.

Books We Love acknowledges the Government of Canada and the Canada Book Fund for its financial support in creating the Canadian Historical Brides series.

Funded by the Government of Canada

Chapter One

May 1867

The Cariboo gold rush may have brought sudden prosperity to Victoria, thought Rose Chadwick as she elbowed her way through the crowded streets, but it didn't beat the treasure she had waiting for her at home. Clutching the shawl wrapped around her shoulders in one hand, and her skirts in the other, she bounced up the stairs leading to Mrs. Beadle's Rooming House, the finest one on Vancouver Island. Her high-top buttoned boots clicked on the wooden porch, the door hinges squealed as she swung it open, and the fragrance of stewing beef enveloped her as she stepped inside. Her stomach growled, reminding her breakfast had been long ago.

Mrs. Beadle popped out from the kitchen at the end of the hall and waved at her. She waddled her considerable bulk down the hallway, floorboards groaning in protest. "I thought I heard you come in." She pointed to the front drawing room. "There's a gentleman here to see you."

"For me?" Puzzled, Rose stepped down the hallway until she could see into the room. Her heart sank as soon as she saw the tall man gazing out the window at the bustling street beyond. She'd recognize him anywhere: slicked back blonde hair, neatly trimmed mutton chop whiskers, and twirling his signature beaver top hat in his hand.

"He's no gentleman," she muttered to the other woman, who inspected Rose with an inquisitive gleam in her eye, although the corners of her generous mouth curled up in an affable grin.

"He says he knows you."

Rose shrugged. "A long time ago."

"He says he has an offer for you."

"An offer?" *I bet he does,* Rose thought grimly.

The man turned as she walked into the drawing room. "What do you want," she blurted before he had a chance to say anything.

"What, no hello, no how nice to see you?"

He chuckled, a harsh sound that grated on her ears. Strange to think that once she thought that the most melodic sound in the world.

She snorted. "Because you're the last person I want to see."

"We'll have it your way then and forego the niceties." He smoothed his whiskers with one well manicured hand, swiping first one side of his face then the other. "I have a proposal for you." His black eyes gleamed as he swept his gaze over her, setting her cheeks to burning.

She laughed, a grim little bark that startled the fat orange tabby cat drowsing in the puddle of sun on the top of the settee. Although the floral pattern was faded, the wood arms and legs gleamed with polish. Despite her vast girth, Mrs. Beadle was a fine housekeeper. Rose had considered herself lucky to find a room here.

Until now. Until Mr. Edmund Hewett had found her.

"I'm not interested," she said curtly.

"You haven't heard me out."

"Because anything you have to say is of no interest to me."

"I want what's mine."

Fear chilled her but she pulled her shoulders back and stood up as tall as her five feet, one inch—in her heels—would let her. "I have no idea as to what you're referring to."

"Ah, but you do. I want what's mine and I'm prepared to pay you for it."

She pointed to the door. "Please go."

"I'll pay you but if not—" His eyes narrowed and his mouth compressed. Any pleasantness he may have feigned disappeared. He pulled out a lock of hair, a single golden curl tied with a dirty piece of string. "—if not, I'll simply take what I want. And I'll see to it that not only will you face financial ruin, I'll let slip about your questionable morals."

Her heart plummeted. A wave of nausea rendered her speechless; her mouth worked but no sound came out.

He chuckled again. "I see you understand me."

A bluff was her best chance. She couldn't let him see how he'd rocked her very world to its foundations. "So it's a lock of hair. That's nothing. Again, please leave. I'm not interested in your proposition. Or your money."

"Not just any lock of hair." He held it out and shook it so the little curl bounced. "But I understand you've suffered a shock with my unannounced visit. I'll leave now, but I'll be back tomorrow afternoon for your answer." He tossed the lock of hair on the ground at her feet. "I won't be needing this anymore."

"Don't bother coming back. I'll not change my mind."

He bowed, more out of mockery than respect, and sauntered out of the room. She clutched the back of the nearest chair for support, knees shaking so badly she thought she would collapse. It wasn't until the door slapped shut behind him that she let go and sank to her knees.

How had he found her? She'd been so careful, had changed her surname, had disappeared one night without telling anyone where she was going. How? Because he's a wealthy, wealthy man, that's how. He could afford to pay anyone to find her. Pinkerton's, presumably.

A clattering of feet sounded from the hallway and a small, blonde haired girl with startling blue eyes burst into the room. "Mama, Mama, Mrs. B. told me you were home."

"Here I am, poppet, did you miss me?" Rose straightened the eyelet apron on her four year old daughter and tugged on her petticoat so that its white lace edge peeped out properly beneath her pink cotton skirt.

Her daughter nodded.

"Were you a good girl?"

"I'm always a good girl!"

Rose pulled her close for a moment and shut her eyes to inhale the little girl scent. Sweet and innocent. Unaware of the Mr. Hewetts in the world.

She rocked back on her heels and twirled the braided gold band on her left hand then with shaking fingers reached for the lock of hair on the floor. Perhaps it wasn't.... She held it against Hannah's head. Of course it was.

Edmund had made clear his intent to claim Hannah. The daughter he had never acknowledged as his.

Rose would not, could not let that happen. Hannah was the most precious thing in the world to her. She would not lose her. He said he was coming back tomorrow for her answer.

That gave her less than twenty four hours for her and Hannah to make good their escape.

* * *

Five months earlier

Viscount Harrison St. John ran his finger beneath the collar of his freshly laundered shirt.

The maid who had washed it had used too much starch and it rubbed against his neck, making him even more uncomfortable on what already promised to be an uncomfortable day. His wedding day. A day that should be the most joyous of his twenty six years. So why did he feel as if he faced the gallows? Because, he reminded himself gloomily, this ceremony was no more than a business transaction.

The snick of a latch interrupted his morose thoughts. He turned to look as a door swung open, revealing a glimpse of the winter-cloaked English countryside before Lord Frederick Worthington stepped through, pulling it shut behind him. "She's running a bit late," he said.

Harrison inspected his best man, attired much like himself in a black wool double breasted suit, crisp white shirt and wine red silk tie. His trousers tapered fashionably at his calves and his black boots shone with all the spit and polish his valet could muster. Unlike Harrison, Frederick always looked as if he could step into Almack's or London's Royal Opera House at a moment's notice. Mind you, the fact he possessed a dashing air might also have something to do with it.

An air Harrison knew he could never match. He'd spent a small fortune on his suit, all in the name of "keeping up appearances" but knew his shoulders did not fill out the jacket quite as nicely as did Frederick's, knew the fresh polish he'd applied this morning couldn't really hide the scuff marks and worn down heels of his own boots.

"What?" Harrison pulled out the pocket watch from his vest. "A minute or two. You know how Miss Nancy likes to make an appearance."

Frederick cocked an eye brow; his blue eyes twinkled. "I suppose you're right. Especially on her wedding day when she knows all eyes are on her. Just as she likes." He winked.

"She'll be here." Apprehensive about the upcoming ceremony, Harrison swung his pocket watch. The chain glittered as it arced back and forth in the weak sunlight streaming through the stained glass windows of St. Barrnabas' Anglican Church, the ancestral church of his family and the scene of countless weddings, funerals and christenings.

Frederick peered around the edge of the transept. "The pews are full. This is quite an event for the locals."

"Ah, yes, the old and venerable St. John family has finally found a solution to its troubles." Harrison didn't bother to hide the sarcasm in his voice.

"Cheer up. You'll scare her if she sees the look on your face." His friend clapped him on the back.

Minutes ticked by. The church began to buzz with conversation. Harrison again pulled out his watch. Fifteen minutes late. Surely Nancy would sweep through the door any second now. Then they could get on with the service and, by the end of the day, he would have a wife and the sizeable dowry she brought. The dowry which would save the St. John estate. In the bargain, her industrialist family, in textiles as were most wealthy merchants in Manchester, would acquire the social status they so desperately craved. Simply put, an arrangement suiting all parties involved.

He glanced over at Frederick. His best man frowned and shrugged. Now what? he mouthed. Harrison shook his head. Foreboding tickled his insides. The interior of the church darkened suddenly as clouds covered the sun.

The notes of the organ swelled to drown out the sound of voices. However, it couldn't drown out the titters. Or the guffaws. The organist played on, several hymns followed with a fugue by Bach. He gritted his teeth. He hated Bach, found the melodies much too dour. It didn't seem right, to be listening to music he didn't even like on his wedding day.

Where in blazes was Nancy?

Yet again, Harrison pulled out his watch. Forty five minutes late. He jammed it back into its niche in his vest, not even caring that the chain had gotten tangled up and didn't hang properly across his chest. Where was she? Then the awful truth hit him like a runaway carriage.

She'd jilted him. Left him literally standing at the altar with half of Lancashire as witness.

A door opened behind him and the vicar emerged from the vestry. He plodded towards them, cassock flapping at his feet, sympathy shining from his rheumy blue eyes. He shook his head sadly. "I'm most terribly sorry. I've just received word she's not coming." He held out a thick cream coloured envelope. "For you."

"I see." Harrison grabbed the envelope, his name scrawled across it in Nancy's handwriting. He didn't have to read it to know what it said—her absence said it all. He folded the envelope in half and jammed it into his jacket pocket then rubbed his hands over his face. A great weight pressed down on his chest, making it difficult for him to breathe.

"Deuced uncomfortable situation." Frederick's concerned voice penetrated the roaring in his ears.

Harrison looked up. "How could she?" he whispered.

His friend shook his head and lifted his shoulders. "Women. Who can understand them?"

The quip fell flat, but Harrison appreciated it nonetheless—it injected a hint of normality into this hideous moment. "Yes. Who can understand them," he echoed. His lips twisted in what was meant to be a grin but most certainly came out a grimace.

"You gentlemen are welcome to stay as long as you wish." The vicar patted Harrison's shoulder. "In time this will be forgotten." He shuffled off.

Forgotten? Seriously? Harrison watched the vestry door close behind the vicar.

13

"A stiff drink is what you need," said Frederick.

Harrison shook his head. He doubted he could force anything past the knot in his throat. "What I need is to get out of here."

Frederick nodded. "Of course. I'll finish up here."

"No. This is my tangle." Harrison turned and stepped out of the transept, moving to face the nave. "I must apologize. There will be no wedding."

His gaze skimmed the front pew, over the horrified faces of his parents, the shocked visage of his sister Laura, the dismay on the faces of his intended's parents. Even they, apparently, had not been privy to Nancy's betrayal. He shrugged then walked down the aisle, past the knowing smiles of the few people still remaining in the pews until he stepped out of the church into the drizzling winter day. He noticed nothing, merely moved out from the shelter of the doorway and thumped down the stairs.

He strode down the stone path, scowling at the clipped boxwood hedge that lined it and turned into the road. Now a few flakes of snow mingled with the rain and it dampened his coat until moisture seeped through his shoulders. It should have been uncomfortable but he didn't feel the wet, didn't feel the chill because a slow burning anger gnawed at him.

Jilted. Rejected. Made a laughingstock. All in the name of "saving the St. John legacy." He ground his teeth yet couldn't deny the relief sweeping through his torso, accompanied by a grudging appreciation for Nancy. He'd been prepared to go through with the charade but at least she had the wherewithal to end it.

He blinked away the snowflakes that had landed on his eye lashes, straightened his shoulders and marched on down the road. He would find another way to revitalize the family fortunes.

The headlines in the English newspapers shouted of the riches of the Cariboo Gold Rush. Perhaps that's where he would go.

To Barkerville.

Chapter Two

Rose stood across the street from the bustling steam ship office. "British Columbia and Victoria Steam Navigation Company," proclaimed the weathered sign tacked above the entrance. Covered wagons lined up beside the building, some with horses already in harness, others being loaded with boxes and barrels. Sucking in her breath and with Hannah firmly in one hand and her carpet bag in the other, she stepped forward. With every step across the muddy, rutted street, the carpet bag bumped against her legs as if propelling her into a new life.

She entered the clapboard building and pulled up. Even at this early hour, the ticket office teemed with humanity. Men, for the most part miners by the look of them, clad in rugged trousers, grubby shirts, and heavy jackets. Nearly all sported thick beards and most, she knew, were miners soured on the California gold rush and now moving their way north to search for the "golden gravel" of the Cariboo. A few miners must have brought their wives, for several women stood amongst them, faces weary and eyes bleak as if they already knew the promised riches would not be theirs to find.

Her heart squeezed at their blatant dejection, yet Rose felt the undercurrent of excitement.

Gold fever. A potent ailment.

No one paid her any attention until she took a step or two inside. A whistle sounded, long and low, and someone commented, "Look boys, we have ourselves a lady." Someone else said "Forget it boys, she's mine". Lewd comments and shouts of laughter flew through the air. Her face flamed and she fought the urge to turn around and run away. She looked down to gather her composure. *Hannah. Edmund would not get Hannah.*

Ignoring the comments as best she could, she lifted her head and glanced around to get her bearings looking for the ticket agent. A line straggled away from the ticket wicket and she took her place behind a harried looking woman, bonnet askew over bedraggled dun coloured curls and a half open satchel hanging from her arm. Two young girls stood by her side, one holding a baby.

A clatter of feet sounded; someone pushed into her and she whirled around, ready to berate the rude person only to see two young boys backing away. Twins by the look of them. Eyes full of mischief, they sidled around her and moved up beside the woman.

She glared at them before turning to speak to Rose. "I am so sorry," she said, "these two are in such a state this morning. We're off to Yale and they seem to think we'll be digging for gold. Where are you headed?"

"Barkerville." She'd decided on the booming gold rush town because of its remote location five hundred miles north east of here. Much larger than Victoria and almost as large, it was said, as Chicago. A young woman and a little girl should be able to avoid discovery quite easily there.

"By yourself?" The woman gasped and fanned herself.

"My daughter and I are joining my husband. He's got a claim out there." An out and out lie, but only Rose knew that. She pulled a rumpled letter from her skirt pocket and waved it in the air, then jammed it quickly back into her pocket before anyone could notice the decidedly feminine handwriting. She'd written the letter herself.

Because she had no husband and probably never would.

"Oh dear, where have those two rapscallions gone? Girls, stay here." Without waiting for an answer, the other woman darted off. She soon reappeared, holding the two red haired youngsters by their ears, one in each hand. "We'll leave you behind if you don't behave," she warned. "We'll take your sisters and the baby, but you'll stay here, see if you don't." She released them and pushed them into place beside the girls. Those two, obviously used to the high jinks of their brothers, rolled their eyes and shook their heads.

Her words had the desired effect, for the boys folded their hands in prayer and looked up with soulful eyes. It didn't last. Soon they were scuffling again, this time pushing into Hannah, who started to cry. Sobbing, she hid her face in Rose's skirts and tightened her little fists in the folds of woolen fabric. "Mama, I don't like it here. I want to go home."

"Shhh, poppet," soothed Rose. "Let me see." She leaned back and pretended to inspect the little girl. "Hmm, nothing that a hug from Dolly wouldn't solve." She unbuckled the carpet bag and pulled out a porcelain faced doll. Sniffling, Hannah took it and wrapped both arms around it. Pressed against the safety of Rose's skirts, she glared at the two boys.

The woman waggled her finger at her sons. "Your father won't be pleased to hear of your shenanigans."

This time they looked suitably chastened.

Rose stifled a giggle at their woebegone expressions. She turned to their mother. "You'll have your hands full. How far are you going?"

"To Yale. My husband has taken a position there. In the Anglican church, the Church of St. John the Divine. Why don't you travel with us? It's on the way to Barkerville. "

"Oh, I couldn't impose on you." She glanced down at Hannah, who still eyed the two young boys suspiciously.

"It's no trouble. I'd like the company."

I'd like the company too, thought Rose. She'd already been noticed by a number of men. Perhaps her idea to travel alone was not quite as sound as she thought.

19

The boys started scuffling and the other woman reached out and snagged them and gave them a shake. "Samuel, Peter. Remember what I said." She sighed then shook her head. "Those two need their father to knock some sense into them." She turned and held out her hand. "Mrs. Elvina Sheepshanks."

"Rose Chadwick." Rose grasped Mrs. Sheepshanks' hand. She may appear frazzled, yet she had a firm grip that conveyed a no nonsense personality.

"Next!" The station agent called out and the other woman moved up to the wicket.

Soon it was Rose's turn.

"I'd like passage for me and my daughter," she said to the bored looking man behind the desk.

He looked at her over a pair of spectacles perched on the end of his nose. His forehead glistened with perspiration and he wiped it off with a grubby handkerchief. "To—?" The question hung in the air between them.

"Barkerville," she whispered.

The ticket agent cupped his hand behind his ear and raised his eyebrows.

"Barkerville," she repeated more loudly.

"That's a rough place for a young woman to be going."

"Not at all." She shook her head. "My husband is a miner. We're going to join him." Funny how much easier it was to spit that out second time around.

"I can't get you to Barkerville. We go as far as Yale. From there you'll want the Barnard Express. But the *S.S. Onward* is plumb booked full so you'll have to wait."

"But I'm to travel with the Sheepshanks family. The lady in front of me. She just bought her tickets. How can the ship be full?"

"Sorry, there's no room."

"You mean to say Mrs. Sheepshanks bought the last tickets?" What rotten luck and not an auspicious start to her getaway. Her heart started to pound at the thought of failure before she'd even left Victoria.

The clerk nodded.

"How long till the next departure, then?"

"We can get you to Vancouver later this afternoon."

"This afternoon? Is there nothing sooner?" Her voice squeaked and she cleared her throat. "I can't wait until this afternoon."

Edmund said he would come back for her answer this afternoon. She'd hoped to be long gone from the island by then. Would he think to look for her here at the steamship office? What would Mrs. Beadle say if he asked her about Rose's whereabouts?

She gripped the edge of the counter and leaned forward. "Please, I must be on the morning ship."

The clerk shrugged. "Sorry, it's full. We don't like overloading the ships because of safety and all." He shuffled his papers and looked pointedly behind her. "Next?"

Rose still clutched the counter, her fingers locked into position. No, she couldn't give up. She must make the clerk understand her desperation. She glanced around the crowded room wildly looking for—what? She didn't know.

Mrs. Sheepshanks came over, this time carrying the baby. Her other children were nowhere to be seen, but she didn't look at all concerned over their absence. "You're white as a sheet. Is there a problem?" She leaned in, patting the baby's back all the while.

"There's no room," said the clerk. "Now you two hurry along." He frowned and made a shooing motion with one ink stained hand.

"No room? Nonsense. Look at the size of her. She can squeeze in with us. Her little girl can sit on her lap." Mrs. Sheepshanks pursed her lips and impaled the clerk with a lofty stare. "I'll take full responsibility for them both. I'm the wife of the Reverend Sheepshanks and he's expecting me. You wouldn't get in the way of the Lord's work, would you?"

"Well, if that's what you want." The clerk sighed heavily and flicked his gaze upward.

"It is."

With a satisfied nod, Mrs. Sheepshanks smiled at Rose, who unclenched her fingers from the edge of the counter and reached for her coin purse tucked into an inside pocket of her carpet bag. "How much?"

"Not enough," muttered the clerk before naming to what seemed to Rose like an outrageous sum.

"Thank you." Rose counted out the coins and handed them to the clerk. He tossed them into the drawer; she heard them drop one by one with muffled "clinks" as he sorted them according to denomination. It seemed forever while he counted and made out the tickets and she glanced repeatedly over her shoulder to the door, expecting to see Edmund at any second.

Finally, the precious papers were in her hand. Passage was more expensive than she expected and took almost half of her savings from her job as shop girl. She hoped she had enough to buy tickets from Yale to Barkerville.

At least she would be leaving Edmund behind, and soon she and Hannah would be safe from his threats. She squeezed her coin purse with shaky fingers, trying not to notice how thin it felt all of a sudden.

However, it wasn't until she boarded the sternwheeler that she felt truly safe. She took Hannah and together they moved to the rear of the top deck. The paddle of the sternwheeler kicked up froth in the harbour as the ship pulled away from the wharf. People shouted; others waved. Hannah waved back and Rose smiled at the sight of her daughter's chubby hand poked through the railing, flapping her fingers against her palm in an imitation of a wave. As they moved into the channel, she took one long look back at the town receding in the distance.

And froze. Edmund stood at the rear of the throng on the wharf. Had he seen her amongst the passengers? Immediately she dropped to her knees and put her arms around her daughter.

And Hannah? Had he seen the little girl at the railing?

* * *

A tremendous crack sounded and the stage coach Rose and Hannah rode in tilted precariously and came to an abrupt stop. Rose gathered Hannah into her arms and grabbed the leather loop overheard to keep them from falling into the other passengers. Not that there were many: just her, Hannah, a man dressed in a fine suit who professed to be a banker and who mumbled his name during introductions so she had no idea what to call him, and the Hodgkinses, an elderly couple traveling to visit their son. A miner, they solemnly declared as if a miner in Barkerville was something special, when Rose knew there were hundreds, if not thousands, all with the same goal in mind—to strike it rich.

They looked at each other. "Well, that's odd," said Mr. Hodgkins and his wife tittered, a shrill nervous sound that grated on Rose's ears for she'd already heard it a dozen times today. Every time, in fact, the coach lurched over an uneven rut, or the horses strained into their harnesses to haul the contraption uphill, or the wheels hit a patch of rocks.

Was it only a few days ago they bid goodbye to the Sheepshanks and boarded this coach for the final stage of their journey? It seemed longer, for today a restless Hannah continually pushed Rose to the limits of her patience.

"Nothing to worry about, folks." The sing song voice of George Dibbs, the "Barnard's Express Line" driver filtered through the roof. "We broke a wheel. Those Royal Engineers might have thought they built the eighth wonder of the world, but she's a rough road from Quesnel to Barkerville."

The banker poked his head out the window. "What are we to do?"

"Well, I'd say, start by getting out." Dibbs chuckled as if he just uttered the most profound witticism.

The passengers clambered out, Rose and Hannah last of all.

"I'll take your little girl." The driver leaned in and held out his arms.

Rose handed Hannah down to him then wiggled along the listing bench. Grasping the door frame in both hands, she swung her feet through and jumped onto the pot-holed road. She stretched her arms overhead, glad for the respite from the jolting, swaying stage coach.

"I'll send my helper back, but it'll take some time to get a new wheel from Quesnel. I suggest you folks start walking. It's not far to Cottonwood House, at most three or four miles. You'll get there faster and will probably all be tucked in for the night before I get this coach going again."

Dibbs's helper, a skinny teenager, touched his fingers to the brim of his hat. "On my way, boss," and off he ran.

"What of our luggage?" Mrs. Hodgkins fanned herself with one pudgy hand. "Is it safe to leave it behind?"

"Hard to say. I'll be here to keep an eye on things, but you never know who might come along."

"Right." The banker strode to the back of the coach and pointed to the baggage boot. "There's a small bag I'd like to take with me. I'll trust the other with you."

"We'll take what we can, but I'm afraid we'll have to leave our trunk behind," said Mr. Hodgkins.

"Are you sure, dear?" twittered his wife.

"There's only so much we can carry." He patted his wife's shoulder. "Maybe once we reach the post we can make arrangements to send someone back for it." He too walked to the rear of the coach.

Rose with Hannah in tow trailed behind Dibbs who sidled around the coach and quickly unstrapped the leather cover on the luggage boot. She stood back, waiting her turn while the others crowded around pointing out their bags.

The banker immediately struck off down the road at a brisk pace, soon followed by the Hodgkins, leaving Rose on her own. She didn't relish the idea of having no company while walking, and she eyed her carpet bag uncertainly. She hated to leave it behind, but the unwieldy thing would be difficult to carry any distance. For now, she would grab their shawls, for here in the mountains it cooled down quickly once the sun set. It shouldn't take too long for them to catch up to the Hodgkins.

"I'll leave my bag with you, but could you please take it down for me so I can take what we need for tonight?" She pointed out her bag.

"Yes ma'am." He swung it from the boot and placed it at her feet. He eyed her from top to toe and she felt herself flush at his blatant inspection. She'd not paid much attention to him, but now she noticed his shifty manner and dark, secretive eyes.

"Thank you," she said stiffly, reaching for her bag. He pulled it back and held it away from her. His intent was clear—if she wanted the bag, she would have to approach him.

"You're a pretty little thing," smirked the driver. He let go of the handle and the carpet bag thumped into the ground behind him. He took a step forward, arms outstretched. "How about a little kiss?"

Rose's skin tightened and she glanced around wildly for Hannah. Her daughter picked wild flowers at the side of the road, a few steps away. "Hannah, come here."

"Leave her be. She's happy." Dibbs took another step closer, close enough for him to grab her forearm.

Rose tugged and tried to break free, but the man tightened his grip and pulled her toward him. "One little kiss," he said and made a smacking sound with his lips.

A wave of rage rolled through her. Here was another man who saw her as easy prey and thought to take advantage of her. A red haze shrouded her gaze and, hauling up her skirts with her one free hand, she kicked him heel first in the groin as hard as she could. A handy trick imparted to her by one of Mrs. Beadle's other tenants, a sweet young teacher who'd had enough unwanted attention of her own and who was happy to share a few tips with the only other woman in the rooming house.

Astonishment rippled through his eyes for a split second, then he doubled over. For good measure, she kicked him again in the knee. To her surprise, she must have hit him just right, for he fell over, landing sideways in the middle of the dusty road.

Frantic, she grabbed her bag and dashed towards Hannah, yanking her daughter away from the ditch and leaving a little pile of crushed flowers in their wake. They headed down the road as fast as she could maneuver the two unwieldy packages—a carpet bag, much too big for her to carry comfortably, and a recalcitrant daughter who wailed with every step. "Mama, my flowers!"

"That is a bad man and we have to run away."

She glanced over her shoulder. He still lay huddled on the road although he'd managed to roll over. He gazed at her through narrowed eyes. Shivers racked her shoulders at the naked anger she saw on his face.

She'd made an enemy and she had no doubt he would come after her hard once he recovered. Or maybe not, she reassured herself. He did have a team and stage coach to consider. It didn't matter; fear sped her down the road.

How far was it to Cottonwood House?

Chapter Three

"Gee up." Harrison flicked the reins of the four mule team, and the wagon he drove lurched to an unsteady roll guided by the deep ruts of the Cariboo Trail. Ruts so deep, in fact, he scarcely needed to direct the animals, for the canvas covered conveyance could only follow the trail. Despite the hat jammed as far down on his head as possible and the shirt buttoned up tightly to his chin, mosquitoes whined around his face incessantly, and he alternated his time between swatting at them with one hand and holding the reins with the other, switching hands when the hand holding the reins became too tired.

"Mules," he snorted. He, Viscount Harrison St. John, who once prided himself on owning the finest four and carriage in Lancashire, was reduced to driving a team of mules. Egads, how Frederick would laugh if he saw him. Harrison could hear him now, "Oh dear, how the mighty have fallen." Then his friend would break into peals of laughter.

A smile broke across his lips at the thought, and his mood lightened. If nothing else, what an adventure he embarked on in the wilderness of British Columbia. Such a change from the insipid, well mannered lands of England, for the terrain here in the colony was as beautiful as it was wild, with soaring mountain peaks, forests so thick you could lose a man two paces in, and tumbling, rock strewn rivers foaming white with rapids. Danger lurked within the beauty, though, for on his way through the Fraser Canyon, more than once he'd witnessed men, horses and wagons venture too close to the edge of the trail and topple off the mountain side into the dangerous waters of the Fraser River below. He'd breathed a huge sigh of relief when they made it safely over the highest and most dangerous point in the canyon, Jackass Mountain.

No overt danger lurked here, though, on the recently constructed road from Quesnel to Barkerville. Or perhaps boredom proved to be the only danger, for the pace was slow and the road uneven. He stifled a yawn and hunched his shoulders up and down a couple of times to assuage the vague ache in his back.

The midday sun shafted through the trees, dappling the road ahead of him with shadows. The squawk of crows broke the silence, and he looked around. Noisy crows usually meant a disturbance of some kind. He tilted his head back and spotted a hawk circling high overhead. Presumably that was the thing that had disturbed them. As if in agreement, several crows flew up and, swooping and circling, harassed the larger bird. At least it gave him something to watch for a while until the hawk flew off, followed by the crows making sure their game continued.

He drowsed then, only jerking awake when the wagon slammed to a stop. The four mules stood stock still for no reason that he could see. Blasted creatures.

"Gee up." He slapped the reins, but the mules stood there, ears flicking forwards and backwards, eyes trained up the road where it disappeared around a bend.

"Gee up!" This time he shouted and grabbed the long handled whip propped against the seat beside him. "Or I'll use this." He waved the whip menacingly. The mules ignored him and he gritted his teeth. His prize team had been far more biddable—a good gee up and slap of the reins and off they'd go.

"Go, you blasted creatures. You're not fit for dog food." He brandished the whip, catching the rump of the lead mule, Nancy. He'd taken perverse pleasure in naming the mule after his former fiancée. It had turned out to be a fine choice—this animal proved just as wilful.

Nancy didn't move, merely looked over her shoulder at him and bared her teeth, stubborn as…well, a mule. Despite his annoyance, he chuckled. What did he expect?

"Harrison, what have you got yourself into?" He slid off the wagon bench and landed on the road with a dull thud and puff of dust. He stomped up to Nancy and looked the animal in the face. "You should know I sold my coach and four for you." He tugged on the mule's traces. She braced herself and refused to move. "Come now," he grunted, pulling as hard as he could, letting loose a string of curses that would wither his mother's ears if she only knew.

The mule eyed him, not at all bothered by the foul language. Nor, apparently, were the rest of the team. They all regarded him with innocent eyes as if they knew full well they annoyed him, but that didn't bother them a whit.

Footsteps sounded from behind his wagon and, out of nowhere, a well dressed man carrying a leather case hurried past him. "Good day." He tipped his hat and continued on at a fast pace.

"Good day." Bemused, he tipped his head to one side. Where had the gentleman come from? And plainly in a hurry, for he didn't even bother to wait for Harrison's response.

The man disappeared from sight and Harrison turned his regard again to the mules. He had no idea how to make them go and, frowning, he crossed his arms. How much longer would he have to wait for the creatures to decide to move?

He waited, tapping his foot all the while. A few minutes later he heard voices, and an elderly couple came into view from behind the wagon, from the same direction as the banker.

"How close are we to Cottonwood House?" the man asked as they drew abreast.

"What are you doing here?" Harrison's astonishment made him rude. "Not that it's my business," he hastened to add, "but we are rather in the backwoods here."

"One of the wheels on our coach broke a ways back. The driver suggested we walk to Cottonwood House. He claims it's only a few miles away."

"I think so, although I'm not entirely sure. It's my first time through and I'm not familiar with the road. I'd offer you a ride but my mules have balked." He tried to make light of it. "I can't think how to make them go."

"They'll go soon enough when they're ready. Mules don't like to be told what to do. You have to convince them they want to." The elderly man laughed. "I wish you good luck with them. If you'll excuse us, we're bound for Cottonwood House."

"We do thank you for the offer but it's a pleasant walk." This time his wife spoke. "I'm afraid my bones have been rattled to bits by this rough road." She giggled, an irritating squeak that set Harrison's teeth on edge, and he wondered how her husband could tolerate it day in and day out. That man, however, smiled at his wife and offered her his elbow. "Come, dear."

With a wave, the two plodded on. Harrison watched them too until they disappeared around the bend.

He returned his regard to the mules and tried a different tack. "You heard them. Cottonwood House is only a few miles away." He made his voice as pleasant as he could. "Fresh hay, water, perhaps even a carrot or two."

Unimpressed, the mules still didn't move. In fact, they ignored him to once again turn their gaze up the road, the route both the banker and the couple had gone. As one, their ears swiveled in that direction.

"Have it your way, then." He yanked off his hat and, still clutching it in his hand, wiped his brow with his wrist. "Please let me know when you're ready to move, will you?"

He put his hat back on, slapping it carelessly on the back of his head before turning to look up the road. "What are you looking at? I don't see anything." He resisted the urge to give Nancy a well-deserved slap; instead patted her on the neck. The mule merely rolled her eyes at him as if she knew very well his only desire was to give her a good whack. He let loose with another string of curses. Not that it accomplished anything, but at least it gave him some satisfaction.

He didn't see the young woman and small girl trudging beside the wagon trail until they came past his wagon. The duo presented a pathetic sight for their bedraggled bonnets slumped on their heads and dust covered the hems of their skirts.

The sight of them shocked him into silence. Were they also passengers from the broken down stage coach? Then he felt himself flush. How embarrassing to be caught cursing at his mule team.

"I must bid you good day," he said, drawing himself up and reaching to his neck to straighten his tie before remembering he'd taken it off in an effort to keep it clean. He bowed instead. Hopefully she would only consider his good manners and not his crude language. He bent so low his hat plopped off and landed upside down in the middle of the road, displaying the sweat soaked band and the outline of three coins within the band.

Harrison snatched it up quickly. Hopefully the young woman hadn't noticed the outline of the coins. Gold coins. His emergency finances if necessary.

She didn't reply but flashed him an irritated look. Not only did anger shade her eyes, but also fear and agitation. Then he noticed her taut face, flushed and shiny with perspiration as if she'd been hurrying some distance.

For some reason he couldn't tear his gaze away from her. His perusal must have embarrassed her because, although she avoided meeting his eyes, a blush coloured her face, highlighting the graceful cheek bones. He turned to look at the little girl. She'd been crying, for tears long past left tracks on her dusty cheeks and her lips trembled as if she struggled to stay silent.

"Is it only the two of you? On foot?" Amazement shaded his questions.

Head high, she ignored him and the duo moved past. Then he noticed the woman dragged some sort of a bag behind her from a leather belt looped through the handles. A decidedly feminine, flowered carpet bag, incongruous and out of place in the wild surrounding and soon to be in tatters on the rough surface. Already it showed signs of wear along the bottom edges.

"Is everything fine?" His question fell on deaf ears. Although he found their silence odd, he couldn't force them to converse.

He watched the two. They quickened their pace after they passed his mule team, and soon they too disappeared around the bend in the road.

Harrison turned his attention back to his team, but he couldn't stop thinking about them. For one thing, women of his acquaintance weren't nearly as hardy as these two—he couldn't imagine the self-important Miss Nancy Simpson making her way on foot through this forest, or any forest for that matter, British Columbian, English or otherwise.

What had driven them then, a young woman and her young daughter, to forge their way through this swampy wilderness? Judging by their demeanors, he could only conclude something foul had befallen them. Why hadn't he done the gentlemanly thing and offered them a ride?

Because he didn't want anything to do with women if he didn't have to, that's why.

Because women weren't trustworthy as he very well knew. Memories of that day in the church five months ago crept into his mind— even now, humiliation roiled in his belly at the thought.

But most of all because her beautiful smoky grey eyes had touched a chord in him. An unwanted chord.

Shaking his head, he climbed up onto the wagon and settled onto the bench, giving the reins an experimental slap. The mules still refused to budge and he gritted his teeth. "Gee up."

Their ears twisted in unison backwards then forwards, but they remained rooted to the road. It wasn't until a good half an hour later that the slap of the reins gave him the results he wanted. The mules moved. Finally, he thought, with any luck they would reach Cottonwood House before sunset.

When he rounded the corner, two things caught his attention: the fresh pile of bear scat on the trail. Which would explain why the mules had stopped; they had sensed the bear. Doubtless the bear had moved on with the human presence and, once gone, the mules resumed their trek.

The second thing was the carpet bag half shoved behind a fallen log by the side of the road. The leather belt dangled from the handles and a sudden breeze sent it swinging to and fro.

His heart sank at the forlorn sight, and he placed his hand on the rifle stashed beside him before scouring the woods with keen eyes, looking for any indication of their presence.

Naught could be seen of the young woman or the little girl.

Did the bear attack them? He scanned the woods again, looking for signs of disturbance but could see nothing out of the ordinary. No. The location of the bag behind the log indicated it had been placed there deliberately. Then where were they? Why did he feel as if it was his fault they'd abandoned the carpet bag? He didn't know them, had no desire to know them. Too, she very plainly had indicated she had no desire to know him either.

So then why did he feel culpable? In his mind's eye, he imagined her reproachful gaze and it gave him a sense of unease as if he there was something he should have done. Perhaps the young woman had found the bag too heavy and continued on to Cottonwood House without it. In that case, she would look for help and come back. At least he could grab it and bring it along, saving her a trip. He'd hand it over to her at Cottonwood House.

That should assuage his guilt a little.

"Whoa." He pulled hard on the reins, set the brake and jumped off the wagon.

It was then he saw the fresh blood spotting the dust in the road.

* * *

"Hurry, Hannah, we must hurry and catch up to Mr. and Mrs. Hodgkins." Rose knew she pushed her daughter to her limits, but apprehension of being alone in the forest urged her to move on as fast as they could.

39

"I'm trying, Mama. I can't go any faster." The little girl continually caught her toes on exposed roots, stones and even the ruts, and only hanging onto Rose's hand stopped her from falling on a regular basis.

"We'll stop for a minute, poppet. I have a piece of licorice for you for being such a good girl."

Rose fished the candy out of her pocket and handed it to Hannah, who sat down before popping it in her mouth. A beatific look came over the little girl's face as she sucked on it, and a smile crept across Rose's lips at the sight. How well she remembered the purity of childhood when the simple things made one happy and the responsibilities of adulthood were an ephemeral notion belonging to the future.

She sank to her knees, welcoming the break. The early summer heat pressed her into the ground and for an instant the thought of continuing on to Cottonwood House seemed daunting. She untied her bonnet and used it to fan herself. Then she put it back on her head, tying the ribbons neatly below her chin before rolling up her sleeves.

A crash sounded from the forest to her left, followed by an uneven rustle as if something— or someone—forged through the bushes. Rose leapt to her feet, moving in front of Hannah to present a barrier to whatever it was. She glanced at Hannah—her daughter had heard it too and she sat still, eyes wide and licorice forgotten. She scuttled on hands and knees to the safety of

40

Rose's skirts and Rose placed her hand on top of her daughter's head. Knees watery, heart pounding, she inspected the dense underbrush, looking for any sign of movement.

For a crazy instant, she convinced herself it was the coach driver. Don't be silly, she chided herself. The forest was nigh impassable. He'd come charging down the road if catching her was his intent. She glanced back the way they came. Nothing. No one came, not even the wagon with the mule train.

It must be a wild animal, and she remembered the fresh bear scat they'd passed a few hundred yards or so back. A grizzly perhaps, judging by the size of the pile, easily enough to fill a bucket. Frantic, she wracked her brains in an effort to remember what to do in case of a bear encounter.

Relief washed over her when she saw the deer. Two of them broke free from the woods and bounded in front of them to disappear into the woods on the other side of the road with more crashes and rustles. She laughed then, more of a weak guffaw, but the sound of her own voice reassured her and her knees grew steady again.

She patted Hannah's head. "Clumsy creatures, aren't they? They're not quiet at all."

"No." Hannah shook her head. "But bunnies are." She slurped on her licorice.

"Yes, bunnies are quiet, aren't they? Come, we have to go." Rose held out her hand to Hannah. "We have to get to Cottonwood House before night falls. I think I have another piece of licorice in my pocket." She patted her skirts. "Yes, I feel it. You may have it once we stop for the night."

Hannah obediently stuck out her hand and Rose grabbed it then seized the leather strap she'd tied on to the carpet bag, deciding it was much easier to drag than to carry. Squeezing her daughter's hand firmly, she started off again.

The rest had done them both good, for they started off along the road at a brisk clip. At this rate, Rose thought, they'd catch up to the Hodgkins or, better yet, reach Cottonwood House in an hour or less. She waggled Hannah's hand. "You're as fast as a pony," she exclaimed. "The licorice must be magic."

"I'm a big girl. I like running." Hannah grinned and took her eyes off the road to look up at Rose.

She promptly tripped on an exposed root. The force of the trip loosened her grip on Rose's hand and arms flailing, she landed face down in the dusty road with hands splayed on either side of her. She was silent for a split second, then a great wail tore out of her, followed by another, and another.

Aghast, Rose knelt beside her. Guilt rolled through her, punctuated by Hannah's howls. This was all her fault. All of it. She had decided to leave Victoria, to take her daughter through the British Columbia wilderness to a rough and tumble gold rush town. She had angered the stage coach driver and pushed Hannah beyond the reasonable limits of a four year old child to put as much distance between them as she could.

"It hurts," Hannah girl. "Kiss it better."

"Where does it hurt?" She gathered her daughter in her arms and gently pulled her up to sit in her lap.

"Here." Hannah pointed to her head. "And here." She pointed to her shin.

"Shhh," soothed Rose, examining her daughter's head. Other than a pink spot on her forehead that would probably darken to a bruise, that part of her seemed fine. Next Rose inspected Hannah's calf. Her stocking had ripped and blood oozed from a wicked gash, dripping onto the dust in the road. She'd landed on something sharp to leave a gash like that, no doubt the exposed edge of a stone.

It would need to be washed and bandaged. Rose tore a couple of strips off her petticoat and dug around in her pocket for her handkerchief. Wetting it would be easy enough, ponds and swampy patches lined the road almost in its entirety. Which is why mosquitoes pestered them both mercilessly every minute, but right now, pesky insects were the least of her worries.

She pulled out the last piece of licorice and held it out. Hannah snatched it and put it in her mouth. Her sobs subsided into the odd snuffle while she worked the candy between her teeth.

"I shan't be a moment." Rose waved her handkerchief in Hannah's face. "This needs to be wet so I can clean your leg."

She poked her way through the undergrowth, pushing aside branches which snagged her skirt with every step. No sooner would she free her skirt, than the next shrub would grab it. In a fit of inspiration, she pulled the fabric up between her legs so it wouldn't catch. The ground beneath her grew soggy and her feet sank into the bog up to her ankles, leaving a line of mud on her boots when she pulled them free. Ugh. She hated dirty boots. The road dust was bad enough; now she had sticky mud to deal with.

Finally she reached the edge of the pond and she dunked the scrap of fabric in the water. She wiped her face with it, dunked it again and used it to splash water onto her arms as high as her elbows. The cool liquid refreshed her. With renewed determination, she struggled her way through the dense bushes back to Hannah.

"Is the licorice good, poppet?" She dabbed at the gash. Hannah started to cry again and Rose tied the strips around her leg before dropping a kiss onto it. "Is that better now?"

At Hannah's shaky nod, Rose got to her feet. The severity of the gash hindered Hannah, and Rose knew she wouldn't be able to walk. That meant Rose must carry her, but she couldn't carry both the little girl and her bag. She supposed they could wait for a wagon or cart or something so Hannah could ride, but to stay here wasn't safe. Not with a bear in the area that could smell fresh blood. And while waiting for someone, what of the driver she'd kneed?

What he appeared first? No, they couldn't wait here.

That meant she would have to leave the bag behind. She hated to do it, but she had no choice. She shoved it as far as she could behind a fallen log but not before fetching Hannah's doll from the side pocket.

"You carry Dolly and I'll carry you both," she said, thrusting the doll into Hannah's arms. With a weak smile, Hannah took it. Rose picked her up and set off down the road.

As she tramped on, she thought back to the man driving the wagon and mule team. Despite her current predicament, she grinned at the consternation on his face over his stubborn team. He seemed to be a gentleman, however, for he spoke with the cultured tones of the British upper class, and he bowed, the first time she'd ever seen it.

She hadn't inspected him too closely, but she did remember his smile—it neatly framed his strong white teeth. He was clean shaven, too, so different from the hordes of men on the road.

She'd noticed his wagon was packed full, so much so that outlines of boxes and barrels poked through the canvas. Did he intend to tackle the Cariboo's hidden gold riches like so many others on this road? The rough and tumble miner's life didn't seem to suit him, though.

Somehow, the thought of his likely failure saddened her.

Chapter Four

"I'm thirsty, Mama." Hannah held up her doll. "And so is Dolly."

"I'm thirsty too." Rose swept the hair off Hannah's forehead and tucked it beneath her bonnet. "We don't have anything to drink. Can you wait?"

She felt Hannah's brow again, brushing her fingers against it to gauge the temperature. Not feverish, she decided, but the little girl needed a drink, and not from the swampy pond they walked beside. Although that water might be good for animals, it wasn't something they should be drinking. They needed a fresh source, a creek or something.

"We'll go a little farther and find a stream. Then we'll take off your socks and shoes so you can dip your toes. Yes?"

Hannah nodded.

The creak of wagon wheels and the clop of hooves sounded in the distance behind them. Terror surged through Rose. Was it the stage coach and the despicable driver? It could not be that the coach had been repaired already. Only a couple of hours had passed since the accident. Fear for their safety made her irrational, she decided. Or perhaps it was the English gentleman and his mules? Nevertheless, who

46

knew what vehicle approached and, more importantly, who was on it?

She shuddered at the remembrance of the stage coach driver's leering gaze and darted into the woods to hide.

"Shhh," she admonished Hannah, placing the tip of her finger on Hannah's lips. 'Let's pretend we're playing hide and seek."

Eyes round, Hannah nodded.

Rose peered out from behind the tree they hid behind. The canvas topped wagon with the mule team hove into view. To her astonishment, she spied her carpet bag on the bench beside the English gentleman.

Unsure of what to do, she set Hannah down and watched the wagon approach. Surely he realized the carpet bag belonged to Rose? Or had he thought it abandoned and therefore fair game? Either way, the only way she could reclaim it was to confront him. Although perhaps not the wisest course of action, considering her situation, but unlike the stage coach driver, the Englishman seemed a gentleman. Too, how could anyone with such a nice smile be anything but courteous?

She stepped out into the road "Excuse me, sir."

He leaned back on the reins, pulling the team to a stop, apparently not surprised to see her, for his face remained placid and inscrutable, although a spark of wariness and yes—perhaps relief—glinted in his eyes. Perhaps he was pleased to see her.

He set the brake and climbed down. He rotated his shoulders a few times before moving closer.

Rose stood her ground. "You have something that belongs to me." She lifted her head to look him straight in the eye, daring him to deny it.

He dipped his chin. "Indeed I do." He looked around. "Have you lost your little girl?"

"No, she's not lost. She's sitting in the shade over there." So, he remembered seeing her with her carpet bag and remembered Hannah. At least he paid attention to his surroundings.

"May I give you both a ride?" He smiled and his deep brown eyes crinkled at the edges.

Oh, how badly I want to accept his offer. She ached all over. Her feet hurt, not only from wearing thin soled footwear on the rough road but also because her wet boots chafed and a blister formed on one heel. Her arms cramped from carrying Hannah, and her head throbbed from the heat. But could she trust him? An image of the Barnard's Express driver clouded her vision and shivers darted up her spine.

"We can't possibly impose and I can't afford to pay you." She shook her head. "Besides, I already have passage to Barkerville once our coach gets repaired. We'll walk to Cottonwood House and wait there."

He pointed to Hannah. "She's hurt. I dare say she's not able to walk far, if at all."

Rose gazed at the bandage on Hannah's leg. Her heart sank. Blood seeped through it, leaving a series of blotches in a line. Goodness, the gash was worse than she thought and would require a doctor's care. Assuming she could even find one in this godforsaken wilderness. Cursing it served no purpose, she reminded herself. They were here by her choice and her choice alone.

Hannah had crept up to join them and Rose reached out to stroke the blood stained bandage before grasping Hannah's little chin in her fingers. "Does it hurt very much?" she murmured.

Lips quivering, Hannah nodded.

"You're Mama's brave little girl." She dropped a kiss on her nose.

"Please, let me take you to Cottonwood House," he urged. Sympathy lined his face and he held out a hand. "Let me help you up."

Rose glanced up at him. He must have spotted her uncertainty and thought to help. But she had no means to repay him for his kindness. Plus, she was wary of being alone with any man, even a man who appeared to be well mannered.

Regretfully, Rose shook her head and was about to decline again until she looked at him. He gazed back at her, and his eyes were the colour of burnt chocolate, soft and warm. A few freckles dusted his nose and he gave her a close mouthed smile. It gave him a mischievous air.

Her misgivings melted away. She needed help and this man offered it. Somehow she felt she could trust him.

"Thank you." She inclined her head. "I'll pay you when I can."

Because she certainly couldn't pay him now.

Only a few coins remained in her purse, which would pose a different problem altogether once she and Hannah reached Barkerville.

* * *

Harrison knew the young woman sitting on the planked seat on his right was apprehensive of his offer of a ride, knew too her apprehension of being alone with him. Certainly she would have refused if her daughter hadn't been injured.

"You and the little girl are almost as big together as that carpet bag of yours," he teased. Perhaps a jest or two would lighten her mood.

She didn't answer, merely slanted a glance at him and shifted a little farther away. She sat on the very edge of the bench, as if by taking up the smallest amount of space possible, she would be less beholden to him.

"You'll fall."

"Thank you for your concern, but I won't." She braced herself with one foot against the foot board, clenching one fist on the edge of the wooden seat as the wagon rattled over a rock. With her other arm, she clutched her daughter close.

Perhaps small talk would help her relax a little. What had happened to her to make her mistrust men so? Surely she could see he was no monster?

He turned to her and lifted his hat. "I am Harrison St. John, late of Manchester. And you are—?"

A gust of wind took her skirts and splayed them against his leg. She gave him an annoyed little look and pulled away her skirts, tucking them under her legs to stop it from happening again. "Rose."

"Just Rose? Aren't you forgetting something?"

Startled, she looked at him. "Forgetting something?" Her brow wrinkled.

He gave her a charming smile, the one Nancy said always made her heart melt. Now why did he have to remember that? Angry at himself, he compressed his lips.

His passenger darted a glance his way and must have misinterpreted his tight mouth as annoyance with her. She sat up and pushed a stray lock of hair beneath her bonnet before answering.

"Rosamund Arabella Ruth Chadwick," she said primly.

"That name's bigger than you are," he chuckled. "How about if I call you Rosamund?"

"No!" She almost shouted. "I hate the name Rosamund."

Startled, he held up one hand. "I must beg your pardon." He looked at her again. "Rose it

51

is, then. But that's not what I meant." He looked pointedly at the gold band on her left hand. "Mrs....?"

"Oh." A flush coloured her face. "Yes, of course. Mrs. Rose Chadwick."

"But I shall call you Rose."

"If you must."

"I have to call you something."

"Do you?" She turned her head, gazing into the forest lining the road. "Pleased to meet you, Mr. St. John."

However, her tone indicated she was anything but. As did her choice of salutation. Mr. St. John? Viscount St. John would be more like it, but of course she wouldn't know his title and he wasn't about to divulge that bit of information. Since arriving in British Columbia, he realized titles meant nothing here.

"What's your daughter's name?" He sought to make idle conversation. She still didn't seem comfortable in his company.

"Hannah." She spat out her answer, plainly loathe to converse but too polite to ignore him.

"What are you doing out here alone?" He checked the road ahead for obstacles and adjusted the reins before shifting his gaze back to her.

"Alone?" She glanced down pointedly at the little girl now fast asleep in her arms. "I'm not alone."

"You know what I mean." His face grew hot with embarrassment at his own impertinence. Her being here really was none of his business.

"No, I'm afraid I don't know what you mean. Being alone implies being with oneself." Once more she glanced down, pulling aside the little girl's bonnet to drop a light kiss on the tousled blonde head. "As you can see, we are two." She straightened her daughter's bonnet before glancing over to him, eyes ablaze as if she dared him to contradict her computation.

"Most young ladies would have a man—"

She interrupted before he could finish his sentence. "I'm not most young ladies."

Now why did that statement intrigue him? Because her independent air appealed to him. Then he remembered the ring on her left hand. He inspected it with what he hoped was a surreptitious glance. The ring glinted in the sun, reminding him she belonged to another man. His burst of fascination fizzled like a rubber balloon pricked by a pin.

"Where's your husband?"

"What?" She turned a startled gaze on him then her face grew wary. "Oh, my husband. He's…ah…a miner in Barkerville. We're on our way to join him."

"We share a common destination, then."

Her eyebrows raised and she nodded. "I see." Once more she turned her head to stare into the forest to her right.

He craned his neck to see what had caught her attention but saw nothing, only more trees. Mostly coniferous, the straight needles in fact, quite uninteresting compared to say, the elongated oval leaves of a horse chestnut, a common tree in England.

Very well, he'd done his best to engage her in conversation but if she preferred to ignore him, he could quite happily reciprocate. Silence fell between them and the next time he glanced over, Rose slept, chin resting on the top of Hannah's head. He took the time to study her profile.

Her feathery black eye lashes fanned across her cheeks, a soft and feminine display belied by her determined chin. He remembered the grey shade of her eyes, eyes he imagined could be silvery or stormy depending on her mood. That elusive curl had freed itself once more from the confines of the bonnet and it fluttered in the breeze. He couldn't quite decide what colour it might be. Butterscotch, he thought, shot through with darker strands of cocoa. He snorted. How silly to compare the colour of her hair to his favorite sweet, butterscotch.

But his gaze crept again to the lock of hair waving in the breeze. Gently he reached over and tucked it behind her ear. She didn't stir. Poor thing must be exhausted, what with carrying her bag and shepherding a young child over the rough and dangerous wagon track that made the Cariboo Wagon Trail. Not even the constant lurch and sway of the wagon over the uneven road kept her awake. A protective surge washed over him, right down to the tips of his boots. Until he remembered the gold ring.

She belonged to another man, a man with whom she had a daughter together. He pushed away the irrational disappointment at the thought. He should be pleased she was married, for she would have no designs on him; plus she had someone to look after her once she reached Barkerville.

All he had to do was deliver her and her daughter to Cottonwood House and then he could relinquish his duties.

* * *

Rose knew Harrison thought she slept, knew too he inspected her thoroughly. So thoroughly, her skin tingled with the intensity of his gaze. She thought back to their conversation. He seemed courteous, and she found the way he blushed from time to time sweet. As if the boundaries of politeness came in uncertain waves of scarlet. In all of her twenty-four years, she'd never known a man to blush as readily as he did. Certainly Edmund never had.

She remembered the startled look on Harrison's face when she'd denied him permission to call her Rosamund. She didn't feel it necessary to explain that Rosamund is what Edmund had called her. Maybe one day she could bear to be called by her full name, but not now. Not yet. That man had destroyed her faith in others of his kind.

No sooner had she finished that thought than Harrison had leaned over. She half expected him to accost her, and it took all her resolve not to jerk away and let him know she was awake. She didn't want to talk and feigning sleep was the only way she could think of to avoid conversation.

Only he'd tucked her hair behind her ear with a feather touch. But oh, that touch. Even now, she could feel the tingle in her skin as the tips of his fingers brushed across her temple. She brushed her own fingers across her cheekbone, as if swatting away a fly but in reality trying to dispel the sensation of his fingers on her flesh.

She thought back to when he bowed to her in the middle of the dusty road. How discomfited he'd been when his hat fell to the ground. He'd picked it up quickly, but not before she saw the coins tucked away in the sweat band. She recalled her own almost empty coin purse.

Those three coins would certainly solve her monetary woes, but did she have the nerve to steal them?

No, she decided. Desperation would not make her stoop to unsavory levels of conduct. Besides, Harrison had been nothing but kind to her and didn't deserve to be robbed of his goods.

But still the image of those three coins danced in her head.

Chapter Five

The wagon crested a hill and Rose saw a small fertile valley spread out before them lined on either side by forested hills and bisected by a narrow river. The road wound down and snaked along beside a tiny settlement consisting of a two-story log house, and several log outbuildings. Barns and sheds, Rose presumed. Cattle, mules, and horses roamed fields marked by split rail fences, and crops of grain and potatoes flourished. A few wagons and another coach were pulled over to one side. All in all, a very prosperous looking place.

"That must be our destination." Harrison shook the reins, but the team needed no urging. Sensing food and the end of a long day, the mules broke into a trot. The wagon rattled and bounced down the road, along with all its contents, including Rose and Hannah.

"Hang on to me," urged Rose, "and I'll hang on tight for both of us." Hannah curled her arms around Rose's neck. Rose hunched down, bracing her feet as best she could against the clattering foot board. Surely her bones clattered too, she thought, clenching one fist around the lip of the bench, holding Hannah tight with the other arm.

"I think Nancy is ready to call it a day." Harrison chuckled. "For once, I think I am in agreement with her."

"Nancy?"

"The lead mule. As long as she's happy, the others go along with her." He applied pressure to the brake and tugged hard on the reins. "Happy or not, I would like to arrive in one piece."

The mules ignored Harrison and charged down the hill. Rose, certain the wagon was sure to tumble, spilling all three of them on the ground, could do nothing but hang on. Beside her, Harrison whooped and hollered. She dragged her eyes from the road long enough to risk a quick glance. The pace bothered him not a bit; rather his grin stretched from ear to ear and he looked to be thoroughly enjoying himself.

"What happened to arriving in one piece," she said through clenched teeth. They hit a rock and her bottom left the seat for an instant before landing with a jarring thump.

"The wagon is new, built of the finest materials, or so I was told. Besides, think how much earlier we'll arrive now, perhaps in time for dinner." However, he applied the brake a second time. "Whoa," he shouted and this time the mules complied. They slowed a little, enough so Rose could settle back onto the bench. Within minutes, they pulled up in front of the road house.

"Why don't you and Hannah go inside," suggested Harrison as he helped them down. "I'll see to the team and I'll bring in your bag."

"Thank you." Rose smiled. "And thank Nancy for the timely arrival."

Harrison laughed and tipped his hat before disappearing around the side of the building.

Rose noticed the blood on Hannah's bandage had dried somewhat and had turned an ugly brown. She held out her hand. "Can you walk, poppet?" Hannah nodded and slipped her small hand into her mother's. Rose gave it a little squeeze of encouragement. "Let's go inside, shall we?"

She inspected the house as they drew closer—a small log cabin jutted out at a right angle from the rear of the two-story log building, forming an overall "L" shape, and mullioned windows flanked the front door. Tucked beneath the gable style roof were more windows that must be bedrooms, Rose surmised. A burst of laughter from an open window drew her closer and through the glass, she thought she recognized the Hodgkinses. As if to confirm her presumption, Mrs. Hodgkins' memorable titter followed another burst of laughter. Rose had indeed arrived at Cottonwood House. The door swung open before Rose could lift her hand to knock.

"That was a wretched walk, was it not?" A visibly perspiring Mrs. Hodgkins regarded them both before her eyes dropped to Hannah's injured leg. "Oh poor thing," she gasped. "Come in, we must clean that up. May I take her?"

At Rose's nod, the elderly woman snatched up Hannah and bustled off through another doorway. Rose trailed along behind and found herself in the kitchen.

"There's a washstand out back if you want to wash the dust off your face." Mrs. Hodgkins handed her a bucket. "The pump's back there too if you wouldn't mind filling this. After raising four boys, I've seen more than my fair share of cuts and scrapes," she said, correctly interpreting Rose's skeptical expression. "That wound needs to be washed and the bandage changed."

"I would like to wash up," Rose admitted. "It's been a hot and dusty day."

"Off you go then and don't worry about your little girl." Mrs. Hodgkins already busied herself with unwinding the bandages. She held up one of the bloodied strips, still edged in lace. "It's a shame you had to ruin such a pretty petticoat."

Rose shrugged. "One does what one must."

"I'll need more water than I have here." She pointed to a small wash basin half filled with clear water. "Before you go, could you please hand me the soap? It's over on the windowsill."

Rose handed her the soap, then slipped out the rear door to head to the water pump. The creaky pump handle required a few hearty tugs before water spewed out, splattering her feet and leaving water stains in the dust on her boots.

The sight of her brand new boots in such a forlorn state brought the sting of tears to her eyes. She blinked several times. What was the matter with her? An injured Hannah sat inside under the care of a stranger. If anyone had reason to cry, it was her daughter.

Rose swallowed hard against the tears and worked the handle a few more times to fill the bucket. Quickly she splashed some water on her face, wiping it off on her rolled up sleeves. Cupping her hands, she scooped some water from the bucket and sucked in a few long, satisfying draughts.

Then she worked the handle again to top up the bucket. She'd filled it too full, and when she picked it up, more water slopped onto her boots. The cool, clear water had restored her good humor, because this time she rolled her eyes and shook her head. They're boots, she told herself. Boots were meant to be durable and utilitarian, and if a little water ruined them then they were probably worthless and should be tossed. She'd take them off and wipe them down when she had a chance and they'd be good as new. They had to last, as she simply didn't have the resources to replace them.

By the time she returned, Hannah's bare leg was propped up on a stool and Mrs. Hodgkins leaned over it. "Hmm, it's not too deep," she declared. "It won't need stitches, but it will need to be kept clean and tightly bound for a few days until the skin begins to heal. She'll have a bit of a scar but nothing to worry about." She patted Hannah's head. "A few minutes more and then we can join the others for supper."

"Supper?" Rose echoed stupidly.

"Yes, along with your bed, you get a meal."

Rose gulped. How much would that cost?

A large woman with greying hair and careworn hands came in. "You're the new arrivals, are ye? Welcome to Cottonwood House. We've beds aplenty upstairs. I can imagine you're wanting nothing more than a solid meal and a good night's rest."

"How much?"

The woman tipped her head to one side at the abrupt question. She looked Rose up and down then looked long and hard at Hannah. "A dollar for you, fifty cents for your girl." The tone of her voice implied she'd named a fair price and was not open to negotiation.

Rose's heart sank. A dollar fifty. That was all she had left. She would arrive in Barkerville with literally not a penny to her name.

However, Hannah needed a good meal and a good night's rest in comfortable surroundings. With a sigh, Rose counted out the coins and handed them over, then folded her empty coin purse and tucked it into her pocket.

She still had her ticket to Barkerville, she consoled herself. She hated the idea of getting on the coach with that miserable driver again, but she had no choice. She and Hannah simply could not walk that far, and she certainly couldn't afford a ticket on a different coach.

The stage coach arrived sometime during the night. It was parked right in front of door when Rose stepped outside the following morning. The driver was nowhere to be seen, but the horses waited patiently, harnessed and ready to go, and Mr. and Mrs. Hodgkins and the banker fellow stood in line, ready to board.

The driver strolled into view from the side of the road house. He'd obviously made use of the pump out back because water dripped from his face wetting the front of his shirt, and he slicked back his sopping hair before putting on his hat.

He came to a halt beside the coach door and opened it before extending a hand to Mrs. Hodgkins to help her in. "Here you go, ma'am" he said with a slimy grin. She eyed his wet hand with some distaste, then ignored it to grab onto the door jamb herself. With an audible sniff, she clambered inside. The driver frowned at her before turning to her husband.

"Sir." He tipped his hat for Mr. Hodgkins, who nodded and followed his wife inside, then the driver tipped his hat once more to the banker.

"I understand it's a day's drive to Barkerville?" asked the banker. "One more day in this coach is about all I can stand."

He meant it as a jest, but the driver saw it as anything but, for his fists clenched and he puffed out his chest. "This here coach is the finest Barnard has to offer."

The banker held up his hands. "No offense intended," he said and he swung himself inside. The driver glared through the open door and a muscle worked in his cheek as if he clenched and unclenched his teeth repeatedly. If he's already annoyed, Rose wondered, what would he say when he saw her?

Now only Rose and Hannah remained and she waited for the driver to notice them. He seemed to be ignoring them, so she shuffled forward, getting her ticket ready to show him. "Excuse me." Her voice quavered and she cleared her throat. "Excuse me."

The driver turned and his eyes narrowed. "You're not getting on this coach," he growled. He turned back to it and slammed shut the door with so much force the coach shook, which elicited a squeal from Mrs. Hodgkins. He made as if to move to the front but Rose stepped in his way.

"I have my ticket to Barkerville. You must honor it." She waved it in the air.

Before she could react, he grabbed the ticket and tore it into tiny pieces. They drifted on the wind, swirling away like her hopes.

"I don't see a ticket." With that, he turned on his heel and mounted the bench. Before she could even blink, the stage coach jerked to a start, leaving Rose and Hannah standing in front of the road house.

Numb, Rose could only watch as the coach drove off at a good clip, a cloud of dust the only evidence of its passing. The jingle of the harnesses and the clip clop of the horse's hooves died away, leaving them in a silence broken only by the two tone whistle of a chickadee.

"Mama?" Hannah tugged on Rose's hand. "I thought we were going with Mrs. Hodgkins."

I did too, thought Rose. She looked down at the earnest little face tipped up to hers. "I've changed my mind. We'll find another way to Barkerville."

Another way to Barkerville? What was she thinking? Her heel throbbed from yesterday's blister. She had no money and an injured little girl unable to walk, not to mention a large carpet bag containing their only belongings. How could she manage the journey?

Her knees collapsed and she sat down hard on her bag. She had no idea what to do.

Chapter Six

Harrison patted his mouth with his napkin and folded it before placing it on the table beside his empty plate. "My compliments to the chef."

The owner of the road house looked at him with a muddled expression.

"Cook," he explained. "Chef means cook. I dare say this is the finest breakfast I've had since leaving England."

"We smoke our own bacon here." She smiled proudly. "Best food this side of Victoria, so I've been told."

"It is indeed." He pushed back his chair. "Thank you, and I shall be on my way." He bowed and her jaw dropped. A flash of amusement lightened his mood. Doubtless, she'd not seen too many of his ilk here.

Whistling, Harrison ducked out the rear door and soon had his mules harnessed. He climbed onto the wagon and shook the reins. Nancy must have been feeling amenable today, for the team started up at an amble. Not the fastest but at least they were moving.

As he rounded the front of the road house, he spotted a forlorn figure sitting right outside the front step. Two, actually, once he got closer.

Rose and Hannah. Blast it; didn't their stage coach just leave? Why weren't they on it?

He contemplated driving past them—Rose had made it clear yesterday she didn't much care for his company. Perhaps he could pretend not to see them, but generations of St. John breeding wouldn't let him ignore the two. As much as he hated to stop the wagon, he couldn't leave without checking on them. He rolled his eyes skyward, then pulled the wagon to a stop.

Two sets of eyes regarded him: one set full of hope and one set full of despair. "I thought you had a ticket on the stage coach that just left," he said.

"So did I."

He could scarcely hear Rose's reply, so thin was her voice. "What will you do?"

"I don't know." She shrugged then clasped her upper arms. "I don't know."

The way she said it pierced his heart. "You're welcome to ride with me."

"I've already told you I can't pay you, so thank you, but no."

There it was again, her independent air. How could he make her understand he expected nothing from her, that the deed itself provided sufficient compensation? "Your company is payment enough," he said finally. "Besides, we'll be there by this evening." He held his breath for a moment, waiting for her answer.

She looked at him as if a day in his company would be a test of her endurance. That stung, and he couldn't keep the brusqueness from his voice. "Never mind, then. I'll be on my way." He slapped the reins. "Gee up." The wagon lurched to a roll and had only gone a few feet before she spoke, panic evident in her raised voice.

"No, wait. We can't stay here. There's nothing for us."

He stopped again, Nancy giving him a baleful glare over her shoulder. "You're right, you can't." Concern for Rose forced him to action. He hopped off the wagon and, without waiting for her permission, grabbed her carpet bag and tossed it in the wagon. "Up you come." He smiled, first at Hannah, then at Rose before swinging Hannah up onto the seat. He held out a hand to Rose. She, with a resolute set to her chin, paid no attention to him and scrambled onto the bench unassisted. Her obvious show of self-reliance made Harrison grin, but he quickly stifled it when she looked at him.

"Thank you. Once again we are indebted to you." Rose placed Hannah on the bench between them then adjusted her skirts.

Yes, she had a suspicion of men, he thought, for she'd positioned Hannah as a barrier. At least she trusted him enough to place her daughter in the middle. That must mean something. She needn't fear, though; he had no desire to draw the ire of her husband. A miner. With a pickaxe, no doubt and the wherewithal to use it to protect what belonged to him.

They rode in silence until Harrison decided to strike up a conversation. He'd spoken the truth when he said her company was payment enough. The road bored him to tears: endless trees and ponds, really nothing more than swamp. "You said your husband is a miner? That seems to be what one does in a gold rush town, doesn't it?"

"I suppose."

"I plan on becoming a miner myself. Hopefully a successful one. It's cost me a small fortune to get supplies and equipment." He poked a thumb over his shoulder. "The wagon's full. I couldn't cram another thing in it if I tried." He chuckled. "It's quite an adventure for an English boy."

"How did you hear of Barkerville?"

"The newspapers. Mr. Barker is an Englishman. And you?"

"I lived in Victoria. The gold rush was on everyone's mind. Hundreds of men passed through on their way to the Cariboo, so our little harbor town is not so little anymore. Outfitting for the miners is a big business."

"Indeed. Including me."

"You don't seem to be the type."

"What type is that?" He looked at her to gauge her reaction.

She cocked her head. "You're too…ah…refined."

"Refined? Being refined doesn't make me weak. On the contrary, a sense of purpose and a moral code will help immensely. I aim to find my fortune and return home."

"Where's home?"

He slanted a glance at her. "If I told you, would you know?"

A little sound escaped her mouth, half giggle, half sigh. "I suppose not, although I would guess you're English?" At his nod, she continued. "No need to explain where exactly in England you're from. Geography was never my strongest subject at school."

"What was?" To his surprise, he was eager to hear her response.

"Arithmetic. I like numbers. They're simple, either you're right or you're wrong. There's no in between."

"True." Arithmetic. An unlikely answer for a young woman.

They drove on for a few minutes in silence. A large uncovered wagon pulled by a team of horses appeared over a slight rise in the distance and plodded towards them, headed in the opposite direction. He pulled his own wagon to one side to make room for the other to pass. The slouching driver waved as he drove by, a friendly gesture in this unfamiliar land. Harrison returned the wave,

Rose spoke once the clatter of the other wagon died away. "What was your favorite subject?" The way she said it, he knew she asked simply to be polite, to pretend an interest in someone she really had no interest in knowing. Or perhaps she found the road as monotonous as he did. As he'd struck up the conversation to begin with, he may as well give her an answer.

"History," he replied. "The classics. Greek. Latin. Shakespeare."

"That's more than one." Humor brightened her words as if she were on the verge of a giggle. Harrison liked her answer—he admired a quick wit and a clever jest.

"Then doesn't that make me well-rounded?" However, there was well-rounded and then there was well rounded. Like Rose. Her curves and petite stature appealed to him, and he wondered what she would feel like if he pulled her close. Which he would never contemplate actually doing, but he found the idea intriguing. As intriguing as the awareness that her feminine softness hid steely determination.

She lifted her left hand to brush away a fly, and the gold band on her ring finger flashed at him. He thrust away his inappropriate thoughts. She trusted him, and he would do all in his power not to abuse that trust.

Besides, she had a husband.

* * *

The wagon slowed as the road neared a fenced grave, enough that Rose could read the headboard: Charles Morgan Blessing.

"Lonely spot to be buried," Harrison commented and he doffed his hat as they drove past.

Rose nodded. "It is." A chill tiptoed down her back at the forlorn sight, a reminder of the

71

fragility of life in this wilderness. She craned her neck for one last glimpse before the road twisted away.

They stopped to eat beside a creek that gurgled alongside the road for a short distance before meandering off into the forest in a tumble of stones. When Harrison offered to share his lunch, Rose finally had to admit to herself she liked the young Englishman. Rather a lot, actually. More than she should.

"We couldn't possibly," she protested when he brought out the package wrapped in paper and tied up with brown string. "That's your meal, and I would feel terrible if you went hungry. Already we can't thank you enough for taking pity on us."

He weighed it in his hands, hefting the package up and down a few times. "This is more than I can eat. The cook at Cottonwood House is a generous sort. Besides," he waggled his eye brows at Hannah which made the little girl laugh. "I daresay you'll never be a big girl if you don't eat lunch."

When he put it like that, what could Rose do but acquiesce? Especially seeing Hannah seemed to like him too.

"Thank you." A warm flush of well being for the proper gentleman who looked after them so gallantly rolled over her.

"You're welcome." He unwrapped the package and handed Rose half of a sandwich, a generous slice of cheese tucked between two thick slices of bread. Baked this morning, judging by the crisp crust and squashy interior. Her mouth started to water, and she bit into it with vigor.

The other half he handed to Hannah. He stepped away to let them eat in peace, grabbing a bucket from the back of the wagon and filling it with water for the mules.

They'd finished their food by the time he came back. He rummaged through the crumpled paper and triumphantly held up a ginger snap cookie. "Look what I found." With a flourish, he handed it to Hannah. "I won't ask your mama," he said with a conspiratorial wink. "She'd only say no, and I think you've been such a good girl you deserve a sweet."

How good he was with Hannah, thought Rose. Her heart warmed at his kindness to a little girl far from home.

Then he peeled and sectioned an orange, which he laid out on the paper before picking up his own cheese sandwich. It didn't surprise her when he offered half of the orange to Rose. She shook her head. "Now I will say no. You must eat it."

"Mama?" Hannah tugged on Rose's sleeve. "Could I play in the water? You said I could yesterday. You said when we stopped I could take off my shoes."

"You're right, poppet, but now we're with Mr. St. John. We mustn't impose on him." *As if we haven't imposed enough already.* He didn't appear to mind, though; in fact seemed to be enjoying their company.

73

"By all means, you must dabble in the water. May I?" He looked at Rose and pointed to Hannah's feet.

Hannah regarded him with wide eyes and glanced to her mother for reassurance. When Rose nodded, Hannah leaned back on her palms and stuck out her feet. He pulled off the small leather shoes and stripped off the little girl's socks. Then he swung her up in the air, dangling her over the creek, swinging her back and forth, catching the water with her toes every time. Hannah's delighted squeals quashed any misgivings Rose had.

"How is it you are so at ease with Hannah?" Rose raised her voice over the sound of the burbling water.

"I have a younger sister, Laura. Not so many years ago, she was just about Hannah's age. She tagged along every chance she could and, actually, she still would if our mother hadn't forbid her from doing so." He chuckled. "She still comes for the occasional ride with me, though. Astride, not side saddle. It's our little secret." He swung Hannah one final time, this time spinning around himself before depositing her on the ground. He dropped to the ground beside Rose and propped himself up on one elbow.

"I can put on my own socks. And shoes too," boasted Hannah. "See?" She proceeded do so, one sock twisted backwards and the other inside out but both on her feet. Then she pulled on her shoes. Whether by luck or design, she put them on correctly, left on left, right on right. "I can't tie a bow tie. Mama does that for me."

"I see a very clever girl doing very grown up things." He leaned over to tie her shoes at the same time Rose leaned over to do the very same thing. They bumped heads and Rose caught a whiff of leather and sandalwood. She jerked back. "Excuse me."

"It was my fault. I must beg pardon." He shifted away and his cheeks reddened.

An awkward silence fell between them, so Rose proceeded to tie Hannah's shoes. "Watch me, Hannah. See the bunny ears? And then you tie them like so."

Hannah jumped up. "I want another cookie."

"That's not how you ask. You must ask Mr. St. John if you may have a cookie please." Rose corrected her before realizing she'd given tacit approval. How very forward of her, of them both really, but it just affirmed her growing estimation of the man. Plus, he'd let Hannah dip her feet in the water, even playing with her which made Rose like him even more. Dangerous, that.

Dangerous and so very, very inappropriate for a supposedly married woman.

Rose gathered herself and stuffed her thoughts back into their proper place in her mind before picking up Hannah. "Shall we move on?" She didn't look at Harrison as she asked and, without waiting for an answer, she lifted her daughter into the wagon.

Without looking at him, she gestured towards the lunch remains. "It won't take me a second." She shoved what was left—a slice of fruited cake and a sandwich of what looked to be ham—into the centre of the crumpled paper and folded it up as best she could. The string was nowhere to be seen, so she simply held out the package to Harrison. "Yours."

Harrison took it from her, a slight turning up of his lips the only sign he knew of her sudden discomfort in his presence.

Rose climbed up and plopped herself beside Hannah. She stared straight ahead, lips compressed, waves of awkwardness roiling her stomach.

She couldn't get to Barkerville soon enough. The sooner she left Harrison's presence, the better off she would be. If only to let her unruly emotions die down.

* * *

"Looks like we've arrived," said Harrison as a cluster of buildings came into view. Once again the mules, sensing the end of a long day, picked up their pace and the wagon bounced and rattled down the last little bit of the Cariboo Trail.

Rose hadn't known what to expect but her first view left her numb. This was Barkerville? The town that gold built? This jumble of wooden, mostly single story buildings tottering on stilts alongside a wide, muddied creek?

Surrounded by steep hills stripped bare of trees? How unattractive, brutally so.

The road through town was in poor shape, rutted and puddled with patches of drying mud. In consideration for pedestrians, raised wooden walkways fronted every building like planked skirts. Rose could only conclude the creek must flood frequently. Her poor boots, already soaked through once since embarking on the trip, would certainly be put to the test here.

The closer they came, the more her heart sank. What had she got themselves into?

Harrison's voice penetrated her thoughts before they became too morose. "Where shall I leave you? I presume your husband has given you instructions?"

Rose expected the question and had an answer ready. "Ah, I believe he said something about a hotel."

"Hotel? There's bound to be more than one in a town of this size."

They entered the town proper. Every building they passed had its own staircase tumbling to the rough road and signs poked out at right angles from the walls: Stables, Bakery, Tin Shop, Brewery, Stoves, Restaurant. The clutter of structures gave Rose the impression that someone had flung a handful of giant dice willy-nilly.

"Whoa." The mules continued their brisk pace. He spoke to them as he pulled back on the reins. "Slow down, will you. I know you think you're getting carrots, but I can't guarantee that."

Rose racked her brains. They drove past several small houses and then the Barnard Express Office. The stage coach had already arrived. It stood in front, nearly blocking the road. Thankfully the driver Dibbs was nowhere to be seen in the vicinity. Or the Hodgkinses and the banker, for that matter. She looked down the street but couldn't spot them. Doubtless they would cross paths soon enough. Although strung along the creek, the town didn't look all that big.

They squeezed past the coach and continued on slowly until they rolled past the Hotel de France. The two story clapboard building with tall mullioned windows flanking the front door and a small balcony off the upper floor had a sophisticated air which Rose found appealing.

"Oh, here," she blurted. "The Hotel de France, that's where he told us to go." She could only hope the Hotel de France provided respectable lodging and not lodging for women of ill repute to ply their trade.

As soon as they stopped, she hopped off the wagon and held out her arms. "Come Hannah, we're here."

With her daughter clasped in her arms, she climbed up the few stairs leading to the hotel's verandah, then watched as Harrison plunked her bag on the boards beside her. He chucked

Hannah under the chin. "Be a good girl for your mama and papa."

Hannah nodded. "I will be a good girl for Mama. But I don't have a papa. You could be my papa, couldn't you?" A yearning note filled the little girl's words and her brow wrinkled. She gazed at him with wide blue eyes.

Surprise lined Harrison's face until his good manners took over and he smoothed his face into a mask. He jammed his hands in his pockets and tilted his head to one side.

Rose squeezed shut her eyes for a brief instant. In Barkerville less than an hour and already her tale of being a miner's wife stood in jeopardy. "Hannah," she gasped. "Don't make jokes. Of course you have a papa." She clapped her hand over Hannah's mouth. Drat. Would Harrison believe the little girl? Or did he believe Rose's story about meeting her husband here in Barkerville?

Harrison looked from Rose to Hannah back to Rose. He didn't give any indication that he noticed the blush she could feel sweeping her cheeks. He also didn't give any indication who he believed.

Suddenly Rose couldn't get away fast enough. She put down Hannah then reached over for the bag. She stretched out her arm to open the door but it swung open before she could grasp the door knob. Of course, Harrison had beaten her to it and opened the door for her.

She fair tumbled over her own feet to get inside. Then, remembering her manners, she turned to thank Harrison. Still holding the door, he regarded her with a steady gaze and the intensity of his scrutiny made her uncomfortable. "Thank you very much," she said stiffly. "We are most grateful." Another flush warmed her cheeks and she cursed herself for being so silly.

He extended his gloved hand and, after a brief hesitation, she took it. He bowed slightly. "My pleasure."

"I will mention to Mr. Chadwick how kind you've been." A lame attempt to bolster her story but worth a try.

"Of course." He inclined his head but one corner of his mouth lifted. "Good day to you, Mrs. Chadwick."

Did she imagine a slight inflection on the Mrs. indicating he knew very well Mr. Chadwick did not exist? Of course not. Certainly he would have questioned her immediately if he thought Hannah spoke the truth.

He let loose the door and it swung closed. Through the window, she watched him climb back onto the wagon and drive off down the uneven road, wagon lurching and canvas swaying.

"Good luck to you, Harrison St. John," she whispered. She watched his wagon until it disappeared into the mix of carts, wagons, people, and livestock filling Barkerville's main street, then straightened her shoulders and turned around.

He's not the only one in need of luck, she thought. She could use a large measure of it right this moment.

Chapter Seven

"May I help you, ma'am?" A clerk leaned against the chest-high desk tucked into the corner of the foyer. The man, elderly with a straggly beard and wearing a rumpled white shirt, appraised her from top to toe. His gaze slid down to Hannah and disapproval stiffened his lip.

"Yes." She grabbed Hannah's hand, proceeding to the desk with what she hoped was a purposeful air. "I need a room for the night."

"Only a couple of rooms left," he grunted. "You'll have to share the bed, though." He pointed to Hannah. "This is a fine establishment. Last bunch we had in here, the kids raised a ruckus, running up and down the stairs, shouting, that sort of thing. People were none too pleased, I can tell you. She better behave or else."

The hotel must be reputable if other families stayed here, thought Rose. "My daughter is very well behaved." She clasped her hands, wondering what the man meant by "or else." It sounded dire.

The clerk continued. "Our guests expect only the best here. That means no noise." He shoved the register towards her, along with a worn wooden pen and an inkwell. "Fill this in. Rate is seventy five cents per night. Up front."

"What?" Rose couldn't believe her ears. The clerk wanted payment now. Not only did she not have a cent to her name, she didn't even have the chance to have a few days to look for work. She made a show of fishing through her pockets. "I...er...seem to have misplaced my purse. Could I bring you the money when I find it?"

He frowned. "Awfully convenient to lose your purse."

"Please, I'm sure it's somewhere in my carpet bag."

He folded his arms. "No payment, no room."

Desperate, Rose searched for the words that might persuade him to change his mind. She twiddled the braided gold band on her left hand. The wedding ring that had belonged to her mother. She looked at it, swallowing hard then pulled it off. "How about if I give you this for now? It's gold. When I find my purse, I can pay you properly."

"If it's money you want for gold, go to the assay office down the street. Or the bank." He pointed.

"Please, my little girl is hurt. We've had a long day. Could you give us the night? I'm sure I can find my coin purse. In the meantime, you can hold on to my ring."

He looked at her long and hard, as if scouring her face for any hint of dishonesty.

Rose waited, stomach churning like a swirling eddy on the Fraser River.

"All right. It's not regular, mind, but you seem like a nice lady. I'll expect to see you in the morning." He tucked the ring in his vest pocket.

"Thank you." At least they would have a comfortable place to sleep tonight. She dipped the pen in the inkwell and signed her name. It was only a hotel room. Why did it feel as if she signed away her life? Maybe it was the veiled threat he uttered over Hannah's behaviour that unsettled her so.

Or maybe it was the fact she had no money and had just given away her most cherished item.

"What brings you to Barkerville?" Business complete, the clerk became chatty. He patted the pocket where her ring nestled.

"I...er...we're meeting my husband. He's a miner," she added.

He cocked his head. "A miner? Didn't he know you were coming?"

His implication was clear—what kind of man wouldn't arrange for accommodation for his own family?

"No. I wanted to surprise him. We're not supposed to come until later in the week but the trip upriver went a lot faster than expected." Another lie that flew easily from her lips. She would have to figure out how to redeem herself, she thought wryly. Bald faced lying was not a particularly good habit to cultivate.

"Anyone I know? A lot of miners come here when they're in town."

Rose froze and she stared at the man. "Er...Chadwick. Mr. Harrison Chadwick," she blurted. Goodness, now how did Harrison's given name slip off her lips so easily?

The clerk's eyes narrowed and he tapped a gnarled finger on the desk. "Humph. Can't say that I know him."

Because he doesn't exist, thought Rose. How soon would it be before anyone realized that?

* * *

A sense of loss washed over Harrison as he drove off. He'd truly enjoyed his day with Rose and Hannah. Although the sun still rode in the sky, the lengthening shadows indicated soon it would slip behind the mountains. Or was it the sun was a little less bright, the sky a little darker now that he no longer had their company?

He followed the flow of traffic. Everyone seemed to have a purpose and seemed to know where they were going. He, on the other hand, hadn't a clue.

He flagged down a gentleman dressed incongruously in a silk top hat and a soiled red satin jacket.

"Where can I spend the night?"

"Anywhere you can find a spot to park your wagon. If you head back the way you came, you can get feed for the mules back at Mundorf

Stables. It's expensive but at least your animals won't go hungry."

Park anywhere. It sounded easy enough. He rolled on to the edge of town. Tents and camps spotted the area, and here and there fires flickered, started, no doubt, against the chill Harrison knew would come once night fell. He surveyed the area with distaste: the patchy grass and gravelled bits, the surrounding slopes denuded of trees, the muddy banks of the creek. It did not look in the least inviting.

He swung the wagon around. "Gee up Nancy. We're heading back to the hotel. I want one last night in a real bed."

Nancy flicked her ears back and lifted her head to let loose an ear-splitting bray, which startled a couple of stray dogs and they began to bark, running alongside the wagon to nip at the wheels. With the clip clop of the mules' hooves and the yipping of the dogs filling his ears, Harrison couldn't hear his belly rumbling, but he was sure it did in anticipation of a good meal. He slapped the reins, sending the team back into town at a brisk clip. At this moment, the Hotel de France seemed like paradise.

Or was it the thought of seeing Rose again that seemed like paradise. Stop that, he told himself. She belongs to another man.

* * *

Rose paused in the doorway of the hotel dining room, Hannah in tow. Darkness had

86

fallen and light from the oil lanterns filled the room with a cozy, golden hue. The planked floor gleamed with polish and the scent of beeswax mingled with the delightful aromas emanating from the kitchen. Baking bread. Roasting meat. Simmering broth. Her mouth watered.

"Doesn't it smell good?" She leaned down to whisper in Hannah's ear. Her daughter nodded and lifted up her doll. "See, Mama, Dolly thinks it smells good too."

"We're all hungry, aren't we? Come, let's find a place to sit."

Only one table remained empty, over by the window and she the threaded her way between the other tables to reach it. She waved to the waitress. "Do you have a cushion or something for my daughter to sit on?"

The woman nodded and soon Hannah perched beside the window, face pressed to the glass. Only then did Rose sit down.

She smoothed her hands over the lace table cloth and the rough texture of the fabric comforted her, reminding her of pleasant evenings at Mrs. Beadle's. Tonight she would pretend she had not a care in the world.

Tonight she would not think of her monetary situation. Tonight she would not allow herself to think of Harrison St. John and his winsome smile.

Until she glanced over and saw him, to all appearances the proper English gentleman.

He'd washed his face and slicked back his hair. The road dust had been brushed from his coat and boots, and a perfectly knotted tie butted under his chin. He stood in the doorway uncertainly, twirling his hat in his hands, scanning the room. For what, she had no idea.

His face brightened when he noticed them and with a wave, he made his way over. Her heart started to pound, so vigorously she was certain everyone in the room could see her chest thumping. She wiped her cheeks, hoping her own attempts at washing up had not left smears of dust on them and glanced down, relieved to see no water spots on her bodice. She looked up again to have him standing before them.

"May I join you?" He pointed to the empty chair beside Hannah. "There's not a seat to be had. Or do you think Mr. Chadwick would object?"

Rose stared at him and, for a few seconds, she was unable to catch her breath. What was he doing here? And why was he asking about her grandfather? *Not your grandfather, you dolt. Your pretend husband.* Don't slip now.

"Aren't you looking for a gold claim or something?" She sucked in a huge breath of air. "I am sorry. How rude of me. Of course you may join us and no, I'm sure Mr. Chadwick won't object. How could he when you've been nothing but kind to me and my daughter."

Harrison pulled out the chair and plopped himself down, then placed his hat on the table beside him. "No gold claims for me, tonight.

I'm afraid I've succumbed to the rather selfish desire to spend one last night in a real bed, with a hearty meal under my belt." He leaned over and pointed to Hannah's doll "And who is this?" he asked the little girl. "I don't think you introduced us before."

"Dolly," Hannah said proudly, holding up the doll for inspection.

"Hello, Dolly, I am pleased to make your acquaintance." He shook the doll's hand.

"She likes you," Hannah pronounced. "Doesn't she, Mama?"

"Why yes, of course, she does," Rose stammered, clasping her hands on her lap, attempting to twiddle the ring on her left hand until she remembered she no longer wore it. Flustered, she glanced around the dining room.

The waitress, interpreting Rose's scan of the room as a call for service, came over. "Tonight we're having venison. How does that sound?"

"Delicious," murmured Rose.

"I could find an egg and a slice of bread for your little girl." The woman, thin and sporting a bruised eye, winked at Hannah. "How does that sound, missie?" Hannah giggled and nodded.

Rose smiled up at the woman. "How thoughtful, thank you."

"It's nothing. I got kids of my own. The little ones don't like meat all that much."

"Venison for me," said Harrison. "I've not tasted a good joint since leaving England. And a glass of your finest whiskey," he added then glanced at Rose. "Would you care to join me?"

Rose shook her head. "No, thank you."

"Lemonade, ma'am?" interjected the waitress. "We got fresh lemons today."

"Lemonade sounds delightful." Rose reached for it eagerly when it arrived, complete with a lemon slice wedged on the edge of the glass. A whimsical touch in such a remote valley, but the liquid washed the dust from her throat. She listened to Hannah chat with Harrison.

While waiting for their meals to arrive, Rose looked out the window into the dark street. Here and there lanterns shone from windows of shadowed buildings and groups of grizzled men stumbled down the street. Bursts of hilarity punctuated the bawdy songs they sang, and a shoving match broke out just in front of the hotel.

"It's quite a stimulating town," commented Harrison, following her gaze. "You can feel the excitement in the air. As if everyone is waiting for their El Dorado."

"El Dorado?"

"A city of gold somewhere in South America. It was never found, so it attained somewhat mythical status."

"I see." Rose nodded. "Perhaps El Dorado is here, then, and not in South America."

"I hope you're right." Harrison smiled, his eyes crinkling, and Rose's heart skipped a beat. "Look, here's an El Dorado of another kind."

He inclined his head in the direction of their waitress, who approached them, plates of venison, potatoes, and gravy balanced on one arm, and a little pink plate with an egg and several slices of bread, crusts cut off, in the other hand.

"*Bon appétit.*" Harrison placed his napkin on his lap and picked up his utensils.

Rose picked up her own utensils. Her own napkin fell to the ground and, chagrined, she leaned down to pick it up. "*Bon appétit?* I'm afraid you have me once again at a disadvantage." *Such a refined man,* she thought. *What a bumpkin he must find me.*

"It's just something the French say. Enjoy your meal." He tucked into his own plate with gusto, savoring the first bite with closed eyes. Thankfully, the buzz of conversation covered the lack of chit chat at their table so the silence as the threesome ate was not uncomfortable.

Meal over, Rose pushed back her chair. "Hannah is tired. I must get her to bed."

"No." Hannah's bottom lip poked out. "I'm not sleepy, Mama. I want to stay here with you and him." She pointed to Harrison and yawned. One little fist rubbed her eyes, first one side, then the other.

Rose knew immediately Hannah needed to go to bed, but how to get her upstairs without her making a scene? The warning of the desk clerk rose in her mind. Hannah must behave.

"If you're not tired, I'm sure Dolly is. Dolly would like nothing better than to snuggle into bed with you."

Hannah looked at her doll. "Are you tired?" Rose tweaked the back of the doll's neck, making her head nod yes.

"Then I'll take you to bed," said Hannah.

"Good girl to look after Dolly so well." Harrison nodded, a mock serious expression on his face. Rose's heart squeezed. How sweet he was with Hannah. What a tremendous father he would make.

"Come back if you can," he said to Rose. "I'll be here. I daresay I fancy a piece of that huckleberry pie I saw over on the sideboard."

"Me too." Rose grinned and he grinned back, leaving her gasping for a moment.

They took their leave, Hannah chattering all the way up the stairs and while Rose readied her for bed. Then the little girl climbed into bed and Rose tucked the doll under the blankets beside her. "Good night, poppet. Tomorrow we'll have an exciting day exploring, won't we?"

"Will we see the man again? I like him, Mama. He's nice."

I like him too, Rose thought. "I don't know, I don't think so. He's going to find himself a gold mine and I think that will keep him busy."

"Oh." Hannah flopped back on the pillows. "Will you sing me a song? The one about the little lamb."

"Of course I will." And she began to sing, "Mary had a little lamb, little lamb, little lamb.

Mary had a little lamb...." She worked through all the verses to the end and by that time, Hannah slept, her breaths coming deep and even. Rose brushed away the hair from the little girl's cheek and dropped a kiss on her forehead.

Rose sat for a while on the edge of the bed watching her daughter. Sleeping was really what Rose should be doing as well. Plus the blister on her heel throbbed and the thought of taking off her boot was an appealing one. Besides, going back to the dining room to visit with Harrison would be the stupidest thing she ever did, for where could it lead? She'd portrayed herself as a married woman. Certainly Harrison was just being kind when he'd asked her to return.

But she knew she would. She wanted to see more of his smile, more of his warm brown eyes and freckled nose. It made him look rather rakish, not at all in keeping with his concise English accent.

She paused in the doorway to the dining room and saw him peering out the window. It wasn't too late. She could retreat and return to her room without him even knowing she'd returned downstairs. She perused his profile for a few seconds, admiring the straight nose and chiseled jaw before moving into the dining room.

Harrison spotted her and his face brightened. He lifted his hand and a flush of well being flowed through her. Perhaps one evening in his company wouldn't be terribly evil.

Chapter Eight

"I'm glad you're here," he said when she sat down again. "Tell me about Mr. Chadwick."

"There's nothing to tell. I expect him to come collect us soon." She reached for her lemonade and took a sip. The tart liquid, so pleasing before, now soured on her tongue.

What a mistake she'd made to invent a husband. It's not that no one believed her. On the contrary, it seemed everyone did. She didn't know how to change her story now.

Rose watched Harrison signal the waitress for another whiskey. He did it with the confident air of someone who expected people to obey him. When he got it, he downed the amber liquid all at once.

"What are you trying to forget?" Her question startled him; he glanced at her then squeezed shut his eyes for an instant before letting loose a bark that should have been laughter but really sounded like the bleat of a wounded dog.

"I don't want to burden you with my woes."

"It's no burden. Consider it repayment for looking after us on the trail."

"You're one of the lucky ones. You're married. You have someone who cares for you."

Rose winced. If only he knew.

He didn't notice her wince. His eyes were glued to the ceiling as if tracing the pattern of every crack and counting every nail head. Finally he looked at her, resignation rampant on his face.

And more. Anguish. Embarrassment and, yes, a touch of resentment.

"I got stood up at the altar. Jilted. In front of family and friends. You know the worst part?" He turned his gaze to her. "She didn't even have the decency to tell me to my face. All I got was a note. A note and a lot of sympathy I didn't want from the fools who still sat in the church waiting for her arrival." He drummed his fingers on the table. "Yet part of me is glad she did it. She had the courage to walk away from a marriage where both of us would have been unhappy. So that makes me feel guilty too."

"You don't need to be sharing this with me."

"It was nothing more than a business deal, so why does it bother me so much?"

"Business deal?" Rose tucked a stray hair behind her ear. What could he mean by that? Didn't one marry for love?

"She's wealthy, we're not. We have the title her family wants, along with the respectability and entrance into the finest drawing rooms." He shifted in his chair. "It's my responsibility to save the St. John name. That's why I'm here. One chance at fortune has slipped away. This is a second chance to restore our family wealth. I shall return home a hero and save everybody."

Rose's throat ached at the bitterness in his voice. How sad. Harrison didn't deserve that shame. "You did nothing wrong. She was the one who wronged you."

He didn't reply, but his eyes narrowed a little as if he considered what she said.

She gestured to the window. "How did you end up here?"

"News of Barkerville and the Cariboo gold rush made news in London. I read it in the *Times*. Considering what happened, this seemed like a good place to lick my wounds."

She searched for the words that could ease his pain. "Your El Dorado. You'll find it here, I'm sure."

He grew brisk. "Let me buy your dinner. It's the least I can do for listening to me."

"There's no need," she started then stopped. In her mind she heard Mrs. Beadle's voice, "Sometimes you just have to take what comes along". And that something that came along could be something good too, couldn't it? Besides, it held her cost at the hotel to the room charge only.

"I insist." He waved to the waitress. "On my bill, please," he said when she came over. "What do you suppose happened to her eye?" he asked as she trotted away.

"Perhaps a husband with a heavy hand." Which Edmund had exhibited from time to time. She shuddered. How she ever imagined herself to be in love with him astounded her. Even in the short time she'd known Harrison, she knew he'd never strike a woman. His handling of his mule team demonstrated that. Although the creatures aggravated him, he did not resort to brute force to bend them to his will.

"I shall bid you a good night. I expect you'd like to return to Hannah." He stood, grabbed his hat and bowed. "I won't see you in the morning. I'm off for an early start."

"Well, then, I wish you all the best, Mr. St. John. For you and your family."

She watched him zigzag his way through the now mostly empty tables. Still she didn't move. She didn't want to lose the spell of the evening spent in his company.

The woman who had served them started to extinguish the oil lamps, moving from table to table until finally stopping in front of Rose. "Lucky lady. Your husband is a real gentleman and your little girl is sweet, so well behaved. I tell you, that ain't easy to do, get a little girl to sit still that long. Try it with a little boy." She rolled her eyes skyward and then laughed.

"Thank you." Rose smiled. "But he's not my husband. We met on the Cariboo Trail. He helped us out. My husband...." She stopped to clear her throat, "will be joining us soon."

"Well, that's a shame. He had his eyes on you all night, though. I coulda swore he was your man. But listen to me prattling on. You must be tired and wanting your bed."

"You're right, I am tired." Rose pushed back her chair, pausing to look outside one last time. The streets were empty now, the darkness complete. A sudden gust of wind rattled the window panes and a forlorn feeling came over her. This land could be inhospitable to anyone, let alone a gentleman more used to life in a proper English mansion than out here in the wilderness.

Sleep did not come easily to her that night. Eyes wide open, she lay on her back beside Hannah. Footsteps pounded down the hallway outside her room; a woman's querulous voice sounded through the door. The wind soughed again, sifting through a crack in the window frame to lift the curtains. The melancholy that threatened her earlier in the dining room after chatting with their waitress came over her again.

Rose would never have a decent man in her life, for how could a decent man overlook the fact she'd had Hannah out of wedlock? Especially a decent man like Harrison, a nobleman no less. He must have a title, although he didn't seem to want people to know.

What about his fiancée? How could she not want Harrison by her side? How could she betray his trust and humiliate him so?

Revulsion flowed through Rose. Hadn't she herself betrayed Harrison's trust by lying to him about her supposed husband? True, it might not be on the same scale as being jilted at the altar, but a lie was a lie.

Certainly she could never tell him the truth about her daughter. She could imagine the disgust on his face if she did, how his lip would curl and his eyes grow cold. He would look at Hannah with distaste when the circumstances of her birth weren't her fault. No. Harrison St. John would never know the truth about Hannah. Tears pricked her eyes at the thought her daughter would never know a father.

Enough about Harrison, she scolded herself. *You have more pressing things to deal with, such as a clerk who expects payment first thing in the morning.* Payment she could not make until she found herself a position; so somehow or other she had to avoid him.

After that, a place for the two of them to live. She needed to build a life for herself and Hannah. That's why she'd come to Barkerville.

* * *

Harrison strode along, arms swinging and boots thumping on the wooden walkway. The brisk morning air cleared his head, and thoughts of the mining venture he was soon to embark on brought a smile to his lips. Plus, the conversation he'd had this morning with the man he shared his table with at breakfast had been a fruitful one. The man, a Scot, steered him to the gold commissioner's office farther up the creek in Richfield. There, he was told, he would get the information he needed regarding claims and what sites were still available.

Not surprising, the office was busy and, after standing back for a few minutes making sense of the crowded room, he elbowed his way to a large roll top desk manned by a harried looking clerk, sleeves rolled up and hat pushed back on his head.

"Wait your turn." The clerk pointed to the end of a line of men winding around the edge of the small office.

The kindly look on his face belied the brusque tone of his words, however, and Harrison tipped his hat. "Certainly," he murmured and he edged his way to what he thought was the end of the line, although it was hard to tell in the churning mass of men. Miners, he could only assume.

Harrison watched the pendulum on the big wall clock. He rocked from heel to heel, sometimes leaning against the wall, sometimes standing, sometimes squatting, every now and then shuffling forward a few paces. Nine A.M....10 A.M....11 A.M.... From time to time he wondered about Rose and Hannah and whether Rose's husband had come into town yet. He hoped for Rose's sake that he had. A rough and tumble gold rush town was no place for a woman alone, let alone a woman with a small child.

It was almost noon by the time he reached the clerk again. The clerk, sleeves now unrolled and buttoned snugly about his wrists, gave him a bored look. "Do you have a mining license?"

"I do." Harrison patted his shoulder pocket. "I bought it in Victoria."

"May I see it?"

Harrison handed over the document and the clerk scanned it. "Everything appears to be in order. It's good for the rest of the year." He pinned Harrison with a penetrating stare. "You know this is non-transferable." Harrison nodded, but the clerk continued, "Sometimes people steal these then they sell them. Anything to make a buck. Just so you know, Judge Begbie doesn't take kindly to people who flout the law here." He folded it and gave it back to Harrison. "Williams Creek is plumb full staked. So is Antler Creek." He stabbed at the map pinned on the wall behind him with one ink-stained finger. "I suggest you try here, at Conklin or here, Stout's Gulch. Or even here, over by Cunningham Creek." He waved his finger over a few other creeks in the vicinity of Barkerville, but Harrison was unable to read the small print on the map, so had no idea what they might be called. "Got your supplies?"

"I do."

"Because a lot of people come here and they're not prepared. They're the ones who lose hope, lose their lives even." He sliced one finger across his throat. "It's dangerous business. Careful when you stake your claim. No more than four men per sixteen hundred square feet. When you stake your claim, come back here to register it. Here's a map, it'll cost you two dollars." He didn't wait for Harrrison's response, simply grabbed a rolled up map from a stand behind him and held it out.

Within minutes, Harrison stood outside the office, map stashed under his arm. He gazed at the few buildings making up Richfield. The faint strains of a fiddle drifted on the breeze, from a saloon no doubt. He looked farther down the creek, catching sight of a few shanties scattered here and there. Slowly he scanned the surrounding valley, the slopes stripped bare of trees, leaving behind a forlorn army of stumps. The creek wound its way through the desolation. Sluices built of hand-hewn wooden planks and ditches spotted its muddy banks, exactly as pictured in the mining handbook he'd spent many hours studying.

The bubble of happy expectation buoying him earlier this morning fizzled away. Up until now, this whole trip had been a lark. An adventure and an excuse to leave not only the stifling confines of England but the expectations he would marry into money. The stories he'd heard about the Cariboo gold rush made it seem as if gold nuggets lay openly on the ground waiting for anyone to stumble by and pick them up.

The eagerness of the failed miner he'd bought his equipment from in Quesnel should have set off warning bells. Instead, Harrison had been overjoyed at the price he negotiated and he'd accepted the man's explanation that "family matters be sending me along home."

Once again he realized success was not guaranteed.

And he played with his very life here in the British Columbia wilderness.

Chapter Nine

Rose dressed carefully the next morning. Somewhere a clock chimed ten times, reminding her she'd not gotten off to as early a start as she would have liked. She'd hated to wake Hannah and instead had let the little girl sleep. Doubtless the journey here took its toll on her. Now she sat playing with Dolly while Rose readied herself. She inspected her image in the small mirror hanging over the washstand in her room, knowing a neat appearance would help in her pursuit of employment.

She wore the same navy blue woolen skirt she'd traveled in, but she'd brushed the road dust from it, dabbing at a few stubborn spots of mud before donning a fresh white cotton blouse, its wide sleeves gathered into narrow cuffs. Instead of the matching jacket, she threw a fur trimmed pale blue velvet bolero over her shoulders. Finally, to accentuate her waist, she cinched on a wide belt made of the same pale blue velvet.

The colour of the velvet stirred memories of her father. "I love that colour on you, Rosie," he'd say. "It makes your eyes look like the lavender grey of rain over the mountain valleys." That was before, though—before Hannah—when she still lived with him in their neat little house on the ranch just outside of San Francisco. But you couldn't turn back the hands of time, so thinking about him served no purpose. She shook her head, then smoothed her hair, pulling loose a few tendrils from the bun at the nape of her neck to curl around her cheeks.

She would do.

"Are you ready, poppet?" Rose patted Hannah's head. Her daughter too, looked her best, blonde curls pulled back neatly into a braid and wearing a fresh striped frock, below which peeked clean stockings. Rose shook out the dust from the little girl's shawl and knotted it about her shoulders.

"Where are we going?" wondered Hannah as they left their room. Rose locked the door, pocketing the key before turning to answer.

"We're going for a walk so we can explore our new home." She took Hannah's hand and they started down the hallway. The bare boards echoed the "clack" of their boots, and inwardly she groaned. It would be difficult to sneak past the clerk if every step they took announced their presence.

"If we don't like it can we go home? To Mrs. B.?"

The innocent question tugged at Rose's heart. Sadly, there would be no returning to Mrs. Beadle's rooming house. If things didn't work out for them in Barkerville, they would have to move on. It didn't bear thinking about. If they couldn't hide from Edmund here in the Cariboo wilderness, where could they go?

But that was a problem for another time. For now she had to avoid the desk clerk because, of course, she had no money. She doubted he would believe her if she told him she couldn't find her coin purse after all.

When they reached the staircase leading down to the lobby, she bade Hannah wait for her. Holding her breath, she tiptoed down a few steps until she could lean over and peer between the balusters. A flush of relief cascaded through her when she couldn't spot the clerk, so she retraced her steps and picked up Hannah.

"I'm a big girl. I can walk down the stairs." Hannah's mouth clamped into a mutinous line.

"I know you can but we need to get outside quickly. There are lots of stairs there, and then you can show me how well you can climb them." Rose whisked Hannah down the stairs, through the lobby, and out the door. She tapped her daughter on the nose. "Wasn't that fun?" She moved away from the entrance before placing Hannah on the wooden verandah and straightening the little girl's shawl. One obstacle down, anyway. She'd managed to avoid the desk clerk. For now.

A whistle sounded, then another. Then a shouted "Hello" and several "Good days". By the time Rose straightened and turned around, a cluster of rough looking men looked up at her from the street. "Oh", she squeaked, grabbing Hannah and pulling her close. More men joined and the group by now numbered perhaps ten. They all gawked at her.

"Need help, ma'am?" One fellow, bolder than the others, vaulted up onto the walk beside her. He swept off his hat and graced her with a gap toothed grin.

"No. I'm fine, really, thank you." Heart thudding, Rose stepped back and glanced around wildly. Where could she hide? And how long would it be before the hotel clerk noticed the commotion and poked his nose out to check? She picked up Hannah, ready to bolt and jumped when someone tapped her arm.

"Don't mind them." The waitress who had served her last night smiled at Rose. "I saw you from across the street and thought you could use a little help. Don't worry, they're mostly harmless. I think. Aren't you, George?" She addressed the man who had jumped up beside them.

"Yep, Gracie, harmless as a newborn fawn." He grinned again, not at all offended by Gracie's bossy manner.

She planted one hand on his chest and gave him a shove. "Then make like a fawn and go hide yourself. Leave the poor woman alone. She's new in town and doesn't need the likes of you scaring her."

"Aw, Gracie, yer no fun."

"And neither is a dirty miner. Off with you." Accompanied by a chorus of hoots and cheers, George jumped back into the street, landing on his hands and knees. He stood up, dusted off his hands and strode off, but not before one last lingering gaze at Rose. Her

107

cheeks grew warm and she knew her red face trumpeted her discomfort for the whole world to see. She looked away, trying to settle her nerves.

Gracie planted her fists on her hips and glared at the lot of them. "Go on, all of you. You'd think none of you had ever seen a woman before. Don't go scaring her little girl, either." She made a shooing motion with her hands. "Go. Or I'll make sure none of you are welcome in the hotel."

"You're a tough one," shouted someone.

"Gotta be to deal with you lot."

A few good natured comments and mutters floated on the breeze, and the men wandered away in groups of two or three. She waited until the entire group dispersed before turning her attention to Rose. She chuckled. "There aren't a lot of women here in town. Anyone attracts attention. Especially one as young and pretty as you."

Rose swiped a hand across her brow. "Phew. Thank you. I didn't know what to do."

"Oh, most of 'em are far from home and lonely for a little female companionship. They're mostly good guys and don't mean no harm. A sharp tongue keeps 'em in line quite nicely, I find." She gave Rose a quizzical glance. "Where you off to? Ain't you expecting your man?"

"Ah...well, yes, I am, but I thought to acquaint myself with the town while I wait for him." She wracked her brains. She could use

Gracie's help in suggesting where she might find employment, but would the other woman find it strange a married woman—a mother no less—wanted to work? She plunged on. "I'm...uh...actually looking for work myself. I've worked in a shop. I'm very good with customers and I can do numbers and...." Her voice trailed away and she shrugged her shoulders. "We're saving up for...ah...a farm."

Gracie's eyebrows raised but she didn't say anything. "Good with numbers, you say? I'd think that would make you wanted anywhere. Especially with your looks. All I can say is start walking and knocking on doors. What are you going to do with her?" She pointed at Hannah.

"She's coming with me. I've no one to leave her with."

"You can leave her with me for an hour or two. It don't get busy in the dining room until later, when the rest of the miners start making their way to town." She held out her hand. "Grace Anne. But everyone calls me Gracie."

Rose shook the other woman's hand. Sinewy and callused, it bespoke hours of honest hard work. "Rose. And this is Hannah."

"Hello, Hannah." Gracie bent down and shook the little girl's hand as well.

Hannah said nothing. Suddenly shy, she stared at Gracie with round eyes.

"You must say hello," said Rose. "It's rude not to." She tugged on Hannah's hand. Hannah hid her face.

"Never mind," Gracie chuckled. Then, "Do you dance?" she asked abruptly.

"Dance? I suppose a little. I can polka. And waltz." Rose tilted her head, wondering why the other woman would ask about dancing. Surely there were no dance halls here.

"There's a saloon down the way. Miners pay to dance, a dollar a dance. You can make good money in an evening. If you can't find the kind of work you're looking for, you might try that. No, wait a second." Gracie propped her fist under her chin and tapped her foot. "Never mind. You're married. I doubt your husband would like you dancing with other men, no matter how well it pays."

"You're right, my husband wouldn't approve." For once her made-up husband served her well. The idea of dancing with strange men every night didn't appeal to her. Plus, she'd vowed long ago not to be a man's plaything ever again.

"I'd best be going." Gracie held out her hand to Hannah. "Are you ready, honey? I think I can find some cookies in the kitchen."

Hannah looked at her suspiciously before glancing up at Rose. At her mother's nod, she took it. "I like ginger snaps," she said.

"I think we have ginger snaps," Gracie said. "If not, how about a lemon drop?"

Hannah shook her head. "I don't like yellow candies. I like red candies."

Gracie patted her cheek. "Maybe we have some of those too."

110

"Are you sure, I mean, I don't want to impose." Secretly, Rose was relieved to have someone to watch Hannah for her. She could make better time on her own.

"It's no bother. She's a well behaved little thing. I saw that for myself last night. When you're done looking, come 'round to the back of the hotel. We'll be there."

"How can I thank you?"

"By finding work." Gracie winked. "Then maybe you can buy me a whiskey. Remember what I said. A sharp tongue will keep you safe." She twiddled her fingers in Rose's direction. "Good luck."

"Right." Rose had no worries about leaving Hannah with Gracie. The woman had a big heart. Maybe when she got back, she would ask her about her black eye. Hopefully it was the result of an accident and not an assault on her person.

Grace walked off, Hannah tottering beside her, looking over her shoulder at Rose, puzzlement evident in her blue eyes. Rose gave her a reassuring wave and turned away.

She had to find work as soon as she could.

Chapter Ten

Rose glanced both ways, trying to decide which direction to go. A few doors away on the other side of the street, she noticed a sign: Oppenheimer & Co. It looked to be a general mercantile and as good a place to start as any. Within a few steps, however, she attracted more attention. Each and every man she passed fell silent. They stopped whatever they were doing and watched her walk by.

Flustered, she picked up her pace, gathering up her skirts to walk faster. However, that move exposed her ankles above her boot tops which elicited more whistles. She dropped her skirts and lifted her chin. It seemed she must run the gauntlet any time she walked down the street. Clasping her hands in front of her waist, she continued on until thankfully, she darted into Oppenheimer's. The door swung shut accompanied by the cheerful tinkle of bells announcing her presence.

A large clothing display blocked the windows of the store front, so not a lot of light came in. She stopped, letting her eyes grow accustomed to the dim interior. Several oil lanterns hung from the ceiling, though, shedding enough of a glow for an inspection of the shop. She only had time for a fleeting glimpse of shelves jammed full of goods before a voice broke through the gloom.

"May I help you?" A stoop-shouldered man with rheumy blue eyes beneath a few wisps of gray hair inspected her. He leaned his elbows on the counter by the cash drawer. A ledger book lay open beside him to one side. On his other side, glass jars of candy marched down the countertop containing the red and white stripes of peppermints, the green of wintergreen, the golden brown of hoar hound and butterscotch. She could hardly wait to bring Hannah and show her the colourful display. But not yet. Not until she found work.

She cleared her throat. "I'd like a position here if you have one available. May I speak to whoever is in charge?"

The man stood and peered down his nose at her. He was taller than she supposed, tall and skinny. "I'm sorry, I have nothing right now."

"Please, I'm good with numbers and I've worked in a store in Victoria. I know what I'm doing."

"Do you have a reference?"

Drat. She'd left in too much of a hurry to ask for a letter of reference from her previous boss. "No. But please give me a chance to show you what I can do."

"I'd like to help you, miss, but my clientele is much too rough for you."

"I'll start for free." Desperation was making her say silly things. She couldn't afford to work for free.

113

"You're an attractive little thing and all, but I don't have anything. Try J.H. Todd down the street." He dropped his gaze to his ledger, using a finger to mark his place line by line.

Rose didn't want to admit defeat. She reached forward and grabbed the ledger. "May I add those for you? To show you what I can do?" Her impetuous act astounded her. What was she thinking, trying to take the ledger from the man? She couldn't blame him at all for not wanting to give her a chance. She wouldn't either, if someone tried the same thing with her. She pulled away her hands and jammed them in her pockets. "Forgive me. I don't know what came over me."

He tugged the ledger closer to him before looking up again. His frosty gaze made her shrivel up inside. "Try J.H. Todd down the street," he repeated. His voice matched his gaze.

"Thank you for your time." Rose tried not to let disappointment cow her spirit. It was only the first place she'd tried, and surely other businesses here could use the help of an eager assistant. She wouldn't let the man see her defeat. One never knew when their paths might cross again. Head high, she left Oppenheimer's.

"You look lost, miss, can I help you?"

Of course. No sooner had she stepped outside the store than she caught the unwanted attention of a young man. A teenager, really, judging by his pimpled face.

She let her disappointment of her unsuccessful foray into Oppenheimer's fuel her

114

tongue. Gracie told her to speak forcefully, so she would. "No." As soon as the word left her mouth, though, she felt bad, for the teen blushed and stumbled back a step or two. "No, wait, I'm sorry. I didn't mean it. You most certainly can help me. Where could I find the J.H. Todd establishment?"

The boy brightened. "That way, miss." He pointed back towards the north end of town.

"Thank you." She smiled at him and he blushed anew.

Rose marched down the street, glaring at anyone who tried to accost her or engage in conversation. Gracie was right. All it took was a brash attitude. She even stomped her heels as she walked. The hollow thud echoed off the boards and it made her feel bigger than she actually was. She passed a barber shop and a doctor's office, a saloon, and a boarding house. If nothing else, the miners here were well served. Isn't that why she came here, because it was a boom town, overflowing with men, with gold to spend and needing places to spend it? That being the case, surely someone would need her assistance.

She stepped inside the J.H. Todd establishment. It was a bit smaller but every bit as crowded inside as Oppenheimer's. Her newfound self-assured confidence didn't help her here either, though.

"You're not strong enough," declared the owner when she asked about a position. "A lot of our goods require heavy lifting, being mining equipment and all. Besides," he slanted a glance towards her. "You're not tall enough. I don't want a lady clambering about the store on a ladder."

"I've worked in a shop before. I can climb up and down a ladder just fine." She pulled herself up. "I may be little, but my work is not. And I'm honest."

He shook his head. "I'm sorry, I can't help. But you might want to try the saloon. They have Hurdy Gurdy girls. You might want to be one of those. Make good money, they do."

"If by Hurdy Gurdy girl you mean a dancing girl, no thank you. My daughter will never see her mother dancing with a bunch of strange men."

The man shrugged. "Suit yourself."

"I will." She marched out of J.H. Todd's store. Hurdy Gurdy girl indeed. Odd, though, Gracie had mentioned dancing girls too. In a town populated mostly by men, women were obviously a popular draw.

She took a few steps away before another wave of disappointment threatened to swallow her whole. She looked up towards the clear sky. Its bright blue colour cheered her spirits a little, that and the smell of cinnamon wafting from a nearby store. "Try again, Rosie," she whispered to herself. "You've only been to two places."

Rose retraced her steps. She was almost at the hotel when she noticed Taylor's Drug Store. She'd stop in here, she decided, then check on

116

Hannah and Gracie. Squaring her shoulders, she stepped inside.

And within minutes, stepped out again. The clerk at the drug store had no interest in hiring her either. "You don't look any older than my daughter," he'd said. "She's twelve. No one is going to take you seriously."

Rose collapsed onto the bench in front of Taylor's store. The nerve of the fellow, telling her she didn't look any older than his twelve year old daughter, when in reality Rose was twenty four. Her appearance had not been a hindrance at her previous position. Because, she reminded herself, Mrs. Beadle knew the shop owner and had arranged for a try out. Perhaps she needed to revisit the idea of a try out, however she needed money to keep going on for a few days. She sat up and smoothed the velvet of her bolero. In hindsight, it was a frivolous item to bring along to a gold rush town and certainly had not given her any luck. Why not sell it?

Of the three establishments she visited this morning, Oppenheimer's was the one that had impressed her the most with its considerable array of goods and natty clothing on display in the front window.

Oppenheimer's with the tall, unfriendly clerk she'd tried to take the ledger from.

Desperation most likely clouded her head, but she would try there first. She got to her feet and made her way back. One fellow with a hopeful expression on his face tipped his hat when she walked by, but the grim set of her face must have warned everyone else to keep clear of her. She arrived back at Oppenheimer's unscathed.

She pushed open the door and, once again, the tinkling of bells announced her presence.

The clerk, still poring over the ledger, looked up. Suspicion filled his eyes when he recognized her. "You again. I told you, I'm not looking for help."

"Would you buy this?" She pulled off her bolero and held it out to him. "I need money. I'm staying at the Hotel de France and am afraid they'll give me the toss if I don't pay for my room. I have a daughter to look after too. She's only four and I don't know what I'll do if I can't stay there."

The clerk slammed shut his ledger and tucked it away beneath the counter top. He eyed the bolero and grabbed it. He fingered it but didn't comment.

Rose knew the garment intrigued him, and she'd had enough experience to know he wanted to barter.

"From San Francisco," she said.

"I had a lady in here just last week looking for something like this."

She pointed to her waist. "It has a matching sash."

His eyes narrowed as he inspected the sash, and Rose could almost see his brain working. "How much do you want?"

"Six dollars, plus two for the sash."

He shook his head and handed back the bolero. "Too rich for me, sorry."

Rose knew what game he played. She expected he would feign disinterest in an effort to reduce the price. "Then make me an offer. Otherwise I'll take it elsewhere." She started to put it on and had one arm through the sleeve when he spoke again.

"Well, it would be a shame to see you out on the street," the man replied grudgingly. "I'll give you three dollars for it. Throw in the sash and I'll give you another dollar."

"Six dollars for the two."

"Let me see it again." Rose tugged off the bolero and handed it over again. The clerk inspected it carefully, checking the seams and tugging on the fur to test the stitching. "Five dollars," he announced. "Take it or leave it."

Five dollars. That should cover the advance at the hotel and give her a few more days to find work. It was better than nothing. "You have yourself a deal, Mr.—"

"Foster. Tom Foster."

"Mr. Foster. I'm Rose Chadwick." She pulled off her sash and handed it over. Tom rooted through the cash drawer and handed over a few coins, which she tucked into her pocket. Transaction complete, the man had a different demeanour. Approachable, friendly, even.

Rose sucked in her breath. "I didn't have any luck at Todd's," she blurted. "Or Taylor's either, for that matter. I'm still looking for work...if you can think of somewhere that might want me. Or here." She made an obvious show of running her gaze around the shelves.

"I can see you have a head for business, but this isn't my store. I'm running it while the owner is away."

"Oh. Sorry to bother you again."

The thump of chair legs hitting the floor sounded. Rose whipped her head around and realized a stocky man had been leaning his chair against the rear wall of the store and watching the proceeding from the shadows the whole time.

"I think you're making a big mistake," he said. He stood up and sauntered over to the counter to stand beside Rose. "Look at her. She'll bring the miners in droves. You've been complaining that business is slow. Having her here will turn things around."

Tom thought for a moment, sweeping Rose with a head to toe gaze. "Yeah, maybe you're right. Maybe a fresh new face is what this place needs."

Rose held her breath, scarce believing what she heard.

"Okay, Rose was it?" At her nod, he continued. "You can start tomorrow. Be here at nine. Pay is two fifty a day, Sundays off."

"You won't regret it, Mr. Foster." Rose smiled. Returning to Oppenheimer's general store had worked in her favor more than she could have imagined, particularly considering how sour the man had been this morning when she first stopped by.

She turned to the other gentleman. "I must thank you for your help."

The man nodded. "My pleasure, miss. Anything to help out an old friend." He gestured to Tom with one pudgy hand. "Tom ain't been too happy with the way things were going here. There's a lot of competition in town these days."

"Good day, Mr. Foster. I'll see you in the morning." Rose floated out of the store, feet barely touching the ground. She had a job and five dollars in her pocket. Maybe she would even be able to buy her bolero back.

Now to find Hannah and Gracie and share her good fortune. She almost skipped with happiness and in no time at all rounded the back of the hotel where Gracie had said they would be. Rose poked her head through the half-open door of the tiny porch. "Hello? Gracie? Hannah?"

Her voice echoed in the empty room. Neither Gracie nor Hannah could be seen. Head reeling, Rose clutched the door jamb.

Where were they?

Chapter Eleven

Harrison strode down the trail from the gold commissioner's office, map flapping beneath his arm. At the edge of town, he dodged a wagon piled high with chopped firewood before pounding up the stairs of the first building with a wooden boardwalk. Anything to avoid the ruts and mud.

In the distance, he caught a glimpse of Rose. For some unwanted reason, his heart leapt at the sight of her petite figure leaning against the front wall of the Hotel de France. As he drew close, he noticed tears streaking her cheeks as she looked around wildly. He began to sprint. Something was terribly wrong.

"Rose! Rose Chadwick!" She turned in his direction. Her tightly clenched fists were pressed into her midriff. The anguished look on her face tore at his guts.

"They're gone! Hannah's gone!" She clutched his arm when he slid to a stop beside her.

"What? Who's gone?"

"Hannah. Gracie said she'd look after her. I trusted her. I never should have left Hannah with her. She seemed so nice."

"Gracie? Who's Gracie?"

"The woman who served us last night. The one with the black eye. I meant to ask her about it. I liked her. I never thought she'd take my little girl and run off." She rattled on. "I was so happy, I found work. She wanted me to buy her a whiskey. I was going to do that for her tonight for helping me out. But she took my little girl. They're gone." She subsided into gulping sobs.

Harrison wanted nothing more than to take her in his arms and press her face against his chest, but he resisted the urge. Instead, he put his hand on her shoulder. "I'm sure there's a good explanation." Even to his ears, his words sounded weak and unconvincing. He cleared his throat. "There's a good explanation," he repeated. "Why would she run off with Hannah?"

"Edmund," she gasped. "Edmund put her up to it."

"Who's Edmund? Oh, of course, your husband." Harrison dropped his hand and took a step back. He rearranged his map, tucking it under the other arm to hide his discomfort. Egads, what was he doing, comforting another man's wife?

"No. No. No," she moaned.

Despite himself, he reached out and patted her arm. "I'm sure you'll find them," he soothed. "Rose, where could they go? We're in the middle of nowhere here." She seemed to take some solace in his words for she stopped moaning and wiped the tears from her cheeks.

"You're right, of course. They can't go anywhere. Hannah can't walk far. She has a gash on her leg."

"Hallooo!"

The screeched salutation caught Harrison's ear and he turned to find the source. Forging their way through the throng on the boardwalk, he recognized the waitress from last night clutching Hannah by the hand. That must be Gracie, then.

"Look Rose, there they are." He pointed with the map. Gracie dropped Hannah's hand and the little girl charged towards them. Rose dropped to her knees and scooped her in her arms.

"Look what Gracie bought me!" Hannah waved a small paper pinwheel in the air. "Why are you crying, Mama? Does something hurt?"

"No, oh, thank goodness, poppet. I couldn't find you and I got scared."

"She was such a good little girl, I thought she deserved a treat." Gracie grinned so widely her black eye almost disappeared in folds of skin. "You were a big help to me, weren't you?" She tapped Hannah's nose.

"I counted." Hannah boasted. "I got it all right, didn't I?" She waved her pinwheel again, the points spinning so quickly they became a blur.

"You do know your numbers." Rose loosened her grip on her daughter and got to her feet, but Harrison noted she kept a tight hold on her daughter's hand. "You'll spoil her," she said to Gracie.

But she said it in such a good natured manner that Harrison knew she didn't mind at all. Relieved, no doubt, to find her daughter safe and sound after all.

"Kids are meant to be spoiled from time to time," replied Gracie. "But she earned it. She helped me count the spoons and then fetched potatoes for me." She fixed Rose with a pointed stare. "Did you find work?"

Rose brightened. "I did. I start tomorrow at Oppenheimer's."

"Bravo," shouted Gracie and she clapped her hands. Then she bent down to Hannah. "Your mama is a lucky lady, see if she isn't."

Harrison's jaw dropped. Rose had a job? Women of his social stature wouldn't dream of working. Didn't she have a husband to keep her? Then why would she work, especially with a young daughter to care for? A burst of sympathy for her tightened his chest and he took a deep breath to dispel the sensation. Life in a rowdy gold rush town wouldn't be easy for her and her daughter, regardless of whether she worked or not.

As if she suddenly remembered Harrison still stood there, Rose turned to him. Her tear-spiked lashes drew his attention and his gaze roved over her shadowy grey eyes before dropping to her mouth. A proud smile curved her lips and his fingers ached to trace the contours. Soft. Her lips would be soft. He licked his own lips in anticipation of— What? He shook his head. A kiss? He couldn't kiss a married woman. He took another step back.

"We mustn't keep you from your business any longer," she murmured. "I do thank you for stopping, but it seems my fears were unfounded."

Harrison nodded and tipped his hat. "All's well that ends well. I'll be on my way, then."

Rose dipped her chin. "Good day. Come Hannah." And she tugged on the little girl's hand and moved away.

Harrison watched the threesome wend their way into the hotel. The mystery surrounding Rose grew. Her comment on Edmund putting Gracie up to abducting Hannah made no sense. What kind of husband would take a child away from their mother? As well, something else niggled at him. Rose wasn't wearing her wedding band. Perhaps she'd simply forgotten to put it on this morning. However, her bare finger sent a signal that would certainly draw unwanted attention.

The whole situation seemed odd. Edmund Chadwick. He made note of the name. If he ever ran across the man, he would have a word or two with him.

In the meantime, Harrison had his own fears. True enough, he had a mining license, a map, and a miner's handbook, but he had no idea how to proceed now. Stake a claim? How did one go about that? Plus, there was the matter of his wagon and mule team. He'd already seen enough on his foray to the gold commissioner's office to know that the rough trails to gold mining country would not accommodate them. Perhaps he'd best start by returning to the stables and seeing what sort of arrangement he could make.

* * *

Harrison entered Mundorf Stables. "Hello," he shouted, scanning the stalls. Most were empty and through the open double doors at the rear he noticed his mule team huddled together in the corner of the pen. Nancy, ears pricked forward, hung her head over the top rail, no doubt plotting her escape. At least they were here, where he'd left them last night, so it appeared the livery owner was a trustworthy sort. However, trustworthy enough to negotiate some sort of bargain remained to be seen.

A red-haired man with a full red beard wandered out from one of the stalls. Harrison recognized him as the fellow he'd shared his breakfast table with that morning.

A grin ripped through the man's beard, revealing front teeth buckled together. "Well, look who's here." He gestured to the map under Harrison's arm. "See you took my advice and went to the commissioner's office." He held out his hand. "We didn't get around to exchanging names this morning. Robert McTague."

The Scottish burr in his voice sounded out of place and Harrison knew from their brief chat at breakfast that the other man had also traveled halfway around the world to join in on Cariboo gold fever. He grasped Robert's hand, giving it a good shake. The other man's firm grip put Harrison at ease immediately.

"Harrison St. John. I made it there but I don't know what to do now. Other than see to my livestock."

"I'm here doing the same thing ma'self. Rode in on my horse but he didn't take too well to the trail. I'm resting him up for now and hoping for the best. Hate to shoot the beast, although I hate to see him suffer too."

"Been here long?"

Robert shook his head. "Maybe a week. But long enough to know this isn't quite what I expected." He laughed. "I've washed a few pans of gravel on some of the abandoned claims and only found enough gold dust ta pay for my food, but I hate to give up. There's naught for me back home."

"Scotland?"

"Aye. Me da's croft is full to bursting, so I thought to make my own way in the world. From your accent, I'd wager you're English."

"Indeed. By way of Manchester."

The other man chuckled. "Well, we won't talk about Culloden, now will we?"

Harrison grinned. "No, I think not." He pointed into the stall. "Is this the fellow you're nursing?"

Robert's face fell. "Aye. That's Brutus."

"I know a thing or two about horses. Let me take a look at him." He ran his hands over the animal's withers, flanks, and on down its legs. "He feels sound enough. A bit bony perhaps, but I'd give him another day or two of rest and some good feed before you decide anything." The horse, a bay gelding, rubbed his nose against Harrison's shoulder, and for an instant he felt a pang of regret for the four he sold to finance his journey here. One day, he vowed, he'd have another set, equally as fine as the first.

"I'd thought the same. Time is the best healer." Robert patted the horse's nose.

"Do you know many people here? Have you met a fellow by the name of Edmund Chadwick?"

"Nae, can't say that I have. But hearsay has it there's upwards of ten thousand men here and up and around the hills. Could be he's not made his way into town for some time. These miners can get caught up with the fever and not wanting to leave their claims unless necessary." He clamped his lips, which made the hairs of his beard stand up around his mouth like a pin cushion, and regarded Harrison through narrowed eyes. "I'm looking for a partner. Two heads being better than one and all that. Until now, I haven't met anyone I'm wanting to spend time with. But I'm thinking a Sassenach might be a good choice. You lot being pigheaded and all." He chuckled and held out his hand again. "What do you think?"

"Partner? You don't know anything about me."

"You've a flair for horses and Brutus has taken to you. That's good enough for me. And like I said, you Englishmen are pigheaded, as far as I can tell. That'll stand a man in good stead out here."

Harrison stared at the other man's outstretched hand. His first inclination was to decline the offer until he noted the trimmed, albeit dirty, fingernails and the calluses on Robert's palm. The sign of honest labour. He raised his gaze and studied the other man's face. Or, rather, only his eyes and forehead, seeing as how his unruly beard covered everything else including his neck.

Robert returned his gaze with guileless blue eyes. "Well?" he prompted.

Still Harrison didn't reply. Here he was, in Barkerville, with a wagon full of supplies and nary an inkling of what to use them for. It might be helpful to have a partner, especially someone already familiar with what to expect. It made sense that the two would be stronger and more productive together. Besides, half of something was better than all of nothing.

He grabbed the Scot's hand. "You've got yourself a partner. Where to now?"

"Let's find a saloon. The whiskey out here is rotgut but 'tis good enough to wet your whistle and raise a toast or two to God and country." Robert chuckled. "And Cariboo gold."

Chapter Twelve

"Thank you." Rose slipped her gold band back on her left hand. Solid and reassuring. it made her feel as if her mother stood beside her in the hotel lobby lending her support. Now that he'd received payment, the hotel clerk dismissed her with a cool nod and returned to his inspection of the guest log.

She and Hannah had a quick meal of beans and bread in the dining room, then the two returned to their room so Rose could check on Hannah's gash.

"On the bed," she directed and Hannah, still clinging to the pinwheel, climbed up.

She flopped on her back and spread her arms. "I can reach across the bed."

"Lie still so I can check your bandage." Rose unwound the cloth strip but had to tug on the last bit as it stuck to the wound.

"Ow." Hannah's bottom lip trembled. "It hurts."

"Shhh, let me look and then I'll kiss it better." Rose bent closer and inspected the wound carefully. The surrounding flesh was red and fresh blood welled along the edges, but it looked clean enough. She dabbed at the wound with a clean cloth and soapy water, wishing she had some liniment.

Hannah sniffled a little but stopped when Rose dropped a kiss on her knee. "You're my brave girl. How does that feel now? We'll leave the bandage off for an hour or two," she said, "and let air get to it so it heals faster. You and Dolly need a nap, and afterwards we'll sit outside in the sun for awhile."

Hannah nodded and soon fell asleep. Rose pulled the room's only chair over to the window and sat down. The blister on her heel ached and she tugged off her boots, wriggling her toes in relief.

She shut her eyes for a moment, remembering the encounter earlier this afternoon with Harrison. How helpful he'd been, solicitous of her even. But she'd been so upset she'd let down her guard and blamed Edmund when she hadn't been able to find Hannah. Harrison had noticed, had jumped to the obvious conclusion that Edmund was her husband. Which is what she wanted, wasn't it? Yet why did she feel a twinge of disappointment at deceiving Harrison?

Elbows on the sill, she let her gaze roam up and down the busy street. The gold rush attracted all manner of men, although she spotted the occasional woman. She noted the newcomers right away. They were the ones with happy expectation rimming their faces and lifting their lips. The ones she could only assume were the successful ones strode along with a devil may care attitude, freshly shaved and dressed in clean clothes. The majority, however, were grubby, down at the heel and faces drooping with fatigue or disappointment; she couldn't decide which.

Her eyes lifted to the surrounding hills. Ugly and bare, stripped of most vegetation, they echoed the misery of lost dreams and dashed hopes. *Please let that not be me!*

After Hannah awoke, Rose carried the chair from her room to the second floor balcony overlooking the street. Grateful for the chance to enjoy the sun and watch the lively town unobserved, she plopped the chair into the outside corner of the balcony where the two railings met, then sat down and folded Hannah in her arms. Leaning against the back of the chair, she settled in.

"How about if we sit here and count the wagons." She pressed her cheek against Hannah's blonde curls. "Look, there's one."

An intermittent stream of wagons and carts rattled by filled with goods and people. So many people, Rose marveled, all filled with purpose. But, she reminded herself, it's what she wanted—to lose herself in the gold rush. She hadn't pictured it quite so rough and isolated, though. However, they were here and, Hannah's gashed leg notwithstanding, mostly safe and sound. Plus, she'd already found employment.

"One, two, three." Hannah pointed with her pinwheel.

"Four, five," added Rose.

"Look Mama. There's a pony with two colours." A pinto horse tied to the back of a

133

wagon piled high with boxes and barrels moved past them at a snail's pace. "Can I have a pretty pony like that?"

"One day perhaps," Rose replied absently, mind now working furiously on her next obstacle.

She needed someone to look after Rose. Mr. Foster had clearly been hesitant to give her a job, in fact, had only hired her at the cajoling of his friend. She could only imagine the reaction if she showed up tomorrow morning towing a four year old girl in hand.

Perhaps she could ask the clerk at the front desk. No, she decided, the fellow had his duties and, doubtless, would not appreciate being pestered by her. She wracked her brains, trying to remember if she'd seen any other women staying in the hotel. No, she hadn't.

Then, all thoughts fled her mind when Harrison strode past. A red-headed man walked with him and the two seemed to be deep in conversation. Harrison tilted back his head and laughed, then the two disappeared out of sight.

His good humor brought a smile to her lips and for a crazy instant she contemplated running out to join him to find out what had made him so happy. She wouldn't, of course. She'd invented a husband for herself, and married women wouldn't run after another man. She peered after him, trying to catch another glimpse of him and, when she couldn't, returned to the problem at hand.

Try as she might, she could only come up with one solution: Gracie. Perhaps Gracie would know someone decent who would be happy to care for a youngster. She jumped up and dragged the chair back to her room before going in search of her friend, finding her in the hotel's kitchen with a wooden paddle in her hand ready to tackle a large pot of soup. Gracie's smile turned to a frown when she saw the exposed gash on Hannah's leg.

"Poor thing," she clucked, dropping the paddle and dropping to her knees to inspect the cut. "Does it hurt very much?"

Hannah shook her head and Gracie looked up at Rose. "It should be bandaged."

"I thought a little sun on it would be good. Besides, someone's already looked at it and said it wasn't that serious." Rose tried not to sound too defensive. The last thing she wanted was to annoy Gracie.

"Liniment would be better."

"I know." Rose lifted her hands. "But I don't have any."

"Dr. Wilkinson has."

"I'm sure he's too busy to see a little girl."

Gracie gave her a dubious look. "He's a doctor. They're never too busy. That's what they do. Fix sick people."

"Do you know anyone who could look after Hannah? I'll pay, of course."

"Other than a doctor?"

Rose grimaced. "You know what I mean. I can't bring her to work with me tomorrow."

"No, you can't." Gracie levered herself up to standing. "I have a girl of my own. She's ten and good with the younger ones. School's out for the summer. It would give you time to find someone."

"Once again I'm in your debt."

"I told you. Buy me a whiskey and we're square. Besides, it's nice to have a new friend. Not too many decent women in these parts."

Rose cringed. Decent women did not bear babies out of wedlock, and she'd try her hardest to make sure Gracie would never find that out. "I take it your husband's a miner as well?"

A shadow darkened the other women's brown eyes. "Was. He was a miner."

"Oh," replied Rose brightly. "What does he do now?"

Gracie shrugged. "He's dead. Couldn't take it no more. He walked up the hills one October day and never came back. He left me alone on the claim in a tent with two little ones and no way of getting into town other than my own two feet. I managed to sell the claim and his stuff and get into Barkerville before the snow flew."

"Oh. Oh." Rose felt her face grow hot. "I thought your black eye was because he beat you." She blurted the first thing that came to mind then kicked herself mentally as soon as the words left her mouth. What a ninny. She'd thought her life had been hard, but it was nothing compared with what Gracie had dealt with. With two children, no less.

Gracie snorted. "I'm clumsy, always been clumsy. I smacked into a door. Kinda wish it was him, though, that beat me. At least he'd still be around."

"I am so sorry," Rose murmured.

"Never you mind. It's all good and I'm here now. I got men calling, so maybe I'll get a beau. When I'm ready. Kinda like being my own woman. Anyway, when I have a chance I'll show you where I live so you'll know where to bring Hannah tomorrow morning."

"I can't thank you enough."

Gracie rattled on. "I'll tell Florence. She'll be happy as anything to earn a little money and that's thanks enough for me. By the time I put food on the table and wood in the stove, there's nothing for extras. She's starting to care about hair ribbons and such." Gracie shook her head and picked up the paddle. "Don't know where she gets that from. It sure ain't from me. I got no time for fripperies."

No, thought Rose. I don't imagine you do. After hearing Gracie's story, she respected the other woman even more. She was a survivor and had a heart of gold. "Gracie?"

"Yeah?" Gracie looked over but continued to swirl the paddle through the steaming liquid. Her thin face shone with perspiration and a few strands of brown hair peppered with grey stuck to her forehead.

"I'm happy to be your friend."

"Take Hannah to the doctor. I don't like the look of that cut. It's too jagged."

I barely have enough money to pay for food and shelter, let alone a doctor, Rose thought. "I will," she said.

* * *

The next morning, Rose left Hannah, lower leg freshly washed and bandaged, with Florence. Gracie's daughter turned out to be a smaller version of her mother, thin and wiry with mousy brown hair. "Mother told me about her leg." She pointed to Hannah's bandage. "I'll make sure she doesn't bump it."

The girl's comment made Rose feel guilty. She hadn't brought Hannah to see the doctor, had instead looked after it herself. After all, hadn't Mrs. Hodgkins, the kindly women from the stage coach, told her it was nothing to worry about?

After kissing Hannah goodbye, she made her way to Oppenheimer's general store. Mr. Foster greeted her with a lukewarm "Good morning", but he spent some time with her, showing her the cash drawer and where to keep the ledger. He also found a wooden box for her to stand on behind the counter.

Which is where she stood now, hands gripping the edge of the counter, inspecting the interior with a critical gaze. Two counters lined the walls, leading to a door in the back wall of the store, presumably where the owner lived. The earthy aroma of tobacco and cigars mingled with the sweet floral scents of perfume. Shelves lined every inch of wall space, stacked with every good imaginable. One shelf held boots and shoes. Another held crockery and hardware. Other shelves contained groceries, including such items as pickles, jams, flour, sugar, tea, salt, coffee, dried beans, and oats. Behind the counter to her right, a locked glass front cabinet displayed liquors and wines. Pots, pans, and coffee pots dangled from the ceiling, and a potbellied stove claimed the central stage. She even spotted stationery stacked high on a top shelf.

The largest section, however, contained tools and equipment: shovels of all sizes, hammers, picks, pitch forks, rope, gold pans, saws, axes, nails, even fish hooks. Everything a man would need to set up a home and mining claim. That such an array of goods could be found here astounded her. Did it all come over the treacherous Cariboo Road? How resilient and courageous of the wagon teams and drivers to make the trip not once but many times.

The door swung open, the bell tinkled its tinny welcome, and her first customer came inside. Only he didn't come to buy anything. He stood and stared at her, eyes round and mouth open. "Oh my, yer a pretty little thing." He took off his hat and smoothed his hair with a grubby hand before plopping the hat back on his head, which made Rose wonder why he bothered to smooth his hair in the first place.

"Can I help you?" said Mr. Foster in a glacial voice. "Are you here to buy, or are you here to ogle my help?"

"Tobacco. And some beans." He glanced at Rose. "And a comb."

So began a steady stream of customers, all of them male, all of them with the same goal in mind—to scrutinize Rose. At first she found it flattering, but soon it became tedious and made her feel as if she were a trinket on display. Mr. Foster cajoled them into buying something and they would. The sales entries in the ledger grew and the cash drawer zipped in and out on a regular basis. At the end of the day, her satisfied boss gave her a thin lipped smile. "You may work out after all. See you in the morning."

"Good night." Rose gathered her shawl and scampered out of the store, eager to share her day with Hannah and Gracie. As she walked, she wondered about Harrison, how he had spent his day, and if she'd ever see him again.

First she made her way to the edge of town to Gracie's tiny log cabin, half buried in the hill up and behind the buildings lining the main street. A log sawed in half, cut sides up, made up the front porch. Rose knocked on the narrow door. "Hello? Florence? Hannah?"

The door swung open and Florence faced her. "Mother's not home yet," she informed her, flipping one skinny braid over her shoulder. "Hannah's been real good today."

Rose peeked in behind her. Though small, the cabin was cozy, with a bunk bed in one corner, a table with mismatched chairs in the other, shelves on one wall and a bench beside the door. Gracie was a good housekeeper, for not even a pin was out of place, and the top of the small wood burning stove in the middle of the floor gleamed. Rose's admiration for her grew

Hannah bustled up beside her, carrying Dolly. "I had fun. We threw stones in the creek. I got mine to the other side."

"I see." Rose eyed Hannah's damp, muddy stockings and water stained skirt. "How did she get wet?" she asked.

Florence shuffled her feet. "Billy pushed her. She fell in. Please don't tell Mother."

Rose's stomach quivered at the thought of Hannah tumbling into the mucky creek. What if she had been swept away? Despite Gracie's assurances, Florence didn't seem capable of looking after Hannah after all. Rose pressed her lips together and didn't answer. "Come Hannah." She grasped her daughter's hand and tugged her towards her. What should she say to Gracie?

First things first, however, Hannah's stockings must come off and her wound tended to. Rose picked up Hannah and rushed back to the hotel, pounding up the stairs with such ferocity it brought raised eyebrows from the unfriendly clerk.

"I'm in a hurry," she puffed and favored him with an icy stare. Once back in their room, she peeled off Hannah's stockings and filled the basin with clean water.

"Does it hurt, poppet?" Rose dabbed at Hannah's gash as gently as she could. Flecks of mud clung to the scab, and she continued to dab until she was satisfied she'd cleaned it as best she could. Then she wrapped another bandage around the little girl's leg. How could Florence be so careless? she fumed. Gracie should be told about the episode, but her new friend was so proud of her eldest daughter, she didn't want to stir any trouble.

Finally she decided to say nothing until she could find someone else to look after Hannah. In the meantime, she would keep an eye on Hannah's cut and hope signs of infection didn't set in.

Chapter Thirteen

The fading sunlight pouring through the windows of the Parlour Saloon illuminated the liquor in Harrison's glass to an amber glow. The liquid sloshed back and forth as he lifted it high overhead. "To us!"

"To us," echoed Robert and he downed his glass in one gulp. He slammed the glass on the marble topped bar and waved at the bar tender. "Another!" he bellowed against the din of shouts and laughter in the saloon.

Harrison swallowed hard, held his breath, and tossed back the fiery spirits before banging down his own empty glass with a hearty "thunk". Rotgut, indeed. But a few glasses of it and a bracing conversation with his new partner gave him a different perspective. "So you're saying I should keep my mules for now?"

"Aye. Lugging a backpack through these hills is back breaking and the mules should be able to follow the trail. Besides, I'm thinking we'll be needing them to pack our gold out. It's heavy, you know." He nodded and leaned forward on one elbow. He slapped his other hand against the top of the bar. "Once we stake our claim, we can take turns heading back into town. One of us should stay there at all times. To avoid claim jumpers." He hiccupped.

143

"Maybe I should sell my wagon?"

Robert shook his head. "Find a place to park it. Once we're done, we'll need a way to get out of here with our stuff. Which, thanks to your wagon, we have." He tugged at his beard. "Still not sure what to do about my horse, though."

"He'll firm up."

"Then I'll ride him out of here like a conquering hero!"

Two more glasses of whiskey materialized in front of them and the men picked them up, clinking them together before downing the contents. "We'll be richer than Croesus hisself," Robert announced.

"Rich!" agreed Harrison.

"Gentlemen, I admire your confidence, but haven't you heard about counting your chickens before they hatch?" The man standing to Harrison's left leaned forward and poked his head around. "It's not as easy as you think. Thousands can attest to that."

The stranger's dour words dampened Harrison's enthusiasm and doubt must have shown on his face, because Robert waggled his finger at the other man's nose. "All we need is a little luck," he retorted.

"Luck doesn't come all that easily."

"Well, then we'll work damn hard." Robert was not to be easily dissuaded. "The new partnership of McTague and St. John or—" he paused and winked at Harrison, "—St. John and McTague will be a successful one, you'll see."

Robert's conviction bolstered Harrison and he glanced to the stranger at his left. "Your words are duly noted, but if we expect failure before we even start, then failure is what we'll have."

The stranger shrugged. "Don't say I didn't warn you." He moved away.

"Tomorrow morning we'll pick up supplies and head into the hills." Robert's cheerful voice confirmed Harrison's zeal. The Scotsman's belief in their triumph in the gold fields was heady and yes, thought Harrison, why wouldn't we find what we seek?

He replied with an eager voice. "I have equipment. In the wagon."

"We'll take stock and top up what we need. I hear Oppenheimer's is the best."

"Whatever you say." Harrison nodded. "Let's go see what I have so we can make an earlier start in the morning. I'm anxious to get started!"

The squeal and scrape of a violin being tuned interrupted their conversation, then the strains of "Beautiful Dreamer" filled the saloon. A lone voice began to sing, a deep baritone that made Harrison's arms tingle with its rich tones:

Beautiful dreamer, wake unto me,
Starlight and dewdrops are waiting for thee;
Sounds of the rude world, heard in the day,
Lull'd by the moonlight have all passed away!

Robert pushed away from the bar and made as if to leave. Harrison held up his hand. "Not until the end of the song." Robert raised his eyebrows but acquiesced, leaning back against the bar and joining in with a surprisingly melodic voice:

Beautiful dreamer, queen of my song,
List while I woo thee with soft melody;
Gone are the cares of life's busy throng,
Beautiful dreamer, awake unto me!
Beautiful dreamer, awake unto me!

The two voices spiraled through the saloon, bringing it to total silence. The silence held for a moment after they finished before a wild crash of applause and huzzahs signaled the crowd's appreciation.

"You have a career on stage if gold mining doesn't prove fruitful." Harrison clapped his friend on the back.

Robert shook his head modestly. "I sing for pleasure. Or in church. I'd rather a hard day's labour beneath the sun any time. Nothing beats the feel of a shovel in your hands, the ache of hard work in your bones and the satisfaction of a job well done in your heart." He grinned. "That's why being a miner suits me just fine."

They left and headed back to Mundorf Stables, but the melody of *Beautiful Dreamer* stayed in Harrison's head. The word play brought an image of Rose to Harrison's mind and one phrase swirled around and around: *Beautiful dreamer, awake unto me.*

The romantic song made him realize he had hopeless feelings for her. How he would love to share those feelings with Rose, to awaken her to love's tender conquest. He took a few more steps in a romantic haze before reality, in the form of a drunken oaf stumbling into him, pummeled him square in the solar plexus. Whether accidently or on purpose, Harrison didn't know, but the blows knocked the breath out of him and he doubled over for a few seconds.

A red haze blanketed his gaze. *Why in blazes did she have to be married?* He threw a punch in return, feeling a satisfying smash as his fist connected with the oaf's nose. His fist came away bloodied.

"Good one," crowed Robert. "For a Sassenach, you're a right fighter!"

Harrison swung another punch, wanting the frenzy of fisticuffs to dull his feelings for Rose, but Robert pulled him away just in time to avoid hitting for a second time the oaf who had started the altercation.

"Let's move on afore this gets out of hand," he said, tugging on Harrison's arm. "The last thing we want is to start out with broken bones and missing teeth. Come on, no time for fighting. We have equipment to organize."

Right. Tomorrow they were heading out in search of their fortunes, Harrison reminded himself. No time for romantic fantasies.

But he turned around to look at the Hotel de France in the distance behind them, slowing down so much Robert had to tug once again on his arm. "What ails ye?"

"Nothing." Harrison's brusque answer brought raised eyebrows from Robert, but the other man didn't say anything. "My wagon's parked out behind the stables. We should have a couple of hours before it gets dark." Harrison focused his mind on the task at hand as the two men broke out into a jog. Regretfully, he pushed away his romantic notions regarding Rose and focused instead on Cariboo gold and the resurrection of the St. John family fortune.

* * *

Precisely at nine A.M. the next morning, Harrison and Robert stood outside the door of Oppenheimer's. Despite the early hour, several men were already lined up ahead of them.

"These gentlemen must be as keen as we are." Harrison said to no one in particular. He flexed his right hand gingerly. Yesterday's blow had left it with an ache and a stiffness he wasn't used to. Egads, he hadn't engaged in a fist fight since his childhood. How that would horrify his mother if she only knew, and she would certainly think the B.C. frontier lead to the demise of his manners, while, in fact, he felt more exhilarated and worthwhile than ever.

"There's a young lady works here now. Well worth the visit, I've heard," said the fellow in front of them, elbowing Robert with a wink.

148

The door swung open. "Gentlemen, watch your step. I'll have no truck with rough housing of any kind," said a tall, thin sour-faced man. Harrison thought him a rather unpleasant fellow, but those thoughts fled as soon as he stepped inside.

Rose was there. Behind the counter. She didn't notice him at first, but finally her gaze roved around the room. It swept past him until a startled look came over her face and she looked at him again. He smiled, pleased to see her answering smile.

"Harrison!" she gasped. "I'd thought you were long gone out to the hills."

"Not quite yet. We're here to pick up some supplies. This is Robert McTague, my new partner." Robert nodded and tipped his hat.

"Pleased to meet you, I'm sure," she murmured but her gaze flicked back to Harrison.

"Still no sign of your husband?"

"No. I'm afraid he must be caught out."

"I'll look for him and tell him you're here."

"I'm sure that's not necessary." Rose cleared her throat. "He'll be along soon enough." A slight frown wrinkled her forehead and she avoided his gaze.

Any mention of her husband certainly made her uncomfortable. It made him wonder if she even missed him and, if so, what an odd situation. Wanting to give her time to collect herself, Harrison eyed the jars of candy lined up on the counter. "I'll take a few of each."

Rose worked her way down the row, placing two or three of each of the candies in the centre of a small square of brown paper. "Is that enough?" When he nodded, she proceeded to fold up the edges and tie some string around it before placing it on the weigh scale. "That'll be ten cents."

He counted out his pennies and handed them to her. With a neat motion, she swiped them into the cash drawer. Then she held out the little parcel.

Harrison shook his head. "It's for Hannah. Tell her I said hello."

"Oh." Her voice squeaked with surprise. She held out the parcel for a few seconds longer, but when she realized Harrison wasn't going to take it from her, she tucked it into her pocket. "How kind of you to think of her. She will be delighted. Thank you."

He didn't move away, just drank in the sight of her. A few wisps of caramel coloured hair framed her cheeks, and the pale blue blouse she wore turned her eyes into smoky lavender. She placed her left hand on the counter top and he noticed the gold braided ring once again on it. She tapped her fingers and the ring jumped up and down with the movement, making it seem as if it reproached him for his observation.

"Is there anything else I can help you with?"

"What? Er...no." Then felt his ears and face grow hot. Of course there was. He and Robert had come to the store to buy food and a few odds and ends. "Well, there is but…ah…I seem to have lost my friend." He backed away, murmuring his apologies, when he bumped into someone behind him. He pivoted on his heel and searched for Robert, finding him in the back corner looking at knives.

"Are you getting sick? You're red as a beet." His friend tapped him on the shoulder.

Harrison shook his head. "I'm fine, I assure you."

"Well, I hear Dr. Wilkinson is a good one. Young but knows his medicine."

"I don't need a doctor," Harrison said. What he needed was to not let a certain young woman bedazzle his thoughts. Of course he couldn't share that with his friend. "Let's get what we need and get out of here."

And thankfully, this time the tall, skinny shop clerk helped them. "Nails. Canvas. Beans, rice, flour, tea, sugar. Is there anything else?" When both Robert and Harrison chorused "no", he packaged everything for them. While Robert paid, Harrison snuck a peek at Rose.

She was helping another customer from her spot beside the candy jars but must have felt his gaze on her, for she met it squarely. Grey eyes met his and the hubbub filling the shop receded until all he could hear was the thud of his heart. Her lips lifted in a little smile and she patted her pocket. "Thank you," she mouthed.

It was all he could do not to leap across the room, vault over the counter and kiss her, but all he could do was smile back. When he did, she bit her lip and looked away. A blush coloured her cheeks a becoming peach hue. She tucked a stray hair behind her left ear and this time the ring out and out demanded his notice. He withered inside. *Mr. Chadwick is one lucky fellow.*

Slowly he followed Robert out of the store, resisting the urge to turn and take one final look. The memories he had already collected of her would have to suffice.

If he ever ran across Rose's husband, though, he would have a thing or two to say to the man for leaving his wife and daughter on their own. If they were his, he'd have waited in town every day until they'd arrived to make sure they were safe. Then he would have stuck around to make sure everyone knew she belonged to him. He saw how men leered at her, how they clamored for her attention, and it made him want to push them aside, every single one and claim her as his own.

He clenched his fists and regretted that he hadn't even said a proper goodbye to her.

Chapter Fourteen

Rose knew the second Harrison entered Oppenheimer's. She'd played coy, pretending she hadn't seen him but, oh yes, she'd caught him from the corner of her eye. A giddy wave of pleasure poured through her at the sight of him.

Happy expectation lined his face and his brown eyes shone, making them the colour of roasted chestnuts at Christmas time. He'd been happy to see her, too, because a wide smile flashed across his lips and he removed his hat. He pushed the hair off his forehead and tucked his hat under his arm before walking over. Then he'd bought sweets for Hannah, and Rose had to grip the edge of the counter for an instant to stop from swaying in his direction.

She was disappointed Tom had been the one to help the two, because she would have liked the opportunity to chat a little with his new friend. She'd heard enough to know the fellow spoke with a Scottish brogue and she was pleased Harrison had found a partner. At least he wouldn't be out tramping through the surrounding valleys on his own. The two of them should have something in common, anyway, coming such a long way from home.

Then the door opened. More customers came into the store, and Rose had no more time to think about Harrison.

* * *

Rose dragged her feet back to the hotel. The busy day had flown by, but now the blister on her heel throbbed and her back ached. It seemed everyone who came in that day wanted something from the top shelves. She'd been up and down the ladder so many times she was beginning to think the customers were just as interested in taking a peek beneath her skirts as actually buying something.

She tiptoed into the kitchen, looking for Gracie who, as soon as she spotted Rose, waved her onto a stool in the corner beside the painted buffet stacked high with clean dishes.

"Phew." She plopped down, pulling off her boot to give her aching heel a break.

"Busy day for you?" Gracie scooted past, balancing three plates on her arms. "It's slowed down a bit in here. I'll have time to chat when I come back."

"I just need to sit for a bit before I pick up Hannah."

Gracie stopped and looked over her shoulder. "Don't go until I come back. There's fresh coffee on the stove. Help yourself."

A Chinese woman clad in a black trousers and a straight black jacket with a stand up collar padded in, carrying two headless plucked chickens by their feet. "Who are you?" Silver hairs sprinkled the black of her braid, but her unlined face made it difficult to guess her age.

She stood and held out her hand. "Rose. I'm Gracie's friend. I'm staying here at the hotel. She…uh…said I could have coffee."

The cook nodded. "Young miss can have coffee. Then go. No like people in my kitchen."

Gracie bustled back in, throwing a stack of plates and cutlery into the wash stand with a huge clatter. "She's my friend, Ming." The cook scowled and flapped her hands, but Gracie ignored her. "Florence told me what happened yesterday. To Hannah. How's that cut on her leg?" She peered at Rose. "You never did take her to the doctor, did you?"

Rose shook her head. "I'm busy at the shop. I don't even have time for lunch."

"I've had a talking to with Billy. He'll leave Hannah alone. You're still good with leaving Hannah with Florence?"

Of course she would give the girl another chance. She owed so much to Gracie, she would give Florence ten chances if need be. As long as Hannah didn't get hurt. And yes, it was easier this way than to try and find someone else to mind her little girl.

"I'm off to get her," she said to Gracie. She wished she had a pair of thong sandals like the cook wore so she wouldn't have to squash her poor blistered heel back into her boot. She tapped Ming on the shoulder. "Where did you get those?" She pointed to her sandals.

The cook lifted her chin. "Kwong Lee Store." She looked as if she wanted to say something else but she turned and began hacking at the chicken carcasses with a large cleaver.

"I don't usually shop in Chinatown." Gracie looked uncomfortable.

"If they have what you want, why not?"

"They keep to themselves. A lot of them don't speak English."

"I hardly think that's a reason to avoid them. Besides, it will be an adventure. Like visiting another country."

"I'm sure it's harmless and all, but I can't leave now, anyhow. Still have dishes to wash and tables to clear."

The cook interrupted them. "It's fine. Tell them Ming said to come. No Chinese man touch English lady."

Rose noted the dubious expression on Gracie's face. "We'll go another time."

"Suit yourself." Gracie shrugged then plunged her hands into the sink full of soapy water and greasy dishes. "See you later maybe."

Rose waved and walked out of the kitchen. In no time, she'd collected Hannah and the two of them returned to the hotel. The desk clerk stared at them as they walked through the lobby, and Rose returned his unfriendly gaze with a stare of her own. She had no idea why the man disliked her so. She'd paid her deposit, hadn't she?

Once in their room, she sat down on the floor beside Hannah. "Time to wash up, poppet. Does your leg hurt?"

Hannah shook her head. "It has a bandage on it. Can you kiss it better? To make it go away faster?"

Rose inspected the gash. The edges were red and the skin surrounding it felt warm and she noticed yellowish fluid draining from it. Guilt washed over her. She would take Hannah to see the doctor tomorrow morning. Doubtless Tom Foster would be annoyed with her but it was a chance she would have to take. Her daughter's health was more important.

After Hannah fell asleep, Rose sat in the chair by the window and gazed at the star-sparkled sky. Was Harrison looking up at the stars too? Was he still in Barkerville, or had he and his partner headed out into the hills?

A shooting star burst across the blackness and before it fizzled away she made a wish—for a little cabin of her own, one she could make into a snug and cozy home for her and Hannah. She glanced around their little room. It served its purpose well enough, with hooks on the wall for their clothing, the bed they shared and the washstand, but the bare walls and floor seemed cold and unfriendly.

While working at the store, she'd heard stories of crowded accommodations—men sleeping on floors, tables, anywhere they could find space, so she should consider themselves lucky they even had this room. But would she ever be able to find somewhere to live in this booming town?

* * *

The next morning, low hanging grey clouds shrouded the hill tops and the moist smell of impending rain filled Rose's nostrils. The change in weather quieted the normally boisterous street and Rose, carrying Hannah piggyback style, strode without incident to Oppenheimer's. She paused outside the door to sling Hannah to the boardwalk.

"I want to see Florence," Hannah said. "I want to play with her."

"You will, but I want to the doctor to see your leg first." Rose placed one finger on Hannah's mouth. "Can we play a game where you'll be quiet as a mouse while I speak to my boss?"

Hannah nodded. "I can play that game." And she clamped her lips together before placing both her hands against her mouth. Rose grinned at the sight of Hannah's eyes, round as blue saucers, peering up at Rose over the hands splayed across her cheeks.

"Good girl." Rose nodded and pushed open the door.

"What is that?"

Mr. Foster's cold voice dampened any hope Rose had that he wouldn't mind her being away from the store for a few hours.

"Who, not what." She pulled Hannah forward. "This is my daughter, Hannah."

"This is a business establishment, not a nursery for little girls."

"She's hurt her leg and I need to take her to the doctor. I hope you don't mind if I miss a few hours of work today. You can dock my pay."

He looked at her, down at Hannah then back up to Rose. His lip curled. "I should have known you wouldn't be reliable."

"Please, Mr. Foster, it's only for a few hours. She fell a few days ago and I'm worried the cut is becoming infected."

"I need someone I can count on."

"You can count on me." Rose squared her shoulders.

His nostrils flared as he sucked in a huge breathe of air and rolled his eyes skyward. "This is why I shouldn't have hired you in the first place. Mothers should be with their children."

"I need this job. I promise this won't happen again."

"See that it doesn't."

"My friend recommended Dr. Wilkinson. Do you know where I can find him?" Rose half cringed, expecting a tirade from Foster.

A vein pulsed in his temple. "Other side of the street."

"I'll be here as soon as I'm able."

Behind her, a grouchy voice sounded. "When's she coming back?" Rose spun around and gave Foster an innocent look. He glared

159

back. They both knew she attracted customers, which spurred business.

"I don't know," replied her boss. "But I can help you."

"You're not nearly as pretty."

"That, good sir, I cannot help. Now, what would you like?"

With a grin, Rose hurried Hannah out of the store.

* * *

Rose found the doctor's office easily enough and she stepped inside to a small vestibule. She was here early, for the room was empty and it made her wonder about his proficiency. Or perhaps no one required his services today, she decided. A sign tacked on the wall above a small bell told her to "ring bell", so she did. She popped Hannah onto the one bench and before she had a chance to seat herself, the doctor came out. He was much younger than she'd expected, perhaps in his early thirties, but his brisk air bespoke competence.

"I'm Dr. Wilkinson. May I help you?"

"Yes." She pointed to Hannah's lower leg. "My daughter fell and has a terrible cut on her leg. I've been keeping it clean but I'm worried it's getting infected."

"You are—?"

"Rose Chadwick."

"Well, Mrs. Chadwick, bring her into the examination room." He stepped back and gestured for her to precede him. "May I?" He pointed to Hannah.

At Rose's nod, he picked up the little girl and swung her onto the examination table draped with a white sheet. He washed his hands in the hand basin in the corner before carefully unwinding the fabric strips on Hannah's leg. He inspected the wound, even going so far as to haul out a magnifying glass. "It's starting to heal, but yes, it does show signs of infection. I'll apply a poultice. Leave it on for a few hours then cover the wound with bandages."

Rose nodded. "Thank you."

He said nothing while he mixed the poultice in a small ceramic pot. "Bring her back in a few days," he said as he applied the moist mass to a strip of fabric. "I might need to apply another one." He wrapped bandages around Hannah's leg to hold the poultice in place then grabbed more gauze from the stack on the shelf which he handed to her. "Use these. They've been washed in carbolic acid so they should be clean." He yanked open a nearby drawer and withdrew a small glass vial. "Here's a bit of liniment to apply when you change her bandages. Do that every day."

"How much do I owe you?"

"Nothing yet. We'll settle the bill when you come back."

Rose's heart sank. She was down to her last two dollars and hadn't been paid yet from her job at the store. In all likelihood her money would be gone by the time she returned to the doctor's office.

Something else bothered her, she thought as she walked away. He'd called her Mrs. Chadwick. But why wouldn't he? Not only did she wear her mother's ring, she had a daughter. Of course he would assume she was married.

At least he hadn't asked her about her husband. Just as well, she supposed, but sooner or later someone would realize she didn't have a husband.

Then what would they think of her and Hannah?

Chapter Fifteen

"Bloody hell, Sassenach, what have you got in these sacks?" Robert patted the leather bags piled up outside their tent. "I told you the mules would be useful. We'd never have managed to haul all this on our backs in one trip." He glanced to the hobbled mules grazing nearby. "Although there may not be enough grass to keep them all here."

"They'll be fine for a few days. Anyway, what you see is everything a man needs to be a successful miner." Harrison hauled out the book tucked away in his chest pocket. "According to this handbook here." He jammed it back in his pocket.

Robert threw him a dubious look. "Reading about it and doing it are two entirely different things." He pointed with his chin towards his own gear. "A gold pan, blankets, shovel, pick and axe are all you really need. Until winter hits. But I hope to be long gone by then."

"Clothing, soap, razor, toothbrush." Harrison pointed as he listed off his own goods, ignoring the incredulous expression on his friend's face. "Gold pan. Sleeping bag. Blankets. Extra socks and boots. Kettle. Pot." Then he pointed to the tools lined up neatly on the ground. "Axe. Shovel. Pick. Although

you're not blind and can see that for yourself."
He patted his pocket. "Compass." Then his hip.
"Knife." Lastly he gestured towards the tent.
"Rifle and cartridges. Books."

"Books? Who brings books out
prospecting?" Robert snickered.

"I didn't bring them all," Harrison replied,
stung at his companion's flippant response. His
books were how he meant to keep in touch with
the educated world. That and his daily toilette.
"Only some of my favorite plays by
Shakespeare. To while away the evenings."

"I intend to be sleeping in the evenings."
Robert stretched and yawned. "Time to build us
a fire and make something to eat."

"Good idea. Now that we've set up camp,
we can have an early start tomorrow."

Robert grabbed his axe and tramped away.
Harrison sank to his haunches and took stock of
the situation. They'd followed the trail from
Barkerville, finding a promising spot up a small
tributary of Cunningham Creek where they set
up camp a few yards away from the burbling
stream. The area was relatively new, for it
hadn't been totally denuded of trees, although a
number of stumps and fallen logs showed
evidence of mining activity.

A few tents and a shanty dotted the banks
of the stream. Some men had been here for
some time, for a sluice had been built, and a
ditch dug to divert water from the creek through
it. Despite the fading afternoon sun, men still
worked, pouring buckets of gravel and dirt at

one end while the diverted stream water ran through the wooden trough. Muddy water cascaded out the other end. It looked like back breaking labour, as evidenced by their fatigued expressions. One of them shouted, plucking a small nugget out of the sluice box and holding it high. "Here boys," he cried. "This is why we're here!"

A chorus of huzzahs greeted his announcement and Harrison couldn't help the frisson of excitement chattering its way up his spine at the raw evidence of gold in the creek. He could hardly wait until tomorrow when he and Robert would begin their own prospecting.

How would they fare with only gold pans and not the sophistication and capabilities of a sluice? Just fine, he reassured himself boldly. And if not, they would build their own.

* * *

Harrison awoke to the pitter-patter of rain on the canvas and Robert's groans. He pried open an eyelid to spy his friend on his hands and knees, head stuck out of the doorway.

"You'd think Mother Nature would give us a bluidy sunny day to start our prospecting," Robert groused. "It's rained so hard the wood will be soaked. I doubt I can get the fire going this morning. Which is a woeful shame, because what a man needs on a day like this is a good strong cup of coffee in his belly."

Harrison crawled out of his sleeping bag and ran his hands through his hair and over his stubbled chin. He'd vowed not to grow a beard, but the prospect of shaving with cold water was not an appealing one. Tomorrow. He'd shave tomorrow, he promised himself.

"There are cold beans in the pot and still some bread," he said. "We have something to eat, that should get us going."

They sat cross-legged in the doorway of the tent, chatting as they ate, sharing stories of the voyage over from their homes.

"Blasted trip that was," Harrison remarked. "Most terrible four months of my life."

Robert nodded. "Aye, I was never so glad to step foot on solid land. You know the worst thing?"

Harrison looked at him and lifted an eyebrow.

"We have to go back the same way!" Robert shuddered.

Harrison laughed. "The fortune in our pockets will sweeten the trip."

"Speaking of fortune, let's get to it." Robert got to his feet and grabbed his shovel and pan. "This is as good a place as any."

"I'll join you in a minute or two." Robert tossed him a puzzled glance and Harrison hastened to explain. "I'd like to comb my hair and clean up."

Robert threw back his head and let loose a round of laughter. "Ye'll be the death of me. I'm the only one out here to see and, frankly, I

dinna care about your hair. Besides." He pointed
to the rain. "Your head's bound to get wet
unless you wear your hat, so why bother with
combing your hair?"

Because I intend to remain within the
realms of civilized behaviour, thought Harrison.
"I'll be right with you," he replied.

By the time he reached the edge of the
stream, Robert had already begun. "Watch me,"
he said to Harrison. His shovel bit into the banks
of the stream and he stepped on its top edge,
levering out a pile of gravel which he dumped
into his gold pan. He knelt down and lowered
the pan into the water and began moving it in
gentle circles. A few large stones tumbled out
and Robert worked the remaining dirt with his
fingers. He contained swirling the pan and
muddy water and sand floated out. Eventually,
nothing remained in the pan.

Robert pointed to the empty pan. "Gold is
heavier, so if we found any, it would still be in
the pan." He stood up. "There's nothing so we
do it again." His shovel clanged as he hit a large
rock and he swung the handle back and forth
until he could bring up another shovel of
gravelled dirt and sand.

Harrison jammed his own shovel into the
shallow water of the creek and tossed the gravel
into his pan. He knelt down. His first attempts at
gold panning brought chuckles to Robert's lips.
"Ye'll get the idea soon enough."

Hours passed. Harrison's knees and
shoulders ached and his hands cramped within

the leather gloves he wore. The rain continued, pelting down continuously and soaking him through and through. He'd thought his boots waterproof, but he'd stepped into the creek so many times they were waterlogged and any hope he had of keeping his feet dry had long fled. In truth, if he didn't find the whole exercise a novelty, he would have been deuced uncomfortable.

The first time Robert bellowed, Harrison wasn't sure what had happened. Had he hurt himself?

"Gold," roared Robert. "A few grains. Take a look, this is what we're after."

He held out his pan and Harrison jogged over to peek inside. A chill and not from the rain, crept over his scalp when he saw the tiny grains. Not many, perhaps five or six, but definitely gold. He pulled off one of his gloves and reached out to touch them, pushing his fingertip hard into the pan so he could feel the golden specks.

His heart started to race and he grew lightheaded. He lowered his chin and closed his eyes for a second to collect himself.

Gold.

"Bluidy unbelievable," murmured Robert with a solemn expression. He reached out with one finger, swiping the grains from side to side. "We only need a few hundred ounces or so of these and we'll be on our way," he joked.

"God willing it will be that easy."

Harrison returned to his own section of the bank and tackled the dirt and gravel with renewed vigor. He didn't feel the cold and wet, for the excitement of possibly finding more gold kept him warm. From time to time Robert would grunt, but by the time it grew almost too dark to see, neither of them had found any more.

"Enough." Harrison tossed down his shovel. "It's almost dark and I don't fancy the idea of tossing gold away because I can't see it properly."

"Just one or two more pans." Fatigue glazed Robert's eyes, but something bright burned in them. Gold fever, Harrison surmised.

"Suit yourself. I'll see you back at camp."

They'd worked themselves around a small bend and disgust filled Harrison when he rounded it to see their tent collapsed into a muddled heap, soaking everything inside. Fools. They'd erected the tent in a depression which had collected rainwater. Everything they owned stood in a few inches of water. His sleeping bag, rifle, everything.

He collapsed onto a nearby stump and swallowed hard against the sudden constriction in his throat. They would have to move the tent to higher ground. That in itself was easy enough but how would they dry everything in the incessant rain? He sat there a few more minutes, waiting for Robert. By then he'd sat still so long he grew chilled.

Still there was no sign of his friend. *Time to fetch him,* he thought. He dragged himself to his feet and stood there, swaying slightly. Hunger poked his belly but the thought of more cold beans repulsed him. What he wanted was some fried bacon and a hot cup of tea sweetened with lots of sugar. Instead of going to look for Robert, he would build a fire and brew some tea. Besides, Robert would surely return on his own volition once it got too dark to see.

Harrison regarded the tent. He sloshed through the water and pulled it upright, tightening the ropes pegged into the ground. It still sagged sadly, but he was able to crawl inside and retrieve their goods, which he stacked beside the stump he'd recently vacated. Sadly he regarded the few tomes of Shakespeare he'd brought. They'd turned into sodden, swollen lumps. He picked up the closest one and read the title—*As You Like It.* He smiled grimly— this certainly wasn't how he liked it.

He shook his head, then pawed through the pile until he located the matches which he tucked into his chest pocket beside the miner's handbook. Then he went in search of wood.

He patted Nancy's neck as he walked by. He'd tied her to a nearby tree and she stood beneath it, head drooping, ears flopped forward, and wet patches on her back. The other mules were tethered a bit farther away and they looked equally miserable.

"I bet you wish you were back at the stables right now," he said. One ear swiveling in his direction was the only indication she heard him, and he patted her on the rump. "Good girl."

He carted a few branches back to their camp and regarded them with an uneasy eye. Everything was wet. Grabbing his axe, he went in search of undergrowth and low hanging dead branches which he found a few hundred yards away. Whack! He let his frustrations with the weather loose with every swing of the axe.

By the time he returned to their campsite with an armful of twigs and small branches, Robert waited for him, the glum expression on his face barely visible through the twilight gloom. "We'll need to move the tent," he said.

"Yes but first I thought to build a fire. Something warm will cheer us up."

"Do ye have matches?"

Harrison dumped the load of wood before patting his pocket. "Here."

"Are they wet?

"They are. I've had them in my pocket, hoping they'd dry out enough to use."

"I doubt it." Robert impaled him with a disbelieving stare. "Ye've never built a fire in your life, have ye?"

Embarrassed, Harrison shook his head. "No." He gestured to the few fires flickering in the distance from nearby camps. "But it can't be that hard."

"Not in your mansion where it's warm and dry and the servants chop the wood and lay the sticks and set the match to it." Robert scanned the area. "There." He pointed to a small thicket of shrubs. "We'll build the fire over there. It

171

should give us a little shelter if the wind picks up."

Robert busied himself with chopping wood and laying the fire, leaving Harrison feeling rather useless. "I'll move the tent to higher ground," he said finally.

Robert glanced over his shoulder and nodded. "May as well put everything back inside too. An' when ye find my clothes, can you bring me my woolen jersey?"

"Of course."

"Do ye have anything woolen? It keeps you warm even when it's wet." The only thing Harrison could think of was his overcoat and when he found it, he shook it out and put it on. Egads, the cold and clammy thing was uncomfortable but once he started to move, he did feel warmer. He found Robert's jersey and tossed it to him.

Then he pulled down the tent, dragging the wet, heavy canvas on the ground behind him. "How about here?" He pointed to a location on a small rise close to the thicket. At Robert's nod, he attempted to erect it and failed miserably. The canvas had a mind of its own and refused to cooperate, collapsing repeatedly. In the background, Robert filled the air with a colourful array of curses as the fire would not start.

Eventually Robert gave up and stomped over to Harrison to give him a hand. "I'll see if I can get a few burning coals from someone," he said after they finished erecting the tent. He took the pot with him. "To carry them," he said, "although my fingers are so cold I could probably carry them bare handed."

He came back and carefully placed the coals in the bed of the fire where they immediately started to smoke. "It's too wet. Do ye have any paper or some such we could burn? Like one of your books?"

Aghast, Harrison stared at him. "One doesn't burn books," he replied frostily.

"One does if one wants a fire."

Harrison handed him the mining handbook.

"Don't you think we should keep this one? It being an instruction book and all."

"This is the only one that's even remotely dry because I had it on me. Besides, one does not burn Shakespeare."

"If ye say so." Robert grabbed the book and glanced through it. "We don't need this page," he ripped one out, "or this one," he ripped out another, "or this." In a short time he had a small wad of paper in his hand and with the help of the coals he'd begged from a neighboring camp, they soon had a cheery blaze.

"We'll take turns keeping this going. We don't want to get cold. A man can't think straight when he's too cold." With the advent of the fire, Robert's good humor returned and he started to whistle. "Where's that kettle? Didn't ye say ye wanted tea?"

Harrison nodded. "And bacon with our beans. We may as well eat it before it spoils."

"Aye." Robert grabbed the kettle and filled it with water, placing it on a couple of stones in the fire. Then he rooted around the small chest of food, pulling out the rasher of bacon and throwing it in the pot. The fragrant aroma of frying bacon swirled through the air. "It's a good thing the sugar was in a tin otherwise we'd have syrup for our tea."

Harrison volunteered to start tending the fire first. Robert sat down, pulling out his folded handkerchief. He unwrapped it to inspect the few grains of gold he'd collected earlier.

"I hope we find more than that," Harrison said. "It's an awful lot of work for a few dollars worth."

"We will, Sassenach. We will," Robert said with a confidence Harrison was far from feeling. He folded up his handkerchief and jammed it back in his pocket before pulling his wet blankets around his shoulders. Much to Harrison's surprise and, despite the unpleasant conditions, Robert drifted off immediately, this time filling the air with his snores.

Harrison settled in for a long, cold night. Total blackness blanketed them, pricked by the sputtering camp fires of the other camps. The sight heartened him. At least they weren't alone in this wilderness. He tugged on his hat, pulling it down over his ears, and turned up the collar of his coat before placing his sleeping bag over his knees. Then he propped up his head with his fists and gazed into the glowing fire.

174

He thought of Rose, the startled expression on her face when she spotted him in the store, how pretty she looked in the pale blue blouse. How he hated being so far away from her, especially knowing the attention she drew from the male populace of Barkerville. He couldn't deny the hopeless attraction he felt for her, an attraction he couldn't act on. He lowered his chin to his chest and shut his eyes against the pressure pricking behind his eyes. Fatigue overcame him, and he slept.

In the dead of night a few hours later, coldness woke him. A cold he'd never felt before, one that turned his bones to shards of ice that pierced his soul. He'd failed to keep the fire going. *You idiot!*

And still the rain pelted down.

Chapter Sixteen

It seemed as if the surrounding mountains had snagged the clouds, for the rain persisted, now entering the third day in a row. Rose tossed her shawl over her head as she clattered her way down the sidewalks towards Oppenheimer's. The blister on her heel had healed finally, so she made good time. She passed a couple of grimy men with canvas sacks of supplies slung over their shoulders and they made her think of Harrison. How was he? Where was he?

When she came to the end of sidewalk, she stomped down the stairs to street level and picked up her skirts so she could hop across the puddles of water collecting on the street to the set of stairs leading up to the next sidewalk. She ignored the rain. Once at the store, she would be warm and dry. It would be busier than usual, for the inclement weather drew in miners from the surrounding area and the town swelled. A few of the lucky ones swaggered into Oppenheimer's to pick out the most expensive bottles of champagne and finest tobacco they could. Others, not so lucky, came to Oppenheimer's to stand by the stove and drive the chill from their bones.

She opened the door to the usual tinkle of bells. "Good morning," she sang out as she stepped inside.

Mr. Foster leaned against the end of the counter drumming his fingers. "I have some business to attend to at the bank. I'll be back shortly. You'll look after the store while I'm away?" He straightened and tucked a leather pouch under his arm. The pouch, Rose knew, contained coins, gold dust and bank notes acquired in the normal course of a day at the store.

"Of course." Rose swung off her damp shawl and hung it on the hook behind the counter.

Her boss nodded and left the store, striding down the sidewalk in his gangly style that made her think of a scarecrow.

For a moment she was alone and she unpinned her hair, combing it out with her fingers before pinning it up again. The door opened, and the first customers of the day came in, two unkempt men, their bushy beards signalling they'd been out prospecting for weeks.

"Pleased to meet you, miss." One of the two lifted his hat.

"Ma'am," corrected Rose. "I have a husband." While at the store, mention of a husband was enough to drive the men into civility.

"The pretty ones always do," he sighed, placing his hand over his heart.

"May I help you?" She stepped onto the box behind the counter and stood on her tiptoes before leaning forward on her elbows in an attempt to make herself look bigger.

"Are you alone?" The second of the two sidled over to the bar. His leering gaze sent shivers across her scalp.

She straightened and pulled her shoulders back. Lifting her chin she said, "My boss is here. He's out back. If you're not in want of anything, please leave."

"I think you have something I might want." Insolence swept over his face and Rose did not mistake his meaning.

"Leave. Or else," she said through gritted teeth. Revulsion filled her as he licked his lips.

"Or else what?"

"Or I'll report you to the authorities."

He turned to his friend. "Hear that, Benson? She'll report us to the authorities." He sauntered around the end of the counter and reached out to grab her arm. She pulled away, teetering on the edge of the box, which only made him laugh. He tugged her closer. "A kiss." He closed his eyes and puckered his lips.

With her free hand, she punched him in the temple. His eyes flipped open and hatred narrowed them to slits.

"You shouldn't have done that," he snarled, raising his fist. Rose cringed, expecting a blow at any moment. She gripped the edge of the counter to stop herself from toppling over.

Benson snatched his companion's upraised fist and pulled it away. "Stop it, Fred. We came in to buy tobacco." He tossed her an apologetic look.

"I'm not paying this harlot for anything." Fred grabbed the display of cigars on the counter top. "Let's go."

"How much do we owe you?" Benson pulled out his wallet.

"We owe her nothing. Now come on." Clutching the box of cigars, he stalked out of the store.

His friend tossed a few coins on the counter. "Sorry, miss...er, ma'am." He tipped his hat and left.

Rose continued to clutch the edge of the counter while her heart slowed. Then she sucked in a huge breath of air.

So far in her admittedly short time here in Barkerville, everyone treated her with respect. The vileness of Fred rocked her and, for a moment, a hazy image of Edmund swam before her eyes. She fought the urge to wretch.

The door tinkled and Mr. Foster strode in. He took in the situation with a glance. "Where's the box of cigars?"

"Gone," she whispered. "Two men stole them."

"That's rather incompetent of you, don't you think?"

"Incompetent? How can it be my fault?"

"I'm taking this out of your pay."

179

"That's not fair. You left me alone. What can I do against two men?"

"Exactly. What can you do? Take this as a warning. Next time, your position here will be terminated." He moved off and began dusting the shelves on the back wall.

She swallowed hard. Tomorrow she had to bring Hannah back to the doctor. How could she ask for more time off now? "Very well." She choked on the words, on the unfairness of it all.

She should look for another job, she thought. Mr. Foster was uncharitable and mean.

The door opened and a well dressed, generously curved woman entered. She marched over to Rose. "I heard about you. You're taking away my business."

"I beg your pardon?" Rose couldn't keep the surprise from her voice. How was she taking business away from this woman? Rose kept to herself and minded her p's and q's at her position here at Oppenheimer's. In fact, she'd never met the woman until this moment.

"Men." She snorted. "Not hanging around my saloon nearly as much as they used to. Now they can come here and look their fill for free. Want a job, honey?"

In a saloon? No. No, she would not stoop to that. She would not stoop to being a plaything for men.

"No thank you." She scrutinized the woman's green silk taffeta day dress with its matching brocade jacket. Stylish, yet not garish, made of fine fabrics and impeccably tailored.

Her saloon must be successful. In short, the woman did not lack for money. "Seeing you're here, may I interest you in some perfume?" She pointed to the locked glass fronted cabinet beside the end of the counter. "We just received a shipment from Victoria. It's the latest in French perfume. Would you care for a sample?"

She reached for the key hanging behind the counter and unlocked the glass door. She took out a pink glass bottle and uncorked the stopper, dabbing it on the inside wrist of the woman who lifted it to her nose for an appreciative sniff.

"Why yes, I do think I'll take it." She opened up her beaded reticule. "How much?"

"Five dollars." Rose's suspicions about the viability of the saloon were confirmed when the lady handed over the money with nary a flinch. Rose wrapped the perfume bottle in some tissue paper and ribbon she found on the shelf below the money drawer.

"I mean it." The woman took the packaged perfume. "I'm Fannie Bendixen. There's a job for you at my saloon, the Bella Union. I run a respectable establishment and my girls don't do what they don't want to do."

Rose felt her cheeks grow warm. The woman's meaning was clear. She didn't run a brothel and any unsavory conduct was strictly in the hands of the girls.

"I bid you a good day." Fannie dipped her chin and strolled out, pausing in the doorway for a moment to unfurl an umbrella.

Rose stared after her, the fragrance of the perfume lingering in the air as if to confirm the woman's offer of employment.

"You may have your faults but you certainly know how to sell." Mr. Foster's voice carried grudging respect.

Rose turned to regard him. His compliment, reluctant though it was, gave a lift to her confidence. Now was the time to mention Hannah and her appointment with the doctor tomorrow.

"I'll…." She stopped to clear her throat and started over. "I'll be late tomorrow. I need to take Hannah to the doctor again."

His face grew red. "What, more time off for your brat?"

She drew herself up and perched her fists on her hips. "Mr. Foster, you know I'm a good clerk. I'm good with numbers and customers like me. So yes, I need more time off for my daughter." She emphasized "daughter". "I'll be in tomorrow as soon as I can."

Her bold words stunned him and he pushed his chin back against his neck looking for all the world like a disapproving turkey. A calculating look filled his eyes as he gazed at her. "I'll say one thing about you," he said finally. "You may be little but you're full of gumption."

Taken aback by his words, Rose didn't know how to respond. So she said nothing, merely lifted her chin in acknowledgement at his compliment.

"Don't let it go to your head, though. If you must bring your daughter to the doctor, then so be it." His brief moment of warmth ended and he turned and shuffled off into the back room, leaving Rose feeling a bit off kilter.

He'd shown a human side just now. Some people were shy, she reasoned, and maybe his crusty exterior hid his vulnerabilities. Maybe it took him awhile to become comfortable with someone new. Maybe the longer she worked here, the more he would come to accept her. She hoped so. She liked working here, but how much better she would like it if she had an agreeable co-worker.

She gazed at the open doorway. Through it, Mr. Foster busied himself sorting through a basket of nails. He must have felt her gaze on him, for he lifted his head and looked back. The familiar scowl scrolled across his face, and any hope she had of some sort of detente fizzled.

Maybe she should reconsider finding another position elsewhere. Just not in a saloon, she vowed.

* * *

Dr. Wilkinson inspected Hannah's leg closely. "I don't think it needs another poultice. It looks to be healing nicely. She'll have a scar, though."

Relief cascaded through Rose. "Thank you, Dr. Wilkinson." She swallowed. "How much do I owe you?"

"Three dollars will cover it."

"I have two dollars. I'll pay you the rest when I can?" She held her breath, wondering what his reaction would be.

The doctor nodded. "It's an expensive place to live with a lot of dashed hopes. Including mine. I came here to look for gold too."

"Oh." She laced her fingers together, forming a solid block with her hands. Someone else with dreams of gold. Like Harrison. She squeezed her fingers, sending a silent plea for his success.

"But it didn't take me long," he continued, "to figure out there was more here for me as a doctor. So yes, I understand the scarcity of money and yes, pay me when you can."

She let out her breath. "That's so very kind. Thank you for your understanding."

He flushed at her words and he turned away to chuck Hannah under the chin. "Be a good girl for your mother."

Hannah looked at him, her eyes wide. Solemnly she nodded.

"Here." Rose fumbled in her pocket for her change purse and passed over the money.

Dr. Wilkinson took it, pitching it into a small metal box. Then he scribbled a few lines in a small notebook, which he lobbed into the box before closing the lid and hanging a padlock from the latch. "That should do it." He tossed her a quizzical glance. "Is there aught else, Mrs. Chadwick?"

She shook her head and gathered up Hannah. "Again, thank you." She stepped towards the door.

"Mrs. Chadwick?"

Rose stopped and turned back. "Yes?"

The doctor leaned against the examination table, arms crossed and a hesitant expression on his face. "I would greatly appreciate a kind word here or there among your acquaintances. I am trying to build my practice."

"Gladly." Rose smiled and left the doctor's office with a light step. Hannah would be all right. A scar was a small price to pay for a mishap that could have been a lot worse.

Hannah tugged on Rose's hand when they passed a bakery. "I'm hungry."

"I know, poppet, but I have no money. I promise we'll come back when I get paid." Her own mouth watered at the aroma of baking. Fruit pies, she thought. Something with cloves. She leaned over and gave her daughter a squeeze. "Let's go see Florence, shall we?"

"Can't I stay with you?"

"No, Mr. Foster is expecting me at the store."

"I don't like Billy. He's mean."

Rose sighed. "But it's Florence you play with, isn't it?"

Hannah shook her head. "Not always."

"What does Billy do?"

"He pulls my hair."

"Does it hurt?"

"Sometimes." Hannah rubbed her head. "Here."

Rose smothered a grin. "That just means he likes you, poppet."

"I like Florence."

"That's good," Rose murmured, gazing into the windows of shops they passed. Stoves here. Boots there. A display of fabric filled another window, and she stopped for a moment. Both she and Hannah could use more clothing and although Rose wasn't the best seamstress, she sewed passably well. Perhaps she could find a sewing machine to borrow. She'd ask Gracie.

"I like being with you better."

"Oh, Hannah." Rose sank to her knees and pulled the little girl into her arms. "You're my favorite person in the whole wide world."

"When can we see the nice man?"

Rose knew immediately she meant Harrison, for he had been kind to her little girl far from home. "I don't know where he is. I don't know if we'll ever see him again."

Pain pinched her heart at the thought. But not seeing him again was for the best. The web of untruths she had spun for herself would certainly bring contempt and dislike to his eyes if he ever found out.

And only reinforce his opinion of women being untrustworthy creatures.

Chapter Seventeen

"Does it ever stop raining in this blasted country?" Harrison tried to ignore the water dripping off the brim of his hat onto his neck.

"At least the mosquitoes are gone." Unperturbed, Robert sat on a large boulder a few feet away on the edge of the creek, concentrating on the eddying water in his gold pan.

"It's rained for a week." Harrison swirled his own pan around and around until it emptied. "The mules are growing duck feet." He didn't even need to look to know he'd find nothing. He placed the pan on the rock beside him and stood up, ready to dig into the gravel bed yet again.

"What are ye doing?" Robert's indignant squawk stopped Harrison in his tracks. "Look." His friend pointed into Harrison's pan. "There are a few flakes."

Harrison sighed. "A few flakes here, a few flakes there." He pulled off his gloves and gave a rueful glance at his wrinkled fingers. He rubbed them together in a vain attempt to warm them before pulling on his sodden gloves again.

"Remember I found this the other day." Robert pulled a pea sized nugget from his pocket. "It's my good luck charm."

"And how much luck has it brought you?"

"I think we need to dig deeper." He pointed up the creek. "A shaft. Like that crew is doing. And we should build a cradle like they have. What do you think?"

"About?"

"The shaft. This claim. Should we stake this as our own or find something better?"

"I don't know if there is anything better." Harrison knew he sounded churlish but quite frankly, he was tired. Tired and wet and cold.

"We've found a bit, wouldn't there be more buried here?"

"All right. Let me get the stakes." Harrison ducked into the tent and rummaged through his chest. He returned to his friend and held them out. "Pound these into the claim and I'll head into town to the commissioner's office to register it," he said. "I'll bring the mules back and look in on your horse too. Unless you'd rather hike into town?" He glanced over at his companion, hoping against hope Robert would be happy to let him go.

"No." Robert shook his head. "I like it out here." He stroked his beard and grinned. "I like the uncivilized look."

Harrison tilted back his head and laughed. "That you do exceedingly well." Relief bubbled through his chest. Robert was amenable to him going into Barkerville to register the claim. Plus, it showed Robert trusted him, and it pleased Harrison to know his partner thought him honest.

Anticipation welled. The thought of a night or two in a real bed and some warm meals lightened his mood. That and he'd go for a shave. A real shave, not the cold water monstrosities he'd been suffering through out here. *And maybe he'd stop into Oppenheimer's and see Rose.*

Because something had been niggling at him. He was beginning to think her husband did not exist. Since leaving Barkerville, he'd asked anyone he'd come into contact with about Edmund Chadwick but no one had heard of the man. True, several thousand men peopled the immediate area, but the camaraderie out here was unmistakeable. Surely someone would have known of him. As well, he remembered Hannah's innocent question asking him if he would be her father and Rose's sudden discomfort.

If she had no husband, what was she doing out here in the British Columbia wilderness? With a young daughter, no less.

The puzzle surrounding Rose deepened.

And he was just the man to solve it.

* * *

The rain lifted the next morning, leaving the mountains cloaked in mist and the trail a veritable bog. Harrison slogged along, pulling his string of mules behind him. They plodded after him, reaching for any blade of grass they could, which meant frequent stops. He tugged

189

them onwards repeatedly but it made for slow going.

Finally he stopped and turned to look Nancy in the eye. She blinked and swiveled her long ears forward as he began to talk. "We're going into town. Where there's hay and maybe some oats for you, so I would suggest it's in your own best interest to step lively." She lifted her head and brayed, a *hee haw* that echoed through the valley and rang in his ears.

"I hope that means yes," he muttered before turning and continuing on his way. His words seemed to have the desired effect, for the animals now trudged behind him obediently. "You're a clever girl," he tossed over his shoulder to his lead mule. "You know exactly what I'm saying, don't you?"

He rounded a bend. A man sat beneath the canopy of a spruce tree just off the trail. The closer Harrison came the more he realized the man was gaunt, nothing more than skin and bones, his clothes hanging like tattered rags from his wasted frame. He'd flung his backpack to one side and leaned against it as he gazed up at Harrison with blank eyes.

Sympathy flooded through Harrison and, despite finally having his mules moving at a reasonable pace, he stopped. The man's hollow cheeks and stringy hair shouted his despair, and Harrison could not in good conscience move on in the face of such misery without attempting to help. "Where are you bound?"

"Barkerville," rasped the man.

"Let me give you a lift on the mules."

Hope blazed in the other fellow's eyes. "You're not joshing me?" He attempted to stand but hunger made him weak and he fell back against his pack.

"No." Harrison shook his head. "I am not. As you can see," he gestured to his mules, "they're not packing anything at the moment. So yes, I'll take you into town."

"I can't pay you."

"I don't want your money."

Tears welled in the man's eyes and trickled down his weathered cheeks. "I've lost everything," he whispered. "Had a good job as a carpenter down south but got bit by the gold bug. Now I've got nothing." His chin dropped to his chest and he continued to cry, a silent display that wrenched Harrison's heart strings. He sank to his haunches for a few minutes to let the other man drain his sorrow and collect himself.

"What you need," he said when the poor soul wiped his eyes, "is a good meal and a hot bath. That'll set you right again." He held out his hand. "Harrison."

"William."

Harrison clasped William's hand and pulled him to his feet. "Let me get you on one of these mules."

With his passenger settled on Nancy and his backpack strapped on the next mule, Harrison continued. They made good time, as it seemed the mules sensed they were heading into

191

friendlier environs. He glanced back to his new passenger.

William slept, head flopping in rhythm to the mule's pace. Poor sod, thought Harrison, ample proof that most men didn't find success out here in the Cariboo gold fields. Camping and prospecting were quite the experiences, though, one he would tell his grandchildren about, but Barkerville too was an experience unto itself.

A lively town where a man could make his own way, and be whoever he wanted to be, no questions asked. A town where an English gentleman could rub shoulders with the grubbiest miner as equals.

A town where people came to escape their past and find their future. People like himself. And maybe people like Rose?

* * *

Rose saw Harrison through the window even before he stepped into the store. His hat drooped over his ears, stubble swathed his chin, and mud not only plastered his boots but his pants well past his knees. Her heart leaped into her throat before it settled back into the cavity of her chest, thumping against her rib cage like a prize fighter looking for escape.

He was here. Looking for her? *Don't be silly,* she told herself. *He's here for supplies, more likely.* Yet a little smile crept across her lips and she patted her hair and straightened her apron. He stepped inside, gaze scouring the store before he spotted her dusting the shelves in the far corner.

"Hello Rose," he said when he reached her. His voice rasped and he cleared his throat several times. "The rain," he said, "has a way of settling into a man's lungs."

"How are you? Apart from the rain and the lungs." Her voice trailed away and she couldn't gather two thoughts together to save her life. She blurted out the first thing that came to mind. "Hannah asked about you just the other day." Then kicked herself mentally. Mentioning Hannah implied a connection. She wasn't sure what kind of connection, but it certainly implied something.

"You're still alone, aren't you?" He pulled his hat off his head and held it in front of him, fingers clenched around it as if it were a life line.

She nodded.

"There is no husband, is there? I've asked around." His voice was solemn, his eyes narrowed slightly.

Her mouth dropped open at his accusation and she sucked in a huge breath of air. How did he know? Why would he care? He must care; otherwise he wouldn't confront her about it. She reached behind her with both hands to steady herself against the shelf.

She glanced over Harrison's shoulder. Mr. Foster frowned and made a great show of winding his pocket watch. Drat, she didn't even have the luxury of chatting for a few minutes. "I can't talk here," she said. "My boss doesn't like me consorting with the customers."

"Later then," he said. "You're still in the hotel?"

She nodded again, head reeling. How had he seen through her ruse? No one else thought it strange her husband hadn't appeared yet. In fact, Gracie had told her to not expect to see Mr. Chadwick for weeks. "They get caught up in the hills and the rest of the world disappears," she'd said.

"Come down to the dining room after Hannah is in bed." His firm tone didn't leave her room to refuse him, and he pounced on her hesitation. "It won't be for long." He winked at her. "I promise." He slapped the hat on his head and stepped away, weaving past the customers lined up at the counter.

It was just as well he left, because her mouth grew so dry she couldn't force her lips to move, let alone form words. What should she tell him? The truth? She shuddered. No. The truth was too ugly to contemplate.

So then what exactly should she say?

Chapter Eighteen

Harrison sat down at a vacant table in the restaurant of the Hotel de France and waved at Gracie. She hurried over. "You're back already?"

"The mules didn't like panning for gold."

"And I'm guessing you didn't either, otherwise you wouldn't be here." She cleared the dirty dishes left from the previous occupants and with her hand brushed a few crumbs onto the floor before straightening the table cloth. "What can I get for you?"

"Whiskey, please. I'm waiting for someone. Rose, actually. We have a few things to discuss."

She threw him a dubious look. "Not sure her husband is gonna like you poking around."

"That is why I'm here."

Gracie's frown told Harrison exactly what she thought about him getting involved in Rose's business.

"It's all above board, I assure you," he said.

"See that it is."

She stomped away and stomped back several minutes later with a large tumbler of whiskey, which she slapped down on the table in front of him with such force a few drops spotted the tablecloth. Not that it mattered, for a number of faded blotches and stains of unknown origin already besmirched the cloth. His mother's housekeeper would have sacked any maid in the household who couldn't launder a table cloth properly. But then, this wasn't England and Harrison rather appreciated any show of civility, stained or otherwise. "Thank you."

"You can thank me by leaving Rose alone." She stomped off again, back stiff and fists clenched.

Her show of support for Rose brought a smile to Harrison's lips. What a staunch friend and ally for Rose to have and a relief to know she wasn't entirely alone in this town. He nursed the drink, glancing at his watch repeatedly. Surely she would come down soon;; it was well past eight.

Then he spied her, standing in the doorway, scanning the room. Her face brightened when she saw him and he lifted his hand in response. He rose and pulled out the opposite chair for her, which elicited a startled look and a breathless "thank you" as she seated herself.

"Hannah's settled," she said. "I didn't tell her I was meeting you. She would have wanted to be here."

"Next time I would be delighted to include her. But I wanted your undivided attention."

"Oh?" She folded her hands into her lap and cocked her head.

Were her hands trembling? he wondered. *Is that why she hid them?* Her face was clear of emotion, although her beautiful grey eyes smouldered with a mix of apprehension and dread.

"You're not married, are you?" He plunged straight to the matter at hand.

She gasped and her face blanched. Then she swallowed hard as if she tried to keep from vomiting.

"No wait." He held up his hand. "I'm remiss in my manners. Would you care for a beverage?" Without waiting for Rose's response, he gestured to Gracie who, still showing her displeasure with Harrison, stomped over again to stand beside Rose. She dropped a hand to her friend's shoulder.

"Is he bothering you?" Gracie asked. She perched her free fist on her hip and scowled at Harrison.

He was hard pressed to keep a smile from his lips. She resembled a brash terrier and he could almost picture a stiff and prickly ruff around her neck, could almost hear the menacing growls. A terrier full of heart, defending its master to the hilt.

Rose shook her head. "Tea," she said, her voice a whispery croak.

That she was fearful did not please Harrison. What was she hiding? Why did the question scare her so? A simple yes or no was all he required.

He leaned back in his chair. "I don't mean to frighten you."

She blinked.

"I find it rather perturbing," he began, "that you have a husband who doesn't show the slightest inclination to greet you and your daughter. I suppose, since meeting up with you on the road, I am feeling a bit protective of you both."

Her mouth twisted and she glanced away. The glow from the oil lamps cast a becoming peach hue to her skin and he fought the urge to reach over and smooth her lips with his fingers.

"So it only makes sense to me that you have no husband," he continued.

She looked at him as if he'd grown an extra ear. She licked her lips and took in a deep breath. "No. There's no husband," she said finally. "I thought it would be better to pretend I have one. I didn't want to draw attention as a single woman."

"Well, that sure didn't work, did it? The whole town knows about you and where you work."

Rose snorted. "I suppose that makes me rather notorious." The corners of her mouth quivered, as if she suppressed a smile.

"You're a widow, then. That makes sense. I can certainly understand inventing a husband for safety's sake and the sake of your daughter."

He reached out and took her hands in his. His fingers tingled where he touched hers and sheer joy pummeled him. He would woo Rosamund Arabella Ruth Chadwick relentlessly until she agreed to be his wife.

Then stopped right there. The last time someone agreed to be his wife, he was left standing at the altar. He pulled away his hands. But he couldn't foist Nancy's deeds onto Rose. She was a different woman altogether, plucky, self-reliant, and devoted to her daughter.

He contemplated grasping her hands again but confusion wrinkled her brow at his previous action, and she bit her lip. Which only had the effect of making him want to kiss her.

Egads, what was wrong with him? He had a simple acquaintance with Rose, yet she intrigued him. Only by spending more time with her would he get to know her better, past the realm of acquaintance and into the realm of friendship and beyond that, matrimony. He scratched his head. Getting to know her better would be impossible once he returned to the claim and Robert. That thought, particularly after the past miserable week, was not inviting at all right now. Yet he couldn't give up already on his dreams of striking it rich, and he couldn't let down his family. He gave a last, regretful glance to Rose's lips.

"Let's order, shall we?" He put his hand up in the air to flag down Gracie who, when she came over, informed them the only thing left was beef stew.

"Beef stew it is," he said.

Rose had the feeling Harrison's suddenly brisk air masked something deeper. She'd seen the considering look in his eyes just now and the way his gaze dropped to her mouth. Ordinarily, a man's attention would have set her skin crawling, but it felt different with Harrison. He was a kind, honorable man and, when he smiled, her insides turned to mushy pudding.

A sudden giddiness came over her. How convenient that Harrison automatically assumed she was a widow. It saved her from making any explanations and it saved Hannah's reputation.

He appeared to enjoy her company, and she certainly enjoyed his but she must be careful. She hated the deception she played but she had no choice. Rose had no place in Harrison's life. He, a fine English lord, and she, a mule skinner's daughter. No. It just couldn't be.

Dinner, when it finally came, tasted like sawdust in Rose's mouth. Harrison chatted a little but he focused on his meal. He waited for her to finish before pushing his chair from the table.

"Good night." He stood and bowed. "May I call on you tomorrow? Before I head back out?"

"Call on me?" It was as if Harrison couldn't make up his mind to keep his distance or not. She looked at him, hoping he didn't notice the heat in her cheeks. "All right," she said. "Only not at Oppenheimer's. Mr. Foster is not the most congenial man." She made a little moue with her mouth.

He chuckled. "Until tomorrow then. I'll pick you up here after work and we'll take Hannah to the bakery."

Rose watched him walk off. She really shouldn't encourage him, for she didn't know his intentions. He seemed to like Hannah and how thoughtful of him to include her tomorrow, but Hannah was not his daughter. Hannah was Rose's responsibility and that's all there was to it.

Harrison disappeared through the doorway but, despite her stern words to herself, she couldn't suppress the yearning. *I'd like to spend more time with him.*

Once more. Just once more she would see him before she pulled herself and Hannah away.

Chapter Nineteen

Harrison bought a copy of the local newspaper, *The Cariboo Sentinel*, the next morning to enjoy while he sipped his coffee. The date, June 10, 1867, startled him. Had it really been five months since Nancy jilted him? He scanned the crisp pages, ignoring the ads but reading the snippets about life in Barkerville tucked in amongst news from beyond the valley. However, the lead story about the Dominion of Canada caught his attention:

"The new power is to be known as Canada, and is to be governed, under the Queen by a Governor General, by and with the advice of a Privy Council, the number whereof is not stated in the Act—that being considered, we presume, a matter of prerogative. The members of the Privy Council are to be styled 'Right Honourables' as in England, the only indication of a titled order given in the bill, or indicated anywhere, as desirable or congenial to the Canadian people."

He remembered an older newspaper article he'd read earlier while sitting on the paddle wheeler from Victoria. It talked about The British North America Act, the legislation passed by British Parliament and signed by Queen Victoria this past March. To take effect on July 1, it would unite the British colonies of Quebec, Ontario, Nova Scotia and New Brunswick into the Dominion of Canada.

Would the colony of British Columbia join the Dominion one day? If so, what a magnificent country, he thought, stretching from the Atlantic Ocean to the Pacific Ocean.

Breakfast finished, he folded up the paper and tucked it into the pocket of his pants then headed over to Mundorf Stables to deal with his mules.

He found Mundorf mucking out one of the stables. The man stopped and leaned on his pitchfork, swatting at a persistent fly buzzing around his ear.

"I've brought my mule team back into town," Harrison said. "You have a fine facility and I'd like to leave them here."

"Starving out in the hills, were they?" He spat into the cart full of manure and dirtied straw.

"Can we negotiate a better price? Two dollars a day per head is a bit steep for my pocket. I could manage it for the few nights we were here before but I'd like to keep my mules. Who knows how long it will be before our claim yields any gold."

Mundorf squinted at him. "I don't run a charity. It costs money to freight in hay."

"But the stalls are empty. You must be looking for animals to fill them." Harrison drew himself up. "I have four mules. How about fifty cents per day per mule?"

"How about you go jump in Williams Creek?"

Harrison tried not to take offence. "Come now, Mr. Mundorf. We're men of business. Surely we can come to some sort of mutual agreement."

"I'm a man of business. You're a miner."

"There's no need to be haughty. How about a dollar a head?"

"Two dollars a head. Read the sign out front."

"How about if I give you my wagon?"

"What do I want with a wagon?" Mundorf pulled at his beard.

"It's worth something."

"Assuming I could sell it."

"Mr. Mundorf, I am pleading for your understanding. I have no wish to part with my mule team, and until my partner and I achieve success with our claim, I have limited funds." He pulled off his hat and turned his back. With his pinkie finger, he pried out one of the three gold coins tucked away in the sweat band. He held it in his palm for a moment, savoring the weight. These coins were his ticket home, but two should be sufficient to buy him passage if need be. He pushed away his regret, turned back to face the other man and held out the coin. "Here. I'm a man of my word."

Mundorf eyed it greedily. "Okay. A dollar a day for three of the mules. That's all I have room for." He hefted the coin in his hand.

"This'll do you for three weeks. And if you're not back by then, I sell them. "

Harrison exhaled. Three mules. Better than nothing. He would simply take Nancy with him; he'd grown rather fond of her. He stuck out his hand. "I thank you."

"Don't thank me." He held up the coin between his thumb and index finger. "Thank this. Money talks." He slipped it into his shirt pocket.

"I'll take a look at Brutus while I'm here," Harrison said. "He belongs to my partner," he added, thinking an explanation might be in order to appease the man as to why Harrison wished to inspect the horse.

"Yep, I still have him. His owner paid up for a month." Mundorf nodded. "He's a fine one and fattening up nicely. You should consider racing him next Saturday."

"Is there a race track nearby?"

"Oh no. Right down main street. It's quite a spectacle. And the prize money's good." He grabbed his pitch fork, stabbing it into the soiled straw. Apparently, he'd had enough of their conversation.

Harrison's skin tingled at the prospect of a horse race. There's nothing he liked better than a jolly afternoon on horseback and well, if that involved wagers, so much the better. He could hardly wait to talk to Robert about it.

Now it was off to the claims office to register their claim, and then it would be time to pick up Rose and Hannah.

205

His step quickened.

* * *

Harrison and Rose, swinging Hannah between them, strolled down the boardwalk to the New England Bakery and Coffee Saloon. Rose and Hannah waited outside and soon Harrison returned with a tray carrying bannock smeared with huckleberry jam, two mugs of steaming coffee, and a mug of milk.

Once again his thoughtfulness towards Hannah struck Rose. Milk. Who would expect a man with no children of his own to buy milk for a little girl? She peeked at him, but he was focused on balancing the tray so he didn't notice. Her gaze ran over his freshly shaven cheeks, then dropped to his freshly polished boots. Everything about him pointed to fine breeding and impeccable manners, and she wondered what he saw in her, a single mother with nothing to her name save the few clothes she'd brought with her and her mother's gold wedding ring.

"Let's go sit by the creek." He pointed with his chin. "Hannah, why don't you take your Mama's hand and the two of you can find a good place to sit."

As they got closer to the creek, Hannah let go of Rose's hand and hopped from rock to rock, crooning a few words every time she landed successfully. "I'm a good girl." Jump. "I like Florence." Jump. "I love Mummy." Jump.

"I'd like a Papa." She turned around and looked at Harrison.

"That's enough Hannah. Wait for me." Rose knew her cheeks flamed and she avoided glancing at Harrison as she studiously picked her way to Hannah. "Shhh," She placed her fingers on her daughter's lips. "We'll have no more talk of Papa," she whispered. She turned to look at Harrison.

He followed more slowly, balancing the tray as he stepped over the jumbled boulders lining the creek. The rushing stream must have drowned out Hannah's voice, for it appeared he hadn't heard her. Rose relaxed.

"Here." Hannah waved her arms. "I want to sit here." She plopped down and sat astride a long, narrow stone with a hump on one end that vaguely resembled a hobby horse.

Rose settled herself close by, tucking her skirts around her ankles and adjusting her shawl. She lifted her face to catch the cool air wafting from the water. Her scalp still prickled from Hannah's comment and, with any luck, the breeze would calm it.

"Gibbs wouldn't believe this if he saw it," Harrison remarked to Rose. He sank to his knees beside her.

"Gibbs?"

"Our butler." He held out the tray. "Could you take this for a moment?"

"Of course." A butler. His family had a butler. How daunting. Rose grabbed the tray and waited while Harrison sat down on an upended

207

stump. He shifted back and forth to find a comfortable position, then held out his hands. Rose handed back the tray.

"Help yourself. There's milk for Hannah."

"I saw that, thank you." She took the mug of milk and held it out to the little girl, who spilled some of it as she repositioned herself on her rock.

"Careful, poppet" warned Rose. "What do you say to Mr. St. John?"

"Thank you," she chirped.

"There's a piece of bannock for you when you finish your milk." Harrison tapped the tray. "But I'll keep it for you until you're ready."

Rose and Harrison sipped their coffee, and soon Hannah slid off the rock. "I can't finish it." She handed her half empty mug to Rose, then looked up at Harrison, clearly expecting her bannock. He made a great show of looking in her mug. "That's a lot of milk for a little girl to drink. I daresay you deserve your bannock now." He made as if to pour out the rest of the milk on the gravel patch beside him.

"I'll take it," Rose blurted. "It's a shame to waste it." Then hoped he wouldn't think her silly. Doubtless in his household back in England, they didn't think twice over wasting milk.

"It is." He looked serious. "Waste not, want not," he added then passed over the mug.

She poured the rest of the milk into her coffee and sipped the creamy mixture while Hannah, bannock in hand, squatted by the water's edge, tossing in twigs and scooping sand and gravel into little piles.

"Have you heard?" asked Harrison.

"Heard what?"

He yanked the paper from his pocket and unfolded it. He pointed to the headline, "'Dominion of Canada'. On July 1, the British North America Act comes into being, forming the Dominion of Canada."

"I didn't know."

"A new and growing country. The perfect place for a man to make something of himself." His face grew animated, and she could see the thought of remaining here appealed to him.

He changed the subject. "What brought you here?"

Rose's heart began to pound. "I wanted to move," she said evasively. "I didn't like my job in Victoria and thought perhaps it was time for adventure."

"You couldn't find work in Victoria?"

"Well, it seemed exciting. To join a gold rush. Talk of it filled Victoria for years."

"Do you like it?"

Rose shrugged. "I'm not very settled yet. The room we have is comfortable but it's not really home. And I'm not too sure about my boss, Mr. Foster. I always feel as if I must tiptoe to avoid annoying him. It makes me feel rather off balance, to tell you the truth.

"You enjoy working?"

"I do. I like being self sufficient and looking after myself and Hannah. Besides, I don't have any choice, do I?"

"I admire your independence."

His compliment warmed her and she faced him. "And you? Are you enjoying your gold mining?"

"Do you want the stark truth or a sugar coated version of the truth?" His voice was wry.

Rose picked up a pebble and tossed it into the stream. "The truth as you see it."

"I'm not sure I like it at all. I like the prospect of striking gold. Who wouldn't? But it's back breaking labour and has destroyed many men. Although I do enjoy working with my hands."

"Wasn't your life easier back in England?"

"Easier in some respects, yes. But I always hated the bowing and the scraping, the platitudes because I am the Viscount St. John. Not seeing the man, only the title and the house." He leaned back on his hands and looked up at the sky. "And the expectation that I would marry for money. I had no say in the matter. It was just what was expected of me. Stiff upper lip and all that rot."

"Then she jilted you. How humiliating."

He grimaced. "More of a blow to my pride. Anyway, that's history. I'm back to the claim tomorrow. It's registered and all, and Robert is waiting for me."

The thought of Harrison's departure brought an ache to her chest. He made her feel cherished and as if she counted for something, a welcome sensation and one new to her. To her father, she had been an unwelcome burden and a constant reminder of the wife who died and left him with a young daughter to raise on his own.

"We really must be going. It's getting late." She gestured to the shadows fingering their way across the rocky ground. "Once the sun goes behind the mountains, it gets dark quickly."

"Of course." He got to his feet and dusted off his pants, then strung the handles of the mugs on the curled fingers of his left hand and tucked the tray under the same arm. He held out his free hand towards her. "Let me help you up."

She took it, liking the feel of her hand clasped in his warm, firm one. She wished she could hold it forever, drawing courage and strength from it. Harrison had said he admired her independence, but the truth was she was scared to death inside. Scared of being unable to care for Hannah properly. Scared of failing here in this gold rush town where opportunity waited for those who took it.

Scared of Edmund finding her again, because this time she didn't know how to fight him—she couldn't keep running forever.

Harrison pulled her up, but when she tried to pull free her hand, he squeezed and wouldn't let it go. He cocked his head and gave her a lopsided grin, and her world rocked for a moment with the rush of pleasure at his

211

attention. She couldn't tear her gaze away from his eyes, warm with admiration. Again his lips dropped to her mouth and, if it hadn't been for Hannah, she would have lifted her mouth to his for one stolen kiss.

Hannah tugged on her skirt and the magic moment was lost. Rose managed to free her gaze and looked down to see Hannah, who waved her half eaten slice of bannock at Rose.

"Can I feed the birds?"

"We can but not until tomorrow because it's time for bed. Why don't you lick off the jam and put the rest of it in your pocket until then?" suggested Rose, holding out her hand.

Hannah shook her head and skipped around Rose to Harrison's side. "Can I hold your hand?"

"Of course not, he has his hands full," exclaimed Rose, mortified at Hannah's boldness.

"I wouldn't if your mama carried the mugs." Over Hannah's head, Harrison's eyes twinkled at her and the mugs clinked as he held them out. What could she do but acquiesce, so grim lipped, she grabbed them and clutched them by the handles like he had.

Then he bent down to Hannah. "You can carry the tray. It's not heavy." As if he sensed Rose's apprehension, he looked up at her. "It's wood, she can't break it."

No, thought Rose. She can't break the tray. But you could break her heart.

The last thing she wanted was for Hannah to become close to Harrison. It would be too cruel for the little girl to think she had a papa, a papa who would one day disappoint her by disappearing back to England.

But who would be the most disappointed? Hannah?

Or Rose?

Chapter Twenty

Mr. Foster again left Rose in charge the next morning while he went to Barnard's Express office to pick up a shipment of flour and syrup. She felt restless and unsettled and, as much as she wanted to deny it, the thought of Harrison's departure gnawed at her like a beaver felling a tree.

Or perhaps it was the sunshine that finally appeared that put her on edge, for the customers in the store also seemed unsettled. The rowdy lot were like little boys, pushing and shoving and jostling for her attention. Despite her repeated pleas to stop, they ignored her. Finally, she grabbed a pot and a wooden spoon.

"Stop it!" She banged the spoon against the pot.

No luck, the caterwauling continued. "I said stop it!" This time she screamed it out.

Still no luck. Finally she hitched up her skirts and hoisted herself up on the counter. "Gentlemen, I've had enough." She banged the pot so ferociously, she left dents, but at least this time they paid attention to her.

Someone whistled. "Lookit those ankles!"

"Oh my lord." The tall man closest to the counter clasped his heart and looked skyward. "I've seen an angel."

Too late she realized her skirt and petticoat had become tangled up and exposed one leg up to her knee, the other to mid shin. That, plus her position atop the counter, afforded the men a perfect vista of her legs.

The jostling began anew as, this time, every man in the store shifted position in order to get a better view. The tall man who had called her an angel rammed the man beside him with a sharp elbow and the unlucky recipient lost his balance, tumbling head first into the display case of fine liquors.

Crash! The glass fronted case toppled to the ground amidst the chink of broken glass. Several bottles broke, and the aroma of fine scotch whiskey and fruity red wine filled the air as rivers of whiskey and wine meandered across the planked floor. The tall man started to laugh and soon the entire shop joined in, laughing at the poor soul nursing several cuts on his cheeks from the broken glass. Blood dripped onto his beard and he rubbed one hand across his face. When he pulled it away, blood smeared the palm. He wiped his palm on his pants and stood up. He glared at the tall man. "We should take this outside," he said. Sudden silence filled the store as the store's occupants watched the unfolding tableau.

Rose slid off the counter and sidled over to see the injured man. She laid a hand on his arm. The last thing she wanted was for the fight to continue outside the store, blocking the door from any other customers. "I don't think that's wise," she murmured. "I think you should see Dr. Wilkinson."

The man shook his head as if to clear it. "Naw. I'll be fine." His lip curled and he gestured to his assailant. "Come on. Outside."

The door opened and the bell's tinkle, normally so cheerful, now sounded ominous.

"What is going on here?" Mr. Foster stood there, thin face glowering and mouth quivering. His gaze circled the crowd and he pointed to the door. "Get out." The men in the store took one look at his face and one by one, they slunk away.

Rose's heart sank. Why couldn't he have stayed away a little longer, at least long enough for her to clear the store and mop up? And maybe give her some time to come up with a reason why the glass case now lay shattered on the floor. She opened her mouth to apologize but shut it again when Foster advanced menacingly and pointed a finger at her.

"You're done. This store can't take the ruckus you've brought in." He stalked behind the counter and yanked open the cash drawer with so much force, his jowls shook. He pulled out a few coins and tossed them at her feet. "Here's five dollars. I shouldn't pay you anything at all. The store was robbed while under your supervision. You've taken time off for your brat and now this."

"Please, give me another chance."

"I can't afford to give you another chance."

"But my daughter...."

216

"That, Mrs. Chadwick, is not my concern. Go find your husband. Find another job. Leave Barkerville. Do whatever you like. But don't come back here." He turned his back to her to survey the damage.

Rose stared at his rigid back and clenched fists, blinking hard to keep back the tears. He'd finally found a way to get rid of her. Her chest tightened as she inspected the coins on the floor.

She had a mind to walk out and leave the money, but practicality won out and she stooped to retrieve the coins. Sudden anger spurted through her. She marched over to the window and yanked her bolero and belt from the display of clothing. "You won't pay me what I'm owed? For something that is not my fault? Then I'm taking this back." She charged out the door, half expecting to hear footsteps pounding behind her, and darted across the street, zigzagging through the parade of wagons and livestock.

Where could she hide?

* * *

As soon as Rose realized Mr. Foster did not pursue her, she stopped and crumpled against the front of a building a few doors away from the Hotel de France. Her heart raced, sweat gummed her palms, and despair rode on her shoulders. With her back to the wall, she slid to her haunches, not caring if the rough wooden siding snagged her clothing, and stared blankly ahead.

She was right back where she was when she first arrived here—with several dollars in her pocket and no work. She owed money to the hotel and to Florence, and she only had a few scraps of food in her room, whatever she'd managed to save from her meals. Enough to feed Hannah tonight but not much else.

Passers-by gave her a few curious stares but they must have understood her state of mind, for they left her alone. She sat there a good fifteen minutes before finally placing her hands on the planks to push herself to her feet. With her palms planted on the wall behind her to give her support, she stood. A string of pack mules led by a Chinese mule skinner plodded their way down the street and mindlessly, she counted them. Ten mules. Then a couple of men on horseback guided a small herd of cattle up the street towards the slaughterhouse in Richfield and she counted them too. Sixteen. Enough to feed a small town. A town in which, it appeared, she did not belong.

A gust of wind swept against her legs, tearing at her skirts and ruffling her hair. She shook her head. *I can't stand here all day.* But standing here was all she could manage because she was empty inside. A failure. Perhaps her father had been justified in banishing her; perhaps Edmund was the kind of man she deserved.

Perhaps she should acknowledge defeat and return to Victoria.

The desire to lay her head on Harrison's chest overwhelmed her and, for a few seconds, she swayed as if on a tilting deck. In her mind, she could hear his words: "I admire your independence."

Rose straightened her shoulders and lifted her chin. Harrison thought her independent. An independent woman would not give up. He expected her to find a solution and she wouldn't let him down.

He wasn't here but Gracie was. Her friend would help her figure things out.

* * *

Rose stepped into the kitchen of the hotel and, ignoring Ming's scowl of displeasure, made her way over to Gracie.

"What happened to you?" Gracie took one look at her and dropped the carrot she was slicing into rounds.

Rose marshalled her thoughts and didn't answer right away.

"Well?" Gracie wiped her hands on her wrinkled apron, leaving faint orange smears on it. She gave Rose an expectant look that brooked no nonsense.

Rose felt as if she were a butterfly pinned to a board. Even if she wanted to bend the truth, Gracie would see through her.

"I lost my job." She choked back the sobs.

"You didn't like Mr. Foster. There are other jobs."

"I don't know. There are so many men here. I attract attention wherever I go, and I'm pretty sure word of what happened this morning at Oppenheimer's will spread." She wiped a tear from her cheek. "No other store will want me. I'm nothing but trouble."

"What happened?"

As Rose recounted the tale, Gracie's lips twisted as if she were hard pressed to keep the giggles inside. "Shame about the booze," she said when Rose finished. "But maybe working in a store isn't right for you. There are other businesses here that you could try." She ticked off her fingers as she listed them. "Bakeries. Restaurants. Post office. Laundries." She gave Rose a calculating look. "Although that's hard work and maybe not right for you." She held up her thumb. "Of course, there are a lot of saloons. Bet you'd do real well in one of those. Fellows are generous once they get a few drinks in them. Mind you," Gracie rubbed her chin, "Hannah might not like that much, with you leaving her in the evenings. Ain't you expecting yer husband?"

Rose stared at Gracie. Here was her chance to clear the air but how would her friend react? "I'm not married." Rose blurted.

Gracie's expression didn't change. "Hmm. I was wondering about him. But I kinda knew anyway."

"You knew?"

"It's the way you look at Harrison. Now I'd look at him that way," she guffawed, "but you're right and proper and wouldn't look at any man but your husband. So I figured you didn't have one."

"There's something else you should know. About Hannah." The burden of deceit started slipping from Rose's shoulders like a prospector's battered backpack. She opened her mouth to explain.

"No." Gracie held up her hand. "I don't need to know anything about Hannah that I don't already know. She's a good girl and she is where she is through no fault of her own."

Gracie did not judge her, did not judge Hannah. A tingling warmth rolled through Rose and she closed her eyes in relief for a second for revealing the truth to at least her friend. That still didn't change her situation, though. "I've nowhere to go." She pulled the coins out of her pocket. "This is what he paid me."

"Cheap bastard." Her friend's voice dripped with contempt. "Like I said, you're best off without him."

"I can pay for my hotel room, but that'll take all I have."

"Come and stay with us for a day or two while you get your head back on straight."

"You don't have any room. I've seen your cabin."

"There's always room for them that needs help."

"Then yes. Thank you." Rose looked down at the braided gold ring on her finger. She walked past the assay office every day on her way to Oppenheimer's. Gold was gold, wasn't it? They would pay her something, anyway. Enough to keep her going for a few more days. The thought hurt, though. Selling it there was permanent. Once she sold it, it would be lost to her forever.

A clang sounded as if someone banged a lid on a pot and Gracie looked over Rose's shoulder. "I best be getting back to work. Ming's getting fretful. Get your things and go to my place."

Rose nodded. "I will." She ducked out the back door and headed over to the assay office.

"How much will you give me for this ring?" Her hand shook as she held it out.

The yawning clerk took it from her and weighed it. He pulled out a ledger book and ran his finger down a column of pre-calculated figures. "Four dollars. That includes our fee."

"That's all?" Rose snatched it back. "Never mind."

"Whatever you say." The clerk shrugged and let out another yawn.

Rose slid the ring back on her finger. Four dollars was not enough to convince her to let go of the only thing she had belonging to her mother.

She made her way back to the hotel and packed up the clothes. Then she cleared her bill and made her way to Gracie's cabin.

"Hannah and I are staying with you for awhile," she informed Florence. Hannah clapped her hands at the news. At least Hannah was happy here. "I'm dropping off our things then I have something I need to do." She dropped a kiss on her daughter's tousled head. "I won't be long, poppet."

She trudged to the Bella Union Saloon, every step feeling as if she slogged through heavy mud. She stood in front of one of the windows and peered through. Fannie Bendixen, the woman she'd sold perfume to, polished tables with a white cloth and beeswax. Today Fannie wore a high necked dress of rose satin trimmed with cream coloured velvet ribbon. Rose glanced down in disgust at her own outfit, the only dress she had brought, a beige and black striped poplin with tight fitting sleeves and a row of tiny ebony buttons down the bodice. Not the most stylish but she'd bought it because she figured the plain style wouldn't attract much notice.

Rose smoothed the skirt a few times, not so much to flatten the wrinkles as to dry her damp palms. Every fibre of her being screamed for her to run away. A dancing girl. A saloon girl. An enticement for men. An object to be pawed and petted.

But everyone told her she could make good money, and she needed to provide for herself and Hannah. Desperation pushed her to it, she told herself. Surely no one would fault a mother wanting to look after her child. She swallowed hard and took a step toward the door. Then stopped.

What would Harrison think when he found out? She shuddered at the thought and jammed her hands in her pockets.

And stared at the brightly painted door to the Bella Union Saloon.

Chapter Twenty-One

The only thing making the day bearable was the sun. It dried out the tent, and Harrison strung out every single piece of clothing he owned on the rope stretched between two trees for precisely that purpose. Warm dry clothing was a luxury he'd missed.

"Are ye finished?" At Robert's humor filled voice, Harrison turned.

"I've had enough of soggy clothing."

"Till the next time it rains." Robert gestured. "Remember those nails and canvas we bought? I'll show ye what I built while you were in town."

Harrison followed his friend down to the edge of the creek. "So this is it?"

"Aye. That's our rocker. A few of the fellows helped me put one together."

He inspected the contraption closely. It vaguely resembled a baby's cradle with an upright handle on one end and a box on top. Beneath the box, canvas covered a sloping and rounded surface.

"How does it work?"

"We shovel the gravel into the box. They call it a hopper." Robert pointed. "See, it has holes in it. When one of us pours in water, the other one rocks it with the handle. The water pours through the holes with any gold dust or, better yet, nuggets." He grinned and gave a thumbs up signal. "The larger rocks stay in the hopper. It's a lot faster than the gold pan. If we're good at it, we can do maybe two hundred buckets a day."

"Impressive," murmured Harrison.

"And we're going to build a shaft." Robert gestured to a small stack of axe hewn logs. "We'll shore it up with that."

"You've been busy."

"I had no one to talk to, may as well work."

"Let's get started then. Perhaps we should take turns on rocking and pouring?"

"Sure." Robert grabbed his shovel and a bucket. "This'll be our test run." He filled the bucket with dirt and gravel from the creek side and dumped it in the box. Then he sloshed into the creek and filled two buckets with water. "Let's go," he said. "Start rocking it. Some guys call this a cradle."

Harrison grabbed the handle and pushed it back and forth while Robert poured in first one bucket, then the second. By the time the second bucket was emptied, larger rocks and pebbles remained in the box while all the sand and finer bits of gravel washed through onto the canvas apron below.

"See any gold? It should be caught on the apron."

"Nothing."

"Again," said Robert. "Empty the hopper for the next batch."

Harrison did as he was told and watched Robert dump another bucket of gravel in the hopper.

"This time we'll be lucky." Robert poured the water into the hopper.

"Brutus is recovering nicely," Harrison said as he rocked the cradle back and forth. Water streamed out the bottom of the box in uneven bursts. "Mundorf suggested I run him in a horse race."

"Horse race? They do that here?" Robert grunted as he wrestled with his shovel in the firm packed beach of the creek. He filled another bucket full of gravel.

Harrison shrugged. "Apparently." He rocked the handle back and forth when Robert poured in the water until only rocks remained in the hopper. "What do you think? Should we race him? The purse could be rich."

"Maybe. Although I hate to leave the claim so soon after getting the rocker built. Seems like we should spend a little time digging."

"Sure." Harrison pushed aside thoughts of racing Brutus. In truth, his desire to return to Barkerville had more to do with seeing Rose than racing a horse. How was she?

Rocks clattered in the hopper as Robert dumped more gravel in it and thoughts of Rose fled while Harrison concentrated on his work. The two of them were getting the hang of it and processing the sand and gravel much more quickly.

The sun was high overhead when they broke for lunch. "After lunch I'll dig and you rock," said Harrison. He welcomed the change because his arms burned with the monotonous motion of rocking the cradle. Digging gravel would also be challenging, but the change would work a different set of muscles, he surmised.

Harrison had dug perhaps his tenth bucket when Robert yelled out.

"Look," crowed Robert. "Gold!"

Collected on the riffles in the canvas was a narrow line of gold dust interspersed with tiny, raggedy edged nuggets.

Harrison leaned on the handle of his shovel and stared at it. "Do you think that's even an ounce?" It was a lot of work for such little reward.

"We'll have better luck the deeper we go. At least we know we have some sort of seam here." Robert scraped the gold into a leather pouch.

By the end of the day, the beginnings of a shaft could be seen outlined in the gravelled bank of the creek. Their little gold mine began to take shape, and satisfaction coursed through Harrison as he regarded it in the fading sunlight, along with amazement at what a man could build with his own two hands. He flexed his hands, liking the feel of the calluses on his palms. "We should have a name for it. Any ideas?"

"Victoria?" suggested Robert. "For the queen?"

"Not very imaginative. How about Witch of Macbeth? You know, '*Double, double toil and trouble*' We're having our fill of toil and trouble here," Harrison joked.

Robert chuckled. "I like it. Witch of Macbeth it is. Or The Witch for short. Because gold practices its own form of sorcery on a man."

"Sorcery indeed."

"Tomorrow we'll start laying logs to shore up the walls." Robert stacked his shovel and the buckets beside the tent.

Harrison nodded. "Let's take a look at what we found today."

Robert pulled out the pouch from his pocket and loosened the draw strings. Carefully he tapped the bag to loosen the contents onto his handkerchief, spread out on a nearby stump. "Beautiful sight," he whispered.

Harrison inspected their gold. Albeit a small reward, it was a start. "Agreed." What was it the Chinese philosopher Lao Tzu said? A journey of a thousand miles begins with a single step? In this case, the building of a fortune begins with a single sack.

He tried to picture St. John Manor, its mellow brick walls cornered by four square towers, but all he could see was Rose. Rose sipping her coffee the evening before he returned to the claim. Rose blushing when he pulled her chair out for her at the dinner table. Rose cuddling Hannah.

How many days before he could honestly say to Robert he wanted to sell out and return to Barkerville? Yet how could he in all good conscience do that when the fate of his family home depended on his success in the Cariboo gold fields?

* * *

The weather held for the following two weeks and "The Witch" extended deeper and deeper. Robert had rigged up a rough ladder and a pulley system to haul up the buckets of gravel. The pile of discarded rocks grew until it resembled a small rocky hill on their claim site.

"You don't think we're covering up the seam, do you?" Harrison mopped his brow and jammed his hat back on his head. He surveyed the burgeoning pile. "I don't fancy the idea of having to move that if we decide to search over there."

Robert clambered out of the shaft. "I don't think so. I think we're doing the right thing building a shaft. Don't forget Billy Barker went down fifty-two feet before he struck it rich."

Fifty-two feet? How in blazes could they dig that deep with the limited equipment they had? As it was, they were only eight feet down and standing in water up to their knees while digging. "On Williams Creek. Not here."

Robert dusted off the sleeves of his shirt and didn't answer.

"My turn down below." Harrison rotated his shoulders and grabbed his shovel. He tossed it down the shaft and climbed down, wincing when the icy water, fresh off the mountains, filled his boots. He loaded the bucket and tied the rope to the handle. "Haul her up," he shouted to Robert.

The bucket bounced and scraped along the wall and Harrison gave it a boost from below. As hard as he tried while filling it, he couldn't keep water out of it, and some of it splashed over the bucket's lip and drenched his shoulders. Egads, could this job be any more miserable? He was beginning to realize the lure of mining for gold became dimmer by the day for him. Yet how could he disappoint his partner? And his family?

"Fill up a few more buckets before you climb up."

With a sigh, Harrison bent his back to the task. The confined space made it difficult to maneuver the shovel. With a muffled curse, he tossed in one last shovelful in the third bucket he'd filled and glanced at the contents. *Why bother?* he thought with contempt, for nothing could be seen in the murky light at the bottom of the shaft.

"Enough!"

A relieved Harrison leaned the shovel against the wall of the shaft and shimmied up

231

the ladder to find Robert shoveling gravel into the hopper.

"I really don't see how we're going to manage going much deeper," said Harrison. "The ladder's too short."

"We'll nail it to the logs and build another one."

"I don't think it's going to be that easy. We don't know how secure the walls are." He pulled off his boots to empty out the water. Then he stripped off his socks and hung them out to dry. He grabbed a dry pair from the line but before putting them on inspected his swollen feet, sickly white in the sunlight. They weren't sore, but they didn't look healthy and the yellowed toe nails stood out against the flesh like slabs of cheese. He rubbed his feet briefly, then put on his socks and boots. Immediately the wet boots dampened his socks and he wondered why he'd bothered to put dry ones on.

Robert must have sensed his misgiving. "Sassenach, don't worry. It'll be fine."

Robert's glib reassurance disturbed Harrison. "What, my feet or the shaft?" The two of them weren't civil engineers, knew nothing about building a structure, especially one that was underground. As far as his feet, he suspected days in cold wet boots had a lot to do with their sad state, and they wouldn't improve until he could don decent footwear.

"Let's finish off with this pile and call it a day. I have half a bottle of brandy stashed away."

"Sure." Harrison nodded and got to his feet. "I'll rock."

It didn't take long to process the last few buckets, yielding a bit of dust and a couple of nuggets the size of grains of rice.

"At this rate, it's going to take us years." Harrison shook his head.

"At least give it the summer. I admit, I thought we'd be finding more. Maybe this creek's not as lucrative as some of the fellows have made out."

The summer. It was now mid-July, so that meant at least another six weeks sitting out here with nothing but back breaking labour, mosquitoes and flies. It seemed daunting to Harrison.

* * *

"Bloody hell." Robert's voice woke Harrison the next morning. "The shaft's collapsed."

Which is what I alluded too yesterday, thought Harrison, but he kept that thought to himself.

"Egads, no!" He dragged himself out of his sleeping bag and poked his head out the tent to see his partner squatting at the edge of their shaft. Harrison made his way over to Robert and dropped to his knees to look over the edge. Below him a jumble of gravel and dirt filled the bottom of the excavation, interspersed with logs sticking out at odd angles. In the middle of the pile, the end of a shovel handle poked up. His shovel. He'd forgotten it down there last night and now it had turned into a forlorn sentinel, standing guard over their dashed hopes.

Harrison didn't know whether to be elated or distraught. On the one hand, weeks of work was destroyed; on the other hand, perhaps Robert would agree the venture was futile. He rolled his shoulders forwards and backwards, trying to work away the sudden tension. "What do we do now?"

Robert's normally cheerful demeanor disappeared, to be replaced by a glum visage and sagging shoulders. "We need a break," he said. "Let's head into Barkerville."

Joy cascaded through Harrison at the thought of returning to town. Hopefully to see Rose. "Together? What about claim jumpers?"

"We'll let Judge Begbie deal with any claim jumpers. He's an honorable man and keeps law and order out here." He rubbed the back of his neck. "Mind you, the way I feel right now anyone is welcome to it."

Chapter Twenty-Two

Wham! The door to the Bella Union Saloon flew open and banged against the wall. Two tipsy men staggered out, followed by a cloud of cigar smoke and the reedy notes of a concertina and an out of tune banjo. Behind them, Rose caught a glimpse of a few couples dancing to a shaky rendition of "The Yellow Rose of Texas".

"Well, look what we have here. Seems like Fanny has herself a new girl," said the shorter of the two. He leaned towards Rose, enveloping her in boozy breath. "Late for work, darling?" To his friend he said, "She's late for work."

"Maybe we should escort her inside. Introduce her all proper like. What's your name?" said the second man, clean shaven and with the barrel-chested look of a wrestler.

"Come on, little darling." The first man grabbed her elbow. "Let's go."

Behind them, Rose spied Fanny making her way towards the door as fast as her girth would let her, a calculating look on her face at the sight of Rose. Any thoughts of working here fled. This woman wanted nothing more than to make money off her, at the cost of Rose's self-esteem. Despite Fanny's comment to her girls being of good virtue, the various states of undress of the ones she'd seen dancing told a different tale.

No, no matter how desperate her straits, she would not work here.

Rose yanked her arm free. "I'm not your darling," she said. "And I don't work here." She backed away, then whirled around and sped off down the boardwalk.

"Don't be shy!" One of them shouted behind her. "How about if we get married?"

"We want to make your acquaintance!" shouted the other. "We're real gentleman and know how to treat a lady."

Humph, gentlemen my eye, thought Rose. She slowed to peek over her shoulder, relieved to see the two leaning against the front of the saloon, cigars in one hand, matches in the other, apparently ignoring Fannie who faced them, shaking her fist.

Over the hubbub of the street, Rose heard her screech. "You two scared away my new girl!" And she let loose with a string of curses that made Rose's ears tingle. Then the woman looked in Rose's direction and waved, making the bracelets on her arm bounce. "Come back," she shouted, this time waving with both arms.

Rose shook her head and didn't wave back.

She continued on her way, ambling down the street, peering into one business after another as she walked by. She needed work and she would find something respectable. Although she'd been here for weeks already, the range of services and merchants still astounded her. Many merchants flew flags from their countries of origin: Great Britain, France, Italy, The

Netherlands, Denmark, Sweden, the U.S., Mexico, and more. The colorful bits of fabric brightened the street and her mood. Maybe Gracie was right; maybe another job would be easy to find after all.

She passed a blacksmith's shop and through the open door came the clang of hammer on anvil, and the flue sucked up a shower of sparks as she walked by. She tried to follow the sparkles, but the late afternoon sunlight was too bright. A couple of larger, black embers fell on the roof of the shanty beside the smithy and she paused for a moment, to make sure nothing caught fire. In the distance the blades of the Williams Creek Sawmill Company whined as they carved their way through logs, turning felled trees into planks and beams for the endless construction of shops, cabins, water wheels and flumes in the area. And always as a back drop, the rushing waters of Williams Creek.

At the edge of Chinatown, she stopped. Hard to fathom but the buildings and shacks here were even more jumbled and jammed together than the rest of Barkerville. She turned back and went down the other side of the street.

A few Chinese merchants had their shops sprinkled in amongst the rest but Wa Lee caught her eye. The sign proclaimed Washing and Ironing, presumably echoed in the Chinese lettering down one side of it. The large sign, freshly painted, hung proudly at right angles so none on the street could miss it.

A laundry. Hard work, true, but there would be no shortage of it because of the dirty nature of mining. Plus, in all likelihood she wouldn't be dealing with customers, she would be in the back and out of sight. She straightened her shoulders and walked in.

"I'm looking for work," she said to the Chinese man behind a short counter. He wore a black cap, a straight black jacket with a stand up collar and a long braid snaked down his back.

"You want to work here?" Amazement flooded his face.

"I do."

"It's hard work. You're small."

"But I'm strong. Please, give me a chance."

"I don't need help."

"I have a daughter to raise. She's four."

"I know. I've seen you walk by with her. Pretty little girl. You lucky lady." He scratched his nose. "For you money is easier to be made in a saloon."

Why does everyone tell me that? she thought angrily. *Don't they know I'd work there if I thought it was the right thing for me, for Hannah?* "But I want to work in a laundry. I like ironing." Which was true, she liked the clean fragrance wafting from the fabric after being ironed, liked the look of smooth fabric and the orderliness of folded, ironed clothes. She used to help Mrs. Beadle at the boarding house and the two had reached an agreement: The other woman would wash and rinse, and

Rose would hang up the wet items and iron them when they dried.

He hesitated. "My wife is sick right now. Maybe try for two, three days. But—" He shook his head. "Is difficult work."

"I'm not afraid of hard work." She sensed his hesitation and plunged in. "I'll be here tomorrow morning."

Face blank, he stared at her, and Rose could almost see his mind working behind the inscrutable, dark brown eyes. Finally he blinked and nodded. "Until Saturday. Then we see."

"Thank you. You won't regret it, I promise."

She almost skipped all the way back to Gracie's cabin.

"I have another job." Rose couldn't stop the grin crossing her face.

Gracie nodded, a satisfied look on her face. "I knew ye could do it. Where?"

"The Wa Lee Laundry."

Gracie's jaw dropped. "What? Working for Wa Lee? Are you right in the head?"

"Why not? He seems nice. His wife is sick."

Gracie frowned. "They don't mix with the rest of us."

"Maybe because we don't make an effort. We agreed I would help out for a day or two."

"Right. Watch out, you don't want to end up in a Chinese house of ill repute."

Rose's eye brows shot up at the warning. "You mean a brothel?" Surely she had misunderstood her friend?

"You heard me."

"Nonsense, Gracie. It's only for a few days. How bad can it be. I don't want to be a saloon girl and I don't want to work in a restaurant. Everywhere I go, men stop and stare at me. Today someone even asked me to marry him. I want something where I'm hidden away."

"Maybe you should get married." A sly grin curled Gracie's lips and she winked when Rose looked at her.

Rose gaped at Gracie. "What?" What was the matter with Gracie, coming out with one outrageous comment after another.

"You heard me."

She fiddled with her sleeves. "I don't want to get married."

"Not even to Harrison?"

Rose's face grew warm. "Enough. We'll have no more nonsense talk about marriage."

"I'm just saying it would solve a lot of your problems and you wouldn't have to hide away with a bunch of wash tubs and a few irons."

"It's honest work."

Gracie sighed. "You like to make things hard for yourself."

"No, I don't. I appreciate you letting us stay here, but it is crowded and we should find our own spot. I'll start asking around at some of the boarding houses."

"Suit yourself, but it's no trouble. Florence likes having Hannah around."

"Hannah likes it too. She's always been on her own and I think she sees Florence and Billy as her family now."

"Will you be putting her in school? We got a real fine teacher here, Mrs. Galloway."

"Perhaps I will. Gracie?"

Gracie looked at her.

"Are you sure you don't mind us staying a bit longer?"

Gracie walked over and hugged Rose. "Not at all. You're helping with the food and the children. Way I see it, we got to stick together out here."

Rose hugged her back.

"I wouldn't forget about Harrison, if I was you."

Of course not, thought Rose. *How could I forget about Harrison?* "He's busy with his gold mine."

"He's got a gold mine here if he would only admit it." Gracie winked.

Chapter Twenty-Three

"I don't think I need a hotel room," Robert said as they entered the outskirts of Barkerville. Thumbs tucked beneath the straps of his backpack, he gestured down the street with his chin. "I'll check on Brutus and maybe sleep in the stables tonight. Seems a shame to spend money on a proper bed. Me ma always told me I could sleep anywhere I could lay me head."

"Suit yourself. I'd like a real roof and a soft pillow."

"Let's meet up in the Parlour Saloon later." His chin swiveled to Nancy. "Would you like me to take her?"

Harrison rubbed his chin, not liking the stubble scraping against his fingers. First thing on his agenda was a hot shave. But not until he'd dealt with his mule. "I'll come with you. Mundorf might not appreciate you showing up with her."

They slogged down the middle of the street. A thunder storm last night had left it a quagmire of mud and manure and, if it hadn't been for Nancy, Harrison would have much preferred navigating the boardwalks.

The news at Mundorf's was not good. "I'm shutting down the stables and livery," he said. "Converting it into a saloon. Gonna call it the

Crystal Palace. But not till the end of the month, so you have a bit of time to make other arrangements for your mules."

Blasted luck, thought Harrison. "Thanks." He gave him five dollars. "I hope this will cover me until you close down?"

"Sure." The coins disappeared into his pocket. He tipped his hat to Harrison. "Pleasure doing business with you."

After making arrangements with Mundorf, he shouldered his pack and checked into the Hotel de France. He poked his head into the dining room hoping to see Rose, but she was nowhere to be seen, only the usual motley assortment of men. He drew a wave and a smile from Gracie, and he wondered about her warm reaction. Last time he saw her, she had no use for him. What had made her change her mind? Perhaps she understood he was no threat to Rose after all. He lifted his hand in return.

At Wellington Delaney Moses' barber shop, he sank deep into the chair and savored the hot towels wrapped around his face. The barber wasn't too talkative, which suited Harrison, and he sat with closed eyes while the man lathered up his shaving brush and circled Harrison's face with it. Then came the soothing strokes of the straight razor followed by a bracing splash of cold water that brought sputters to Harrison's lips. He cracked open one eye to see Wellington hold up a bottle labeled "Hair Invigorator."

"I'd recommend this, sir." At Harrison's nod, he slathered some on his hands and rubbed it through Harrison's hair. "Wait and see how good this makes your hair feel. I only sell it to my favorite customers." He winked.

Harrison chuckled. The man was a smooth salesman as well as a good barber, and he gave him a generous tip, which drew a smile and a knuckle to the forehead from the man.

"Nice business you have here," said Harrison as his eyes swept the room. Shelves full of ribbons, silks, and combs surrounded him.

"Yep," Moses chuckled. "I call this my Fashion Saloon."

"Indeed," Harrison agreed. "I'm sure your goods are the equal of any. Good day, sir." He inclined his chin and left.

On his way to the Parlour Saloon, he peered through the windows of the hotel as he walked past but didn't see Rose. Although she wouldn't be hanging around the lobby, so why did he even bother?

Because he couldn't control his gaze at the slightest chance he might catch glimpse of her.

At the saloon, he found an empty table tucked into the back corner and ordered two glasses of whiskey. He nursed one while he waited for his friend to return. Robert showed up about half an hour later, a glum expression on his face and a water-stained, crumpled envelope clutched in one hand.

"I stopped at the post office. Meant to send a letter home, but this was waiting for me." He pulled out an equally stained and crumpled piece of paper and held it up. "Me da's passed on."

"I am sorry. My condolences."

"Ma wants me to come home. To help with the croft. My sisters can only do so much and my brother's only ten. Too young to be head of the household."

"What will you do?"

"I dinna know." Pain and disappointment filled Robert's eyes. "I hate ta give up here. But how can I ignore my family?"

"You have a decision to make."

"I dinna want to leave here. We've not struck it rich yet."

"Circumstances change. Do what you need to."

"But you're my partner. How can I leave you in the lurch?"

"I'm a grown man, I'll find my way." He picked up his glass. "Let's have a toast to your father, shall we?"

"Aye."

They clinked glasses and Harrison tossed back the fiery liquid in one gulp. "It still doesn't taste any better." He grimaced.

"But it does the trick. I'll get us another one." Robert sauntered over to the bar and soon returned with two more drinks. "I'll think on it tonight."

"Meet me for breakfast at the hotel and let me know what you decide. In the meantime," he held up his glass. "A toast to friendship."

They shared a few more drinks, then Robert left. Harrison couldn't deny the freedom bubbling up through his gut at the thought the mining venture with Robert could end as soon as tomorrow. He would honor the partnership, though, if Robert decided he wanted to stay on.

He checked the time. Oppenheimer's would be closed. He would stop by first thing in the morning as he needed to buy paper, pen and ink. Robert's letter had reminded him he hadn't sent even a note home to his mother since reaching Victoria. He'd make sure to send his regards to his sister Laura. Although sweet natured, her headstrong ways sometimes led her into doing something reckless. Much to his parent's chagrin. A smile curved his lips at the remembrance of some of the scrapes she'd been involved with. Yes, it was high time he wrote home.

* * *

Harrison stepped inside Oppenheimer's the next morning and scanned the interior eagerly. "Doesn't Rose Chadwick work here anymore?" he asked of the same clerk who had worked here with Rose. He was certain the man would know.

Mr. Foster shook his head. "No. Had to let her go some days back. She wasn't working out."

His chest tightened, making it difficult for him to breathe. "Do you know where I can find her?" he finally managed to gasp.

"No. But I suggest try looking for trouble. She's probably in the middle of it."

Harrison stifled the urge to run out and start searching for Rose. He owed his family a letter, so instead he took his purchase and returned to his room. He sat on the bed, using a book to write on. He stared down at the blank piece of paper. He could think of nothing to say. Several times he dipped his pen into the inkwell only to hold the pen up so long the ink in it dried up.

So far the amount of gold they'd found was laughable. The prospect of earning enough to save his family home and good name became more disheartening by the day. And the more disheartening it became, the less he wanted to do it. There were other ways to earn money here in Barkerville such as selling goods and services to the men prospecting and mining in the area. After all, ten thousand men was nothing to scoff at. An idea had come to him when he had given a ride to William. With his wagon and mule team he could provide transport for the goods required to keep Barkerville going.

Or he could always return home and rejoin the marriage market. Plenty of well do to merchants were dying to buy titles for their daughters. He grimaced. No. He would find his own solution.

Finally, he put pen to paper:
Dear Mother

I hope this letter finds you and the rest of the family well. I am pleased to say I've made a safe arrival in Barkerville. The town is bustling with all manner of individuals and it grows daily. The British Columbia wilderness is breathtaking and so different from England that one can scarce believe it is the same planet. I have embarked on a mining venture with a Scottish gentleman I met here. Although the returns are smaller than we would like, we've had some triumphs.

He paused. It seemed silly to write about a mining venture that could end as soon as tomorrow, but he could think of nothing else to say. It was easier to let them think he had some success.

I am enjoying my time here. Do give my regards to Father and Laura and know that all of you are in my thoughts daily.

Your loving son,
Harrison.

As he folded the letter and tucked it into the envelope, he admitted the only one really in his thoughts daily was Rose.

And he didn't know where she was. Had she left Barkerville? In which case, he would never find her. His heart shrivelled at the thought.

* * *

Harrison sat by himself at a table by the front window the next morning, ostensibly to enjoy the sun but really to scan the people walking by in search of Rose. By the time Robert wandered into the hotel dining room, the breakfast rush was already over. The chair scraped the floor as Robert pulled it out and scraped again as he positioned it closer to the table after sitting down. The noise grated on Harrison's ears. It sounded like failure.

Gracie took one look at Robert's face and poured him a coffee. "Thick and black. Looks like you need a jolt of something this morning."

Robert gave her a wan smile and picked up his mug. He looked as if the weight of the world sat on his shoulders. He took a sip, scowled and set down the mug.

"Can I conclude from your demeanor you've made up your mind?" Harrison took a sip of his own coffee, the third of his morning, sweetened with plenty of sugar and milk. It made the drink palatable, but only just.

"I have." He took another swallow and almost choked. "Phew, strong enough to burn the hair off a boar." He wiped his mouth with the back of his hand. "I'm going home. Me family needs me now."

"Of course."

"So I think we should sell the claim. Anything we can get for it will be better than leaving it sit."

Harrison sipped his coffee and tried to think of a response.

Robert scowled and circled his mug with both hands, fingers tapping against it. "I hate to give up."

"Me too, but sometimes 'tis best to quit while ahead. And we are ahead. We're still alive, whole and hearty and we've found gold. Maybe not as much as we would like, but we have had some measure of success. More than a lot of men, I wager."

"Would you like to buy Brutus? I know you like horses."

"Brutus?" The thought pleased him. The beast was a fine piece of horse flesh and a reminder of his genteel life back in England. "Sure."

"It shouldn't take us longer than a few days to pack up our stuff and sell the claim. Then I'll be on my way. I won't bother sending a letter. It would get there the same time as me."

Harrison despised the idea of defeat at the hands of a fickle gold mine, but without a partner it would be futile. True, he could work for other mining ventures, but that would involve the same back breaking labour at a pittance of a wage. Besides, he still toyed with the idea of starting a transport business, although it might horrify his family. He, a St. John, entering into a business undertaking. However, circumstances had changed and he must change with them. Slowly he nodded.

Robert downed the rest of his coffee. "Let's head back to the claim."

"Don't you want to eat?"

"Not hungry." Robert's blue eyes were downcast and, even behind his thick red beard, Harrison could see the droop of his friend's lips.

He reached over and clasped Robert's shoulder. "We're making the right decision. Sometimes it's best to move on and put the past behind us."

Robert gave him a mournful look. Then his usual good humour took over and his beard split into a ragged grin. "I've got a girl back home. She loves me, money or no. Said so before I left."

"You're a lucky man." That's what Harrison wanted. Someone who loved him, money or no. Someone like Rose.

"I'll meet you back at the stables." Dodging tables he trotted off and, judging by the sudden burst of laughter filtering through the doorway, stopping long enough to exchange quips with the clerk in the lobby.

Harrison waved at Gracie and she scurried over, her hair dragged back into an unfamiliar tidy bun and the bruise around her eye faded away. She looked surprisingly attractive, and Harrison wondered what had brought on the contented gleam in her eyes. Maybe she had found love.

Which Harrison hoped to find too. "Do you know where Rose is? She's not working at Oppenheimer's and she's not staying here anymore."

"Why do you ask?"

"I want to see her. To make sure she's all right. She's still in Barkerville?"

Harrison's heart leapt at Gracie's nod. Rose was still here.

"She's staying with me. But she's got herself another job. Foster gave her the boot a while back. Good riddance, I'd say, blaming her for things that weren't her fault. Except—" She stopped and smoothed her hair with one skinny hand.

"Except what?" Harrison prodded.

"She works hard, putting in long hours." Gracie avoided eye contact with him. Apparently wherever Rose worked did not meet Gracie's approval.

Something I hope to save her from, thought Harrison. He had other ideas for Rose. Ideas including him. "We're heading back out to our claim. Please tell her I shall call on her in a few days."

Chapter Twenty-Four

Ready to start her day at the laundry, Rose tied a scarf around her head and rubbed bear grease into her hands. Her job made the skin on her hands red and chapped, and she tried to protect them as best she could. Even so, her hands were a pathetic sight. It was honest work, she reminded herself, and Wa Lee's wife was still sick, so the few days had stretched into two weeks which, at fifteen dollars a week, had been good for her finances.

The long days wore her out and each night, after spending an hour or two with Hannah, she tumbled into bed so tired she couldn't even dream. But she always spared a few moments to think about Harrison. How did his mining venture go? Did he find the success he needed to help his family? Or had he already left Barkerville? That last thought saddened her that he would leave without saying good bye. So then she would console herself that he still toiled away at his claim.

Today, Gracie's prophetic words about Rose making things hard for herself rang in her ears. Oh, she'd started the day well enough, with a tubful of heavy cotton pants and jackets, followed by several tubs of socks and flannels. The problem arose when she washed a tubful of

253

dirty white shirts. Somehow, a red handkerchief had become mixed up with the shirts and when she dumped the wash water, all the shirts had turned pink. Soaking the shirts for a few hours in bleaching powder and water rectified the problem but did elicit several eye rolls from her boss.

"Well, at least everything is disinfected now," she said with a weak smile, which only garnered another eye roll.

After bleaching the shirts, she'd dumped too much bluing in the rinse water and the shirts came out spotted with blue. It made her wish she'd paid more attention to Mrs. Beadle's instructions on wash days at the rooming house in Victoria. But it had nothing to do with Mrs. Beadle's instructions and everything to do with her constant daydreams of Harrison and wondering when she would see him again.

Wa Lee gave her a mournful look when he inspected the blue spotted shirts. "Customers all ask about you. Good you're pretty, you say sorry. Men would be mad if Wa Lee ruined shirts."

So much for her idea of staying out of sight. "I'm sorry. I didn't mean to."

"My wife better now. She'll be here tomorrow. But still you come. We're busy." He dug around in his pocket for a handful of coins. He counted them out carefully, holding some out to her while shoving the rest back in his pocket with his other hand. "You go now.

Maybe find a husband. Then men leave you alone."

A husband? Hadn't Gracie said the same thing? What was it with people trying to arrange her life? Besides, the only husband she fancied right now was Harrison, but that was impossible. He would return to England when he struck it rich, and she doubted he'd take her with him. He'd never marry her when he discovered Hannah was born out of wedlock.

Wa Lee bowed as she took her money and tucked it into her coin purse, patting it through the pocket of her skirt. The weight of it comforted her. She would be able to clear her debt with Dr. Wilkinson and buy fresh bread and milk for Hannah, Florence and Billy. Besides, she wanted to treat Gracie to a bottle of good whiskey. Whatever was left she would deposit into the Bank of British North America just down the street from the laundry. She still hoped to find a place of her own, although living with Gracie and her family was no hardship. It was just that she didn't feel right taking advantage of Gracie's hospitality, for her friend would not take any payment.

But today she was going to indulge herself. She wanted a pair of thong sandals like the ones Ming, the Chinese cook at the Hotel de France, wore. Wa Lee wore them as well, and they looked much more comfortable than her boots. The warm August days made the laundry room stifling hot and turned her feet into pools of sweat.

She left the laundry and headed into Chinatown. The buildings crowded along the road in this part of Barkerville were a little smaller, no more than huts, really. But stove pipes poked through the roofs, so at least the occupants stayed warm during the cold winter days. Chickens zigzagged across the road, reminding her of the day Ming walked into the kitchen of the Hotel de France carrying two plucked chickens. Perhaps this is where she got them.

Rose's eyes couldn't take it all in. She peered between the buildings and spotted a pen with a mother pig and piglets rooting around in a pile of food scraps. A few steps farther she spotted a large vegetable garden planted on rock walled terraces on the hills behind the untidy row of shacks.

She received no more than a few curious stares and no one stopped her. In fact, anyone she approached bowed as she passed by. She passed the Chinese Masonic Hall, a gambling den, and found what she thought was a store. The door was propped open and she paused for a moment, inhaling the scent of incense and cooked meat, trying to make sense of the Chinese lettering on the sign. Beneath the Chinese lettering was the name of the store in English: Kwong Lee Company. A sense of triumph filled her at realizing she had found the store Ming had recommended. She stepped inside.

If the owner of store was surprised to see her, it didn't show. When she told him Ming had sent her, he bowed and left her to her devices. Slowly she turned around in the middle of the floor, inspecting the premises. Goods crammed the shelves from floor to ceiling, from pretty blue and white bowls to opium pipes to clothing to cigars to provisions to hardware and mining tools.

She perused the shelves of boots and shoes and found what she sought. Pointing, she was soon on her way, thong sandals tucked beneath her arm and with still plenty of daylight to play with Hannah.

* * *

Rose tugged off her boots and stockings and slid her feet into the thong sandals. She admired the black velvet straps wrapped around her feet. Woven straw made up the soles and she roamed around Gracie's cabin, making a soft *thwap thwap thwap* noise as she walked on the wide wooden planks making up the floor.

"Those are funny shoes, Mama." Hannah sat on the floor playing with Dolly and her pinwheel. She made swooshing noises as she waved the pinwheel through the air.

"They are but they're comfortable." She wiggled her toes, liking the feel of air wafting between them, so much less constricting than her high top boots and stockings. It felt a little cheeky, to have her toes poking out like little pink sausages. She wiggled them again and Hannah giggled.

The door squealed open and Gracie came in. Billy ran over to her and she ruffled his hair before dropping a hand onto Florence's shoulders for a quick squeeze.

"Harrison sends his regards."

"What? He's here? In Barkerville?" Rose's breath caught in her throat. Harrison had thought of her. Did he think about Rose as often as she thought about him?

"Yep." Gracie took off her shawl and hung it on a hook beside the door. "Says he'll call on you in a few days."

"He will?" Joy surged through Rose. Harrison told Gracie he would call on Rose. She hugged herself and twirled about the tiny cabin on tiptoes. Or as well as she could twirl on tiptoes in the thong sandals. She kicked them off and continued in her bare feet. She held out her hands to Hannah, and the two of them twirled around the room together.

Gracie waited until they collapsed, out of breath and giggling, onto the wooden bench beside the door. "Here for now. Headed back out to his claim though," she said. "Don't think it's going too well."

Rose slipped her feet back into the thong sandals. "Oh dear. He had such high hopes, along with a lot of responsibility."

Gracie looked at her, one eyebrow cocked.

Rose nodded. "He's here to earn money for his family."

Gracie grunted as she pulled off her own boots. "That's not unusual. Ain't that why everyone's here? To feed their families?" She pointed to the thongs. "Can I try those? You look like you're having too much fun."

"Of course you can." Rose slipped them off her feet and handed them over. "He was going to get married, you know. She stood him up at the altar."

"Well, you better not disappoint him then." Gracie jammed her feet into the thongs and took a few steps around the room.

"Gracie!" Rose's cheeks grew warm and she cleared her throat a few times before fishing her handkerchief from her pocket. She wadded it up and threw it at her friend.

Gracie chuckled and dodged it. "I think we all know life isn't fair. But we take what it hands us. If she stood him up, I'm sure she had a good reason. Besides," she picked up the handkerchief off the floor and tossed it back, "now it means you got a chance with him."

"Do you really think so?" Rose knew her voice was wistful.

"Yep. All you gotta do is be patient." She hitched up her skirts and looked down to inspect her feet in the thong sandals. "My toes ain't as pretty as yours," she said. "But I think I'm gonna get me a pair of these."

* * *

Harrison took one look back at the patch of land they'd called home for the past two months. Already, as he and Robert moved away with Nancy loaded to the hilt with sacks and his chest, men swarmed about, one climbing down into the shaft they'd so fondly dubbed "The Witch", two others working the cradle and a fourth stoking the camp fire.

Selling the claim had been easy, made even easier by the fact he and Robert included the tent and much of the tools and equipment they'd used. They'd also bragged about the gold they'd found, insisting to the would-be buyers that pressing family matters called them home, otherwise they wouldn't be selling out.

It seemed to work, for a deal had been struck in no time. He'd felt a moment's remorse over the exaggeration of the gold they'd found but then tempered it with the thought that even though they hadn't had the success they wanted, it didn't mean there wasn't more gold deeper down, just waiting for someone else to dig it out. After all, was it so terrible to sell dreams?

He was astonished at how little regret he felt. He'd learned a lot about himself here in the Cariboo wilderness. Learned that an English gentleman was judged by what he could do, not by his birth. Learned he liked the feel of a tool between his palms and the sun warming his back. Learned he loved the rugged beauty of this land, especially now with the prospect of British Columbia joining the Confederation of Canada.

At the end of it all, and including their gold, they each walked away with $500. After Harrison bought Brutus, he still had $450. Not a fortune but nothing to scoff at either. Robert boarded the stage coach outside the Barnard Express Line and poked his head out to wave as the coach rolled away. Harrison waved back and watched till the stage coach disappeared from sight around a curve in the road.

Then he turned around and inspected the lively, bustling street. The palpable energy stirred his blood. Whoops of excitement rent the air, and an eager buzz surged up and down the street.

Someone or other had struck it big and come into town to display their booty. And, no doubt, leave some of it behind in the pockets of the merchants and saloon and restaurant owners, who indirectly earned their own living from the gold fields. He'd heard tales of men who had come into town and blown every speck of gold they'd found on champagne, cigars, and dancing girls. Then they would head back out again, as penniless as when they first arrived.

However, he himself had earned to enough to stay awhile longer and try and make another start in a different venture.

A venture, he hoped, that included Rose.

Now he just had to figure out how to save his family's fortunes yet remain in Barkerville and win the heart of the pretty young widow who had snared his attention.

Chapter Twenty-Five

A few days later Rose stood outside behind the store hanging up clothes in the afternoon sunshine when Wa Lee poked his head out the back door.

"Someone here to see you."

"Oh? Did I ruin someone else's shirt?" She grimaced.

Her boss chuckled and shook his head. "No. He wants to talk."

"I'll finish hanging these up first." She rummaged around the basket of wet clothes and pinned the last two pairs of pants to the line. Then she wiped her hands on her apron before making her way to the front of the store.

Harrison leaned against the door jamb, back to her, looking out on the street. She didn't say anything, just stood there and sucked in the sight of him as if she'd been stranded on a mountaintop for days without water.

He'd washed and changed, for his combed hair, still damp, curled over the edge of his collar from beneath his wide brimmed hat and when he glanced to one side to watch a wagon piled high with lumber drive by, a couple of flecks of shaving soap dotted his cheeks up around his ears. He'd obviously left the barber's chair before the shave was finished. One hand was rammed into the pockets of a clean pair of pants and his jacket was freshly laundered and pressed.

"Hello," she said.

He whirled around and a slow smile spread across his face. In his free hand drooped a bunch of fireweed and lupines tied with a lace ribbon.

"For you." He held it out.

Rose dropped her gaze to the bedraggled flowers and her heart swelled. He'd picked flowers. For her. No one had ever done that for her before. "Thank you," she managed to gasp, taking them from him and holding them up to her nose to inhale the sweet fragrance. Mind you, they could have smelled like burning garbage and she still would have thought it the most lovely fragrance in the world.

His gaze on her was warm, admiring, and she blushed and inspected his freshly laundered apparel. "You didn't get that done here," she blurted, pointing to his clean clothes.

"No. I wanted to surprise you."

She couldn't deny the well-being curling through her like a fluffy kitten rubbing itself against her legs. All she could manage in response was a weak "oh." Then she pointed to his cheek. "You have...ah...soap there."

He wiped it off. "Are you finished for the day?"

"I think so, but I'll have to check with the owner first." She held up the flowers to her nose once more and took a deep breath to steady herself.

"I'll wait."

She nodded and went in search of Wa Lee who, with a knowing look in his dark brown eyes, gave her permission to leave.

"Where are we going?" She pulled off her apron and hung it on the wall behind the counter and patted her hair.

"I want to show you something. Can you walk in those things?" He pointed to her thong sandals.

Around the world if I had to, she thought. "Yes."

He tucked her hand into his right elbow and his left hand remained resting gently on hers. Rose relished the contact. She squeezed his elbow and he glanced down at her and smiled. Her heart flip flopped and for an instant she couldn't catch her breath. Walking by his side, she felt protected and cherished, and a real lady.

They strolled through town to the north end of Barkerville and a few steps beyond onto the Cariboo Wagon Road. "Here." He took her hand and they climbed a short distance up the hill behind the main street. He helped her sit on a stump, then sat down on the ground beside her.

Barkerville spread out below them in all its rough-and-tumble glory. Shouts and the faint tinkle of music drifted through the air, and smoke curled from several chimneys. The pleasant late summer evening had brought everyone out as clumps of men wandered the road in both directions between Richfield and Barkerville.

Harrison tapped her knee and she turned to him. "I'm thinking of buying some land over there. A bit up the road." He pointed west, in the direction of Quesnel. "I intend to build a small stable and office here. For an express company. Like Barnard's. I already have a mule team and wagon." He paused. "You know, I never thought I'd be considering this. It's not what one of my status usually does."

"There's no shame in owning your own business." Rose looked down to admire the flowers clenched in her fist, then peered over to Harrison. He leaned back on his elbows, gazing at the sky and chewing on a blade of grass.

"It's one thing to marry into business," he said. "It's another thing entirely to be in business." He tossed away the grass he'd been chewing on, sat up and picked a fresh blade. He fiddled with it before tucking it into his mouth. "I'm hoping to earn enough to send money home. At least to assist my family in the short term, maybe give them...us...some time to determine a solution to our financial woes."

"A noble idea," she replied. *What would be the solution for his family?* she wondered. *If he wasn't successful here, would they expect him to find another rich heiress to marry? If so, when would he return to England?* The thought disheartened her and she renewed her gaze on the town below in an effort to push away the waves of disappointment.

"Rose," he said. He caught her hand and she turned to find him gazing at her with a serious expression. "Would you—?"

Her breath caught in her throat. What was he about to ask? Was he going to ask her to marry him? She looked down at her red, work roughened hand caught in his own callused one.

He paused for a moment as if he were about to choke on the words. "Would you consider coming to work for me? I know you're at the laundry and I'm sure that's wearing. I need someone to manage the office and deal with customers. I've seen you at the store and I know you can do it. Besides, it would give you the chance to use your skills in mathematics." He looked at her.

Disillusionment crashed over Rose. She pulled away her hand and looked away. How could she be saddened it wasn't the question she'd been expecting? He'd said nothing about love, about wanting to be with her. True, he'd bought her dinner, had bought beverages and bannock for her and Hannah, had brought flowers for her now, but obviously he was just being considerate. He'd already said he felt responsible for them, seeing as how he had rescued them on the road.

She discounted the flowers. He'd obviously brought those to sweeten his proposal of employment. Her feelings of disappointment were foolish. Even if he asked for her hand in marriage, she would turn him down. Between

Rose's humble upbringing and Hannah's birth, she couldn't accept.

He mistook her silence for indecision. "Please think about it."

The setting sun washed the hills with red, promising another warm day tomorrow. "I will," Rose managed to choke out. "I must be going. Hannah will be wondering where I am."

He helped her to her feet and in silence walked her home.

"There's going to be a theatrical evening at the Parlour Saloon day after tomorrow," he said when they arrived back at Gracie's cabin. "Would you like to attend with me?"

Rose looked at him, confused and unsure of his intentions towards her. Was he trying to woo her after all? Or was it simply a ploy to persuade her to work for him?

He stood there, waiting expectantly, expression hopeful. He'd removed his hat. Usually he twirled it in his hands, but now he held it between clenched fists.

"Yes," she said finally. Because she simply wanted to be with him and consequences to her heart be damned.

Relief rolled through his eyes and he inclined his head. "Until then."

Rose watched him walk away until he dodged between two buildings and disappeared into the jumble of livestock and humanity littering Barkerville's main street.

Fool. You're heading for heartbreak and disaster.

* * *

Gracie took one look at Rose's face when she stepped through the door. "You're looking a little flustered. He asked you to marry him," she guessed.

"No."

"Lost his nerve, did he?" Gracie chuckled.

"I don't know why you're so sure about that." A sudden burst of anger flared up through Rose, then just as quickly died away. Gracie only had Rose's best interests at heart. "He asked me to work for him, if you must know."

"It's a start." Gracie nodded wisely. "Your talents are wasted in the laundry. You can do a lot better for yourself. So what's he planning on doing that he needs your help?"

"He's planning on opening his own express company. Like Barnard's."

"Could work. There's a lot of coming and going hereabouts. I know the hotel is always looking for some new thing or other. To keep the customers coming back. And you know one thing." Gracie skewered Rose with a sideways leer. "If nothing else, the customers will be coming in to see you."

"Right. Just what I want. To be the sideshow of the business."

"You can use your talents. And if one if your talents is looking good, then so be it."

"There's something else. He invited me to attend a theatrical evening with him at the Parlour Saloon."

"Well, now, I've never been, but I think they call themselves the Cariboo Amateur Dramatic Association. Their shows are pretty good." Gracie shrugged. "So I hear."

"So you think I should go?"

"Why not? Hannah's no bother. You deserve a night out." She grabbed the tin plates from the shelves above the table. "Anyway, kids are getting hungry. Time for supper." She turned away and started setting the table.

Her friend had a way of making Rose see things in a different light. Gracie was right. If Rose's looks would help Harrison's business, then what was there to be ashamed about? She would like to be the one to help Harrison. Maybe then he would stay.

And Gracie thought Rose deserved an evening out with Harrison. All of a sudden, she couldn't wait.

Chapter Twenty-Six

Harrison knew Rose had watched him move off, knew because he had felt her gaze on his back. Once he'd disappeared from her view, he rubbed his neck, trying to dispel the prickles her perusal had raised.

He'd disappointed her with his offer of employment. He had seen it flash across her face when he asked. In truth, he had wanted to ask if she would mind if he continued to call on her, but at the last second had lost his nerve. He wanted to do things right by her and Hannah. Some man had hurt her in the past, and he didn't want to repeat that mistake.

Then he'd blurted out his proposal for employment in an effort to cover his discomfort.

As an honorable gentleman, he couldn't renege on the offer. Whether he liked it or not, he was now committed to pursuing his idea of owning stables and a shipping company. Or at least trying. Tomorrow he would pay a visit to Barnard's office and take a look around.

He had a lot to learn.

* * *

Harrison stood back and inspected the building containing F.J. Barnard's Express office. Business appeared to be good, for a large covered wagon was being unloaded, its contents stacked on the sidewalk in front of the building in a ragged pile of barrels, boxes, and sacks. Several more wagons of varying sizes waited behind for their turn at the loading dock. Schedules and waybills plastered the walls, and shouted orders filled the air. To all appearances, Barnard ran a brisk business, and anticipation filled Harrison at the prospect of his own scheme. What better use of his mule team and wagon than for what it was intended?

He crossed the street, dodging a couple of men on horseback and leaping across several puddles. Once inside the busy establishment, he sidled off to one side. The bright room hummed with activity, and Harrison savored the lively atmosphere while he inspected the interior.

A young man with curly black hair manned the counter running through the middle of the room, and behind it an elderly clerk with his sleeves rolled up worked at a roll top desk shoved in one corner. Shelves of books lined the wall above the desk. A small stove stood in the middle of the room crowned with a battered kettle, and guarding the entire area from the opposite wall hung a huge rack of antlers. He'd seen enough of the animals over the summer to know they were from a caribou. The antlers of English deer paled in comparison. Towards the rear of the office, several scales of varying sizes caught his eye. Scales, of course; shipping went by weight.

Harrison waited for a break in the hubbub before making his way over to the fellow in charge of the counter. "May I speak to the manager?"

The young man looked up from the stack of papers he counted, holding his place with an ink stained finger. "And who might you be?" His voice held an Irish lilt and suspicion darkened his blue eyes.

"Harrison St. John." Harrison knew better than to use his title. The young Irishman would doubtless be repelled, not impressed, by it.

"And what might this be regarding?"

Before Harrison could answer, a shout cut through the noisy room.

"Ned!"

He turned in time to see someone, one of the drivers presumably—judging by his sturdy boots, large hat and the whip in his hand—burst through the door and charge towards the counter.

The elderly clerk turned around. "What's your beef, Charlie? Can't you see I'm busy here?"

"The wagon broke down ten miles back. Hit a pothole and cracked both front wheels."

Ned hauled himself to his feet and ambled over. "I keep telling you not to drive so fast. The road's in pretty poor shape, what with all the heavy traffic these days."

"Horses got spooked and got away from me." Charlie shuffled his feet.

"Eh? What spooked 'em?"

"Grizzly. Biggest one I've seen. Pete tried to shoot it but, by the time he got his rifle up, the bear took off into the trees."

"So you left the team hitched to a broken down wagon and hightailed it outta there? With a grizzly in the area?"

"I left Pete in charge. He said he was fine. Besides, that grizzly's been hanging around all summer. Ain't bothered no one yet."

"Let me see." Ned grabbed the bills of lading from the young Irishman and started flipping through them. "Says here you got a wagon full of coffee, tea, flour, potatoes, and cabbage. And some salmon." He slapped the pile back down on the counter. "Don't think we should leave that fish out there. It's packed in ice and all, but it'll be melting. That bear will come back sniffing around for sure." He peered at the blackboard listing drivers and dates on the wall beneath the antlers. "Now what to do," he muttered to himself. "Don't have any fresh teams or wagons available till tomorrow morning. What do you think?" He turned to his young assistant. "Got anyone in mind who could drive out?" His assistant raised his hands and shook his head.

Harrison couldn't believe his ears. Here was his chance. He stepped forward and bowed. "Excuse me for being bold, but may I offer my assistance? I have a wagon and team of four mules which I would be happy to offer for your disposal."

Ned scoured him up and down with a critical gaze. "What did you say your name was?"

"Harrison St. John. At your service."

"Have we met?"

"No sir, we have not. Until recently I've been up around the headwaters of Cunningham Creek prospecting for gold."

"Now you're here in town." He snorted. "You're one of the lucky ones. You must have something to fall back on."

"And, dare I hope, the opportunity to help you?"

Ned stroked his chin and stared at Harrison. "You seem like a right decent fellow and I sure do need the help," he said finally. He stuck out his hand. "I appreciate the offer and I'll pay you for your troubles."

"My sincere thanks." Harrison turned to the driver. "Will you be coming with me?"

"Naw." The driver shook his head. "The wagon's easy enough to find. Just head back on the road towards Quesnel. It's not going anywhere." He chuckled at his own joke. "I'm thirsty, might need to wash away the road dust with an ale or two."

"Then I'll be on my way."

"Maybe you could give me your name and where you're staying. I'll start an account for you." Ned shoved a piece of paper and a pen and inkwell across the counter towards Harrison. "I'm expecting the stage coach any

274

minute, so may as well get our paperwork out of the way first."

"Certainly." Harrison moved off to one side. He couldn't wait to share the news with Rose that he had snagged himself his first job as a transport driver. Certainly an encouraging start to his venture.

Pounding hooves and the jingling of harnesses sounded followed by a bellowed "Whoa." Then the screech of a brake handle being set.

"And here it is. Right on time today for a change." Ned strode to the door and flung it open.

Harrison finished writing down the information, then waited for Ned to come back. Several passengers straggled through the door, but one in particular caught his attention.

A tall blonde haired man with neatly trimmed mutton chop whiskers and wearing a black beaver top hat and expensive suit marched in with the air of someone who expected people to jump at his entrance. He scanned the room with chin lifted at a supercilious angle, then stepped to the counter to speak to the young Irishman. Harrison turned to leave but the newcomer's voice raised and caught Harrison's attention.

"I tell you, I'm in search of a young woman. She would have arrived in early June."

Harrison turned in time to see the Irishman shake his head.

"Come now," the man said, "surely you must see who comes and goes into this wretched town of yours."

"Sorry, sir. Can't say as I do."

"Her name is Rosamund Lang." He held his arm out about chest height. "She's petite, about this tall. Has a daughter. There can't be that many women here."

The clerk's mouth took a mutinous curl. He obviously didn't like being harangued.

Rosamund Lang? Petite with a daughter? It had to be the Rose and Hannah he knew. But wasn't her name Rose Chadwick? Then he remembered her telling him: Rosamund Arabella Ruth and how he'd teased her about her long name. But which was it, Lang or Chadwick?

"If you think of anything, send a message to Edmund Hewett. I'm staying at the Occidental Hotel."

Edmund Hewett. Harrison's world rocked. This must be Rose's Edmund. But hadn't she said she was a widow? Yet here stood her husband, blustering and very much alive. Didn't he say his last name was Hewett? Then why did Rose call herself Chadwick?

He fought the waves of nausea. Surely this was nothing but a horrible coincidence. Yet there couldn't possibly be another young mother named Rose in Barkerville, so it had to be her. What a cruel joke. He'd offered her work, had wanted to call on her, had even entertained thoughts of marrying her. The room spun and he clutched the edge of the counter for support.

"You okay? You look like you've been mowed down by a runaway steam locomotive." Ned's voice penetrated the haze in Harrison's head.

"I'm fine," he managed to gasp. "I'll be on my way to retrieve your goods."

"Great." Ned lifted a hand. "I won't close up till you get back."

But what he had thought would be a good initiation into the ins and outs of a transport company turned out to be a let-down. All he could think of was Rose's treachery.

* * *

Despite Harrison's shock over the incident with Edmund Hewett, the trip to the stranded B.X. wagon went smooth enough. Pete, the assistant driver, turned out to be an amiable sort and once the goods had been transferred to the other wagon, he chatted all the way back to Barkerville. He didn't seem to expect any answers, which suited Harrison just fine. He doubted he could carry a conversation with anyone anyway.

When they arrived back in Barkerville, Ned seemed pleased and told Harrison he would add him to the list of drivers. He also offered to stable the mules for the night.

Head down, arms hanging limply by his sides, Harrison trudged back to the Hotel de

277

France, Edmund Hewett front and centre in his mind. Why had Rose let him think she was a widow?

"Harrison."

He lifted his head and blinked a few times to clear his vision from the road dust of his earlier trip. Smiling, Gracie stood there, carrying a lumpy burlap sack. Potatoes, he assumed.

"Rose sure is looking forward to your evening at the thee-ater." She pronounced it like two words.

He stared blankly at her. Of course. He'd asked Rose to attend the theatre with him tomorrow evening. That certainly couldn't happen now, not with her husband in town.

"Can you tell Rose I can't see her anymore?"

"What? What's happened?" She glared at him. "You can't disappoint her like that."

He forced the words past the lump in his throat. "Her husband's here. Edmund."

Gracie cocked her head, a puzzled expression in her eyes. "She doesn't have a husband."

"Well, sure looks like she does."

"Why don't you ask her rather than jump to conclusions? And by the way." She tapped his chest with a firm finger. "I don't appreciate being asked to do your dirty work. You're a grown man, nothing to be afraid of from a sweet thing like Rose."

"I do not consort with married women. It's not right."

"She ain't married." Her voice was adamant and a small bubble of hope burst through the painful shell around his heart.

Very well. He would take out Rose as planned and get the truth from her. He just hoped he could accept it if it wasn't the answer he wanted.

Chapter Twenty-Seven

Rose fretted all day about what she would wear that evening to the Parlour Saloon with Harrison. Finally, she decided on her navy blue skirt and velvet bolero and sash. It might be warm inside the saloon, but the walk home afterwards would be cool. She rushed home from the laundry to freshen up.

"You look nice." Gracie tapped her foot. "Only—" Her voice was hesitant.

"Only what?"

"Wait a second." Gracie stepped over to her chest and lifted the lid to rummage through it. "Here." She held up a pair of lace gloves. "Wore them for my wedding but never had a chance to wear them since. You may as well use them. Your hands...er...ain't in the best shape."

Appreciation spilled through Rose and tears pricked her eyes. "Thank you," she whispered. "I shall take care of them. I expect Florence will want them for her wedding day."

A knock sounded. It must be Harrison. Rose sucked in a huge breath to steady herself and tossed a tremulous smile to Gracie before opening it.

He didn't smile when he saw her, and his solemn expression scared her. Something bothered him and she wracked her brains trying to remember if she'd inadvertently said something to offend him last time they were together.

"Hello," she said.

He nodded once but didn't answer. Did torment or disappointment darken his eyes?

Hannah pushed herself in front of Rose and tugged on Harrison's coat. "Doesn't Mama look pretty?"

"Indeed." He choked out the word as if he spat out poison.

What was the matter with him? Rose wondered. What had happened to the warm eyed, endearing man who brought her flowers not two days past?

"Good bye, poppet." She dropped a kiss on Hannah's forehead to hide her discomfort. So far this evening wasn't going at all like she expected.

He offered his arm to her and she took it, but the muscles below her fingers were stiff. Harrison was not comfortable in her presence. When would he tell her what was wrong?

She didn't have long to wait. They'd barely reached the still-bustling main street before Harrison spoke. "Someone's looking for you. A man by the name of Edmund Hewett. Do you care to tell me what's going on?"

A sudden weight pressed down on Rose's chest; nausea roiled in her belly. Somehow she kept one foot moving in front of the other.

Edmund was here. In Barkerville.

He'd found her. And Hannah.

Shock weakened her knees and she tripped on a protruding board, falling heavily against Harrison. He caught her and pulled her upright, holding her close for a few seconds against his chest before setting her on her feet. She looked up at him and caught a glimpse of sympathy. Clearly, he understood her distress.

He wanted the truth, and he deserved it. Now that Edmund had followed her here, sooner or later she would have to tell Harrison the entire story. She swallowed hard and gritted her teeth. Best to say it now before she was too lost in love for him. "Not here," she said. "Let's find a quiet spot down by the creek."

She clutched his hand, half expecting him to rebuff her, but he glanced down at her with a gloomy expression on his face and settled her fingers firmly in his.

At the north edge of town, she found a fallen log beside the creek. She sat and glanced at Harrison. He stood, arms crossed and face blank. He was not making this easy at all.

She looked up at him and met his gaze squarely. "I grew up on a ranch outside of San Francisco. I hardly remember my mama because she died of a fever when I was seven. It was always just me and my father. He worked as a mule skinner, horse trainer, groom...you name it, for Edmund Hewett." She stopped to clear her throat. "I was nineteen when I caught his eye, and I believed his words. I believed he would marry me. I know now what a fool I was, but love makes you foolish. At least I thought it was love." She lifted her hands. "He had his way with me and when he discovered I was with child, told me he didn't want a mule skinner's daughter for a wife and that he'd marry someone else. My father disowned me because, in his words, I had brought shame upon the family. I made my way to San Francisco and stayed with my father's sister, my aunt Hannah. She helped me find work, helped me with the birthing, and helped me find my way to Victoria. I named my daughter for her because she showed me nothing but love and didn't judge me."

The *brrrrr* of a woodpecker interrupted her and she stopped talking for a moment. The bird swooped away, its red cap flashing, and she watched it until it disappeared into a patch of woods higher up the hill. Then she looked at Harrison again. His expression hadn't changed, but she saw no censure in his gaze, only interest in her story.

She took a deep breath and continued. "Men and women too, were heading north for the Cariboo gold rush, so steam ships were plentiful and passage was easy to find. Aunt Hannah knew Mrs. Beadle and sent a letter to her explaining my situation. Mrs. Beadle took me in and I lived with her in Victoria. I tried to disappear. I didn't want to have anything to do with Edmund, so I changed my name. I used Chadwick, my mother's maiden name, so instead of Rosamund Lang I became Rose Chadwick. I didn't think anymore about

Edmund until he came to the boarding house a few months ago and demanded I give him Hannah." Her voice turned bitter. "No, worse, he offered to buy her from me, as if she was a plaything to be bartered with. I knew a powerful man like him would win. How could I fight him? So we left the next morning and came here. He didn't want her before, so I don't know why he wants her now. But he won't have her." She lifted her chin. "He won't have her," she repeated.

"Why not tell me the truth earlier? Why did you let me think you were widowed?"

"I didn't want you to think ill of Hannah. She shouldn't pay for my mistakes.

Rose let shoulders droop, then pulled herself upright.

"As for me," she lifted her head to meet his eyes, "I didn't want to have to admit my foolishness."

"Do you really think I'm that shallow?"

"Perhaps not. But you're an English lord."

"Only if I want to be."

Silence fell over the two. Rose looked around, anywhere but at Harrison. She didn't want to see the disappointment on his face now that he knew her story.

"Rose." Harrison held out his hand and she took it. Finally she plucked up her courage to look at him.

His face was gentle, and he pulled her close. "How brave of you and how fierce you

284

are, defending your daughter the only way you knew how. Let me help you."

"Help me?"

He tilted her chin and brushed his lips against hers. "Marry me, Rose. Together we'll make a home for Hannah and I'll make sure the bastard leaves you alone."

Her skin tingled at the touch of his lips on hers and she couldn't collect her thoughts. Then she realized what he'd said. He'd offered to marry her. Not because he loved her, but to save Hannah from Edmund.

"Marry you? I can't!"

He pulled himself away from her, a wounded expression on his face. He still held onto her hands, though, and she took comfort in the warmth, the strength emanating from them. "You don't need to answer me now. Think about it."

"You don't need to throw your life away on me. Not when you can marry anyone." She tried to smile but knew it probably came out more like a grimace. "I appreciate it. No, there's only one way to deal with Edmund."

"And that is?"

"Face him head on. He tried to intimidate me and I ran. Not this time. I need to find him and settle this now." She pulled her hands free and straightened her shoulders. "I can do this on my own."

"No, you're not. I'm coming with you. I know where he is staying."

Drat. Harrison wanted to come with her. Just one more reason for her to love him. But she couldn't let herself. Sooner or later he would be leaving Barkerville to save the family back in England who depended on him.

Chapter Twenty-Eight

The clerk at the Occidental Hotel lifted his eyebrows. "We don't normally discuss the whereabouts of our guests."

Harrison leaned over and grabbed him by the front of his wrinkled shirt. "He's an acquaintance and we have some business to discuss with him. Where can we find him?"

"I think he said something about the Wake Up Jake Saloon," the clerk stammered, face red and forehead lined with sudden beads of sweat.

Harrison released him and stepped back. "That wasn't so hard, was it? I thank you, good sir." He tipped his hat then turned to offer Rose his elbow. "Shall we?"

The clerk straightened his tie. "And a good day to you," he muttered.

Rose smothered a smile at his unhappy expression, then looked up at Harrison. "I'm ready. I think." She clutched Harrison's arm and tried to ignore her hammering heart.

Confronting Edmund in the restaurant was the best approach as she was sure he would not attempt anything with an audience. He liked to think he was a cultured man, and the last thing he would want was to draw unfavourable attention to himself.

Darkening clouds nudged the edge of the mountain tops, brightened by the occasional flash of lightning. The ominous sight sat heavy on her. The upcoming conversation with Edmund did not promise to be an easy one. He'd traveled all this way to find her and wouldn't be dissuaded that easily from his goal of claiming Hannah. But, she vowed, she would not lose her daughter.

Rose pulled her hand away from Harrison's arm once they reached the restaurant. She stopped in the doorway and scanned the room. The Wake Up Jake billed itself as the finest restaurant in Barkerville, and the striped wallpaper, crystal lamps, and polished floor supported their claim. Most tables were occupied by two or more people, but Edmund sat at a table by himself, a fine bottle of wine and a glass half-full of the burgundy liquid in front of him. He read a newspaper.

She gathered her courage and marched towards him. Harrison's reassuring presence followed her. *He's with me,* she thought. Edmund couldn't hurt her now.

Rose came to an abrupt stop by Edmund's table and folded her arms. "Are you looking for me?"

Edmund looked up and deliberately folded the newspaper. "Not you so much. Hannah."

Harrison stood behind Rose and a gentle weight pressed down on her as he dropped his hands on her shoulders. Edmund's eyes narrowed at the gesture and a sly smile curled his lips. "I see you have a champion."

"Something you know nothing about." Rose lifted her chin.

A hush fell over the dining room at the unfolding tableau, and the other diners waited for what he would say.

Edmund regarded her with a condescending eye. "I made you a reasonable offer. Why not take it and forget about your past mistake."

A red haze distorted her vision and she blinked. He blatantly referred to Hannah as Rose's past mistake. She dropped her fists to her waist and leaned toward him. "The only mistake I made was in thinking you were an honorable man."

Edmund pointed to Harrison. "And this gentleman is? He looks nothing more than a disreputable miner to me."

"This is the man I'm going to marry." Because I love him. The thought jolted her and she peeked at him over her shoulder. A forbidding expression cloaked Harrison's face. Forbidding—ferocious even—as if he faced an enemy. He looked as if he really cared about what happened to her and Hannah. Amazement flooded her, leaving her a bit dizzy, and she almost missed Edmund's response.

"Oh, you found someone to marry you, did you?" Edmund hooted. "Oh, that's rich. Does he know about your unsavory background?"

"He's been more of a father to Hannah than you've ever been." Rose gritted her teeth.

Edmund sat there, gloating and so sure of himself. How could she ever have imagined herself in love with this self-centred oaf?

Harrison stepped around Rose. "I know who you are." He pulled her close and looped one arm around her shoulders. "I know the whole story. Rose told me. Unlike you, I look after what's mine."

Edmund regarded him with a languid gaze. "She's yours now, is she? Well, you're welcome to her. Give me the girl and I'll leave you two to your wedded bliss."

"You're not taking Hannah," Rose announced. A knife clattered to the floor, followed by a shushing sound. The audience hung onto every word, the silence so thick Rose could very nearly feel it push against her chest.

"Shall we take this outside?" Menace gave Harrison's voice a hard edge.

"You wish to fight? With fists? Why, how positively barbaric." Edmund chuckled, a nasty sound that set Rose's teeth on edge.

Harrison's arm swept the room. "Look around. See where we are. Do you think anyone cares about a fight between two grown men? Shall we settle it the old fashioned way?" He clenched his hands. "What do you say? Or would you prefer an out and out duel? I know they've been outlawed, but I'm sure we could find a brace of pistols somewhere."

Edmund stared, an incredulous look twisting his features. "I'm not risking my life for this. If anything, fisticuffs it is." He got to his feet. Rose had forgotten how tall he was, taller than Harrison by a few inches. The bout would favour Edmund, and her mouth grew dry at the realization. "You're an easy match for me," he continued, "and I shall have you at my feet in no time."

The scrape of a chair being pushed away from a table reverberated through the room, then another, and another. Several men ambled over to stand behind Rose and Harrison.

"When you're done beating him," drawled one, "then you can take me on. I know this man. We had claims in the same valley. We stand up for our own here."

"Yep." A man with rolled up sleeves flexed his biceps. "I could use a good fight."

"This is going be the most fun I've had in a long time," crowed a third, skinny and with neatly combed hair.

"William!" Harrison reached out and clasped the other man's hand.

"You know him?" Rose said as Harrison clapped his free hand on William's shoulder.

"He sure does," William said. "This fellow showed me kindness, and now I have a chance to repay the favour."

The show of support bolstered Rose and, with renewed courage, she regarded Edmund. He looked as if sour lemons filled his mouth.

"I'm not fighting the whole room," Edmund spluttered. He patted his hips as if he searched for something. Pistols, Rose could only assume, or perhaps a knife.

"What kind of man takes a little girl away from her mother?" A bearded man, taller even than Edmund, and carrying a pipe and with trousers tucked into knee high leather boots, moved up beside William.

"Who are you?" Edmund folded his arms.

"Judge Matthew Begbie."

"He's not known as the hanging judge for nothing," said the man with the rolled up sleeves.

"I'm the father. I have every right to the child as much as she does," said Edmund.

"No, you don't," flared Rose. "You promised to marry me, but you turned your back on me when I told you I carried your child."

"Why do you want her now?" Judge Begbie's measured tones filled the room.

"I can give her a better life on my ranch than she'll ever have here."

The judge shook his head. "That's a matter of opinion now, isn't it?"

"You've never shown the slightest interest in her." Rose's palms itched with the desire to slap the conceited expression from Edmund's face.

"You've done nothing but ignore Rose and Hannah," said Harrison. "You can pack up and leave."

"I know your type," continued the judge. "Think you can buy whatever you want. You say she's your daughter? Then let her decide what she wants. When she's older. In the meantime, this is a decent town with a school, a library, a hospital, music teachers, dance instructors, everything a little girl could want or need."

Edmund's face turned a dull red. "Why don't you mind your own business?"

"Keeping scoundrels out of this town is my business." He pointed at Edmund with the stem of his pipe. "Oh, and we have a post office. You want to get to know your daughter? Then start writing letters. I suggest you leave this fine young couple alone."

"And if I don't?"

"I think I can find something to charge you with. Disturbing the peace. Making threats to an innocent child. Harassing a young woman. My jail's comfortable. You might like it."

"Jail?" Edmund's voice was disbelieving. "You have no reason to throw me in jail."

The judge shrugged. "I just gave you a whole list of reasons. But I can think of more."

A muscle worked in Edmund's cheek. "Very well. I'll forget about Hannah. For now." He turned to Rose. "This isn't over."

"As long as they're in Barkerville, yes it is," said Judge Begbie then he faced Rose. "I trust he won't bother you." He nodded to Harrison. "I bid you a good night, sir." He returned to his table but pulled his chair around. His face glowered as he watched Edmund.

Edmund scowled at Rose and Harrison for a moment before tossing back the rest of his wine and stalking out.

Disappointed mutterings swept the room that the show was over. "That's it boys, I don't think we're needed here anymore." William's jovial voice rang through the room. "How about we leave these two alone?" The men moved off, leaving Harrison and Rose standing alone by the deserted table, the bottle of wine, empty glass, and folded newspaper the only evidence of Edmund's presence.

"I have to go home," said Rose. "I don't trust him not to try and make off with Hannah."

Harrison's face grew steely. "I'll get my rifle and meet you there."

She stepped out of the restaurant and her heart plummeted. Edmund stood not a few yards away, attempting to light a cigar in the evening breeze. She would have to pass him to get to Gracie's cabin. Even if she crossed the street, he would see her. Behind her, Harrison cursed beneath his breath.

Edmund twisted his head and spotted them. He took a long puff on his cigar and pursed his lips, exhaling a thin, angry stream of smoke that soon lost its shape on the breeze.

"Why now? Why do you want her now?" Rose cried out.

A flush mottled his face. "I can't sire more children, thanks to a nasty bout with that damn typhoid," he spat. "I'd planned to head into San Francisco in search of a wife. Who could resist a lonely widower with a young daughter? That way I can leave my ranch to my own flesh and blood and there'll be no questions asked." A muscle twitched in his jaw. "You've ruined it for me."

"So Hannah is nothing more than a prop for your aspirations," growled Harrison. "Get out of here." His murderous expression turned his eyes to pools of black, and he pointed to the Barnard Express office. "I expect you to leave Barkerville tomorrow morning."

Proudly Rose stood beside him. She placed her hand on Harrison's elbow. He fought for her. For Hannah. Maybe he didn't need to profess love for Rose. Maybe that would come in time. Maybe for now, his actions were enough.

Edmund took another puff then tossed away the cigar. "Gladly. This place is a hell hole."

They both watched Edmund walk away, then Harrison pulled her around to face him.

"I'm proud of you," he whispered. "He's a bully and you called his bluff." He took one of her hands and lifted it to his mouth. The faint brush of his lips felt like butterfly wings against the back of her hand and shivers galloped up and down her spine.

Harrison gazed at her and a slight smile curved his lips. Joy and satisfaction filled his eyes, and Rose felt her cheeks grow warm at his intent perusal.

"Who's William?" She blurted the first thing that came to her mind.

"Did you mean what you said? About me being the man you're going to marry?"

Did she? She stared at him long and hard. Then an answering smile lifted the corners of her mouth. "Yes. You told me I could think about it, and I have. If the offer still stands."

"It does."

Then a cold wave of reality hit her. How could she, with a bastard-born daughter, marry a British peer? A peer who only offered to marry her to make her daughter's life easier. She made a mistake in accepting his proposal and would have to tell him. "I'm not of your class." She looked down and started fiddling with the loose ends of her belt. "I don't think I can marry you after all."

"What are you talking about? Do you think I care about that? You are in a class of your own. You're intelligent, fearless and beautiful. You willingly tackled a new life head on to protect your daughter. Any man would be proud to claim you as his own."

"But aren't you returning home to England?"

"No. I'm not."

"But your family. You were to marry into money. To save the St. John legacy." Her voice trailed away.

"You let me deal with my family back in England. Besides," he added, "I don't care what they think of you."

But maybe I do, she thought. "Very well," she said.

"But I would like to get married in the Church of England. I don't want there to be any question about the legitimacy of the ceremony. And it's important to me too. To wipe out the disaster of my last so-called wedding." He gave her a lopsided grin. "Besides, it will please my mother."

Of course Harrison would want to placate his parents in some way. And she, Rose, would be more than happy to do what pleased Harrison. Only Rose's stomach shriveled into a hard ball. "There isn't one here."

Harrison took one look at her face. "It's late and it's been quite an evening. I'll stay with you, Gracie, and the children until we're sure Edmund has left town. We'll talk more tomorrow about our wedding plans."

* * *

Elation filled Harrison when Rose, on tiptoe, pasted a shy kiss on his cheek when he returned her to Gracie's cabin. He stood there for a moment after the door closed behind her, then turned to gaze upon Barkerville below him. Darkness shrouded the little town but the welcoming glow of oil lamps shone golden from a few windows, and the smell of wood smoke wafted through the air. Farther up the valley, towards Richfield, campfires flickered. Not everyone slept yet.

He hated to disappoint his family, but the truth was he didn't want to return to England. Being the Viscount St. John held no appeal for him. He wanted to stay here, in this exciting new land with Rose.

He had an idea for his parents and their financial woes, but they certainly wouldn't like it. It would be a difficult letter to write, but it would have to be done.

Before he wrote any letter, though, he would make sure Edmund never bothered Rose again. He sat down and wrapped a blanket around his shoulders, placing his rifle within easy reach.

Chapter Twenty-Nine

Only Gracie was still awake when Rose stepped inside the cabin. The three children slept, Florence and Billy together in the bunk bed, and Hannah in her little trundle bed beneath Rose's cot.

"There's gonna be a wedding," Grace squealed, dropping her mending. "I can see it in your face." She leapt to her feet and rushed over to hug Rose.

Rose beamed. "I think we're getting married here. But Harrison wants the ceremony to be performed by an Anglican minister."

"Pffft, that's easy. There's one in Yale. Maybe he'll come if you offer him enough money. For his mission and all."

Rose stared at Grace, a memory nibbling at her, then she remembered the trip with the harried mother and children up the Fraser River from Victoria to Yale. She clapped her hands. "Yes. The Reverend Sheepshanks! I traveled with his family on the paddle wheeler as far as Yale. I'll talk to Harrison about it tomorrow."

"Hannah will be one happy little girl. She talks a lot about wanting a papa, you know? To Florence. When you're not around."

"She does?" A sudden stab of guilt made Rose feel as if a blade had been slipped between her ribs. Until now, she hadn't thought Hannah overly bothered by her lack of a papa in her life. She'd always been satisfied with Rose's vague answers.

Apparently not. A wave of gratitude towards Harrison gushed through her and pushed the blade away. She couldn't wait to tell Hannah.

* * *

The next evening Rose and Harrison sat on the edge of the front porch watching Hannah, Florence, and Billy play hide and seek. Hannah's shrieks of laughter when Billy found her warmed Rose's heart. Hannah thrived here.

Harrison's voice broke her gaze. "I checked with Barnard's. Edmund left town this morning."

"If he ever writes Hannah," mused Rose, "I'll save the letters and give them to her one day."

"You know, he didn't even ask to see her, so I doubt very much we'll hear from him again. I think the threat of jail was enough to scare him. He'll find another solution. His kind always do." He took her hand. "I've had a busy day. I bought the property I showed you and registered it with the gold commissioner. I'm really pleased with it. It has a nice stand of trees and a small spring, so the livestock will have plenty of water." He squeezed her hand. "I also called in at the saw mill. Turns out William

300

works there, and he's agreed to help me build a house. Something small for now but it will be up in time for winter. We'll add a shed and small corral for Brutus and the mules, and that will keep us going until next year."

"And I found an Anglican minister," said Rose. "Or, at least I think I have. There's one in Yale, but Gracie suggested that if we offered him money for his mission he would come here."

"Splendid."

"I can write a letter, if you like. I met his wife on the ship."

"Rose?"

Rose glanced at Harrison. He looked uncomfortable.

"Do you have…er…a suitable dress? Not that you don't look pretty in that one," he pointed to her beige and black striped gown, "but don't you want something white?"

"This is all I have."

"Wait." He took off his hat and dug around in the sweatband. He pulled out a gold coin, which he held out to her. "And buy a new dress for Hannah too. I want both my girls looking their best."

Tears pricked Rose's eyes. She blinked them away then looked up at Harrison. Admiration filled his eyes and something else. Perhaps affection for her?

"I'll send the letter tomorrow. Wa Lee won't mind if I take a break to go to the post office. I'm sure they sell paper and envelopes there too."

Harrison nodded. His eyes crinkled at the edges as a small grin tickled his mouth. How she loved this man, his kindness and consideration, his respect for her. And she would tell him so.

Rose screwed up her courage. "Harrison?"

"Rose?" His face grew serious as he waited for her to speak.

She lost her nerve. "Er…it's late, and the children should be off to bed. I'll see you tomorrow."

He still said nothing about love. But then neither had she.

* * *

Rose stepped into the post office and went straight to the wicket. Thankfully, she was the only customer in the store, so she should be able to get in and out quickly. She didn't want to abuse Wa Lee's good nature. After purchasing paper and a stamped envelope, she found a quiet corner in which to compose her missive to Mrs. Sheepshanks:

Dear Mrs. Sheepshanks,

I hope you remember me, my daughter Hannah and I traveled with you to Yale earlier this year. I will be getting married soon and would like your husband to perform the ceremony as it is the wish of my fiancé to be married in the Anglican Church.

Then she thought the note too brief so she added a sentence:

Barkerville is a lively place and not at all fearsome. I look forward to making a home here with my soon to be husband. I hope this letter finds you well,

Yours sincerely, Rose Chadwick

"Should be there by the end of the week," grunted the clerk when she handed it through the wicket. "The stage coach leaves first thing in the morning."

"Thank you." Rose turned to leave.

"Wait a second, miss. You're the one marrying Harrison St. John?"

"How do you know that?"

He grinned. "Oh, the whole town knows. That was quite the little set-to you had in the Wake Up Jake the other night. Everyone's been talking about it."

Rose's scalp prickled with embarrassment. "Yes, I imagine everyone heard about that."

"There's a letter for him. I didn't know he's a viscount, though. Seems like a regular fellow and not uppity at all." He handed it to her. "You may as well deliver it. It will save him a trip here."

"Of course." Rose took the rich cream envelope. *Viscount Harrison St. John, Barkerville, Cariboo, Colony of British Columbia,* read the address. The handwriting was refined and feminine, the paper thick and luxurious. She turned it over, and shock and dismay filled her when she saw the name and address of the sender.

The letter came from England. From Harrison's mother.

Rose stared at the envelope clenched in her hand. Certainly, Harrison had talked about his family but seeing this made them real, brought them closer.

Her first inclination was to toss it away, to keep his family a nebulous entity on the other side of the world. She wouldn't, of course. No doubt Harrison would be pleased to hear from his mother. She folded it, tucking it into her sleeve.

What was in the letter? His mother couldn't know about Harrison's and Rose's impending nuptials. So what could it be?

Don't be silly, she told herself. It's simply a mother sending a letter to a far-off son she missed dearly.

Yet foreboding made her stomach churn and her knees weak.

Chapter Thirty

Later that day Harrison waited at Gracie's cabin for Rose to come home from work. He spotted her as soon as she rounded the buildings lining the main street of Barkerville.

Right away he noticed something bothered her. She trudged toward him up the hill, feet dragging as if she wore shoes of lead, holding something in her hand—an envelope by the looks of it. What could be so terrifying about an envelope?

At the last moment, she saw him and her step faltered. Then she pulled herself up and picked up her pace. "For you," she said when she reached him, handing it to him stiffly like a wooden toy soldier might do. "The fellow at the post office gave it to me when I sent the letter to Reverend Sheepshanks."

He looked at her, then glanced down. He recognized his mother's handwriting immediately and felt a pang of guilt. He'd not had the time to write home and inform them of Rose and Hannah. Mind you, it took at least four months for a letter to reach England, so even if he had written to her it would have crossed paths with this one.

"You have nothing to fear," he said. "It's only a piece of paper, scarcely anything to worry you."

His joke fell flat. Rose kept her face stiff face although her lips trembled.

"It's nothing," he repeated. "It's from my mother. I'll read it right away so you don't have to fret about it."

She swallowed hard and looked at him, eyes wide with apprehension.

He scanned it quickly once. A curse exploded from him. "Excuse me," he muttered, giving her a glance. "I need to read this again."

Rose sat down beside him on the front porch and wrapped her arms around her middle.

Harrison read the letter again. And again, while he tried to make sense of it.

Finally he turned to Rose. "My sister Laura met an industrialist one day while out riding. Someone involved with the railways. Apparently the two met in secret for a number of months before eloping to Gretna Green. According to my mother, they have brought down shame upon the entire family. My father is apoplectic and has threatened to disown her and will have nothing to do with her. My mother wants me to come home to set things right."

The colour drained from Rose's face and his heart squeezed at the despair in her eyes. "Then you must go home," she said.

Harrison shook his head. "No. I'm not going home. This is home."

"Don't you see? You needn't marry me after all." She fiddled with the buttons on the cuffs of her sleeves and didn't look at him.

"Not marry you? Whatever are you talking about?"

"Your family needs you."

"You need me. You and Hannah."

"But—"

Harrison placed a finger over her mouth. "No buts. I'm not going anywhere." A feeling of weightlessness came over him and he looked up as if he would float up into the sky. "In fact, this is perfect."

"I don't think so."

She'd turned away her head and spoke so softly Harrison barely heard her response.

"Rose." Gently he tilted her face back to face him. "Listen to me. This solves everything."

A tear trembled on the lower lashes of one eye. "I don't understand."

He couldn't help it; a smile curved his lips and he had to stop for a moment to collect his thoughts against the elation surging through him. "I came to Barkerville to make my fortune," he began.

"I know," she whispered. "But you haven't. You sold your gold claim."

"The longer I lived here, the more I realized I didn't want to return to England. However my family expected me to, so how could I not?" He took her hand and laced his fingers through hers. "In this country, a man can make something of himself. By himself. For himself. But times are changing at home too. I had thought to write and suggest they consider converting the estate into a cooperative of farms. One they could manage and earn enough to live a comfortable life. I knew they wouldn't like it, although my father has quite a keen mind and could quite easily make it run. But now," a chuckle spilled from his lips, "my sister has solved everything. Not only is her new husband a wealthy man, he has the business knowledge to guide my father."

"You make it sound so easy."

"Oh, he won't like it at first. But once he finds meaning in his life, he'll embrace it. He won't disown Laura. She was always his little sweetheart. Once the shock of her marriage wears off, I dare say in time the situation will right itself."

"You're sure? This is what you want? To stay here with me and Hannah?"

"I've never been more sure of anything in my life. Rose," he cupped her face in his hands, "I love you. You caught my heart the moment I saw you, a daring young woman marching down the Cariboo wagon road with a little girl and a big carpet bag. Only I didn't know it then. But it didn't take me long to realize you were the one for me. So yes, this is what I want. To marry you and make a home in Barkerville for us."

Tears shimmered on Rose's cheeks. "I love you too, Harrison," she whispered and she brushed away the tears and smiled. A late ray of the setting sun flashed over her face, turning her eyes into glittering silver. This was his fortune, he thought, the reason he'd traveled halfway around the world. To find this young woman.

A little girl's squeals of laughter rang out and Hannah raced around the corner of the cabin, pursued by a giggling Florence. The two skidded to a halt.

"Mama, why are you crying?" Hannah's brow furrowed.

"Because sometimes people cry for joy." She reached out and pulled Hannah close. "Mama and Harrison are getting married."

Hannah's blue eyes grew round, and she inspected Harrison with a serious expression on her face. "Now you'll be my papa?"

"Yes," he said. He reached out and smoothed the hair on the crown of her head. "Now I'll be your papa, and I can't wait."

Rose looked at Harrison. *He couldn't wait to be Hannah's papa.* Love swelled her heart and she found it difficult to draw a breath against the sensation.

Best of all, he loved her, Rose, just as she was. He recognized and accepted that her past made her what she was today, recognized and accepted that Hannah deserved legitimacy.

He loves me!

The high pitched *squeee* of a hawk sounded and she gazed upward. High overhead, the bird drifted with outspread wings on the mountain air currents as it circled higher, ever higher. The sun's rays caught it, and it glowed golden.

That's just how she felt—warm and golden with love and happiness, a happiness that just grew and grew till she felt she could touch the sky.

He loves me!

* * *

On a Saturday two weeks later, Gracie helped Rose into her wedding dress. "Here's your something borrowed." She held out her lace gloves. "I figure Florence is still a ways off using them." She winked. "He's a lucky man."

"I'm lucky too, Gracie."

"Love has a way of making everyone lucky. Now let me see," she said. "You got something old." She pointed to Rose's boots. "Something new. That would be your dress. And something blue." She held out a blue silk ribbon. "For your hair."

Rose giggled. "Where would I be without you?"

Gracie shrugged. "I dunno, and it don't bear thinking about. Hold still while I button your dress."

Rose glanced over her shoulder at her friend. Gracie's mouth was twisted in concentration and Rose giggled. "It shouldn't be that difficult," she teased.

"Phew." Gracie swiped her hand across her forehead. "The pearl buttons are pretty and all but they're tiny and hard to work into the loops. But you're all hooked up now." She took a step back. "And don't you look bee-you-tee-full. I'll make sure Billy and the girls are dressed and ready to go. You sit and relax for a few minutes."

While Gracie busied herself with the children, Rose twisted and turned in front of the small mirror hanging on the back of Gracie's door, trying to see as much of her wedding dress as she could. It had a small stand up collar and the waistline sat just above her own. White satin ruffles edged the lace covered skirt and sleeves. She'd had to shorten the skirt but there had been enough discarded fabric that she could edge the sleeves of Hannah's white poplin dress with matching white satin ruffles and make a sash.

She pulled up her dress to inspect her boots. She'd stopped at the shoemaker and had him clean and polish them and they shone smartly. Finally, she threaded the blue ribbon through her hair, letting the ends dangle down her neck.

"We're all ready. You'll do," Gracie said cheerfully. "I think I see the wagon on the street, so we should be going."

Rose picked up the nosegay of late summer lupines Hannah had picked for her and turned to inspect Gracie's Sunday best dress, a long sleeved rose pink silk that put colour in Gracie's cheeks. Today her hair was smoothed neatly into a bun, and she'd tucked a matching rose pink silk flower behind her ear. "You look lovely, too." Behind her, her children stood at attention, Billy, with fresh scrubbed cheeks, looked smart in long trousers and a clean white shirt buttoned up snug beneath his chin.

Florence looked just as smart in a flower print high-waist dress with a white eyelet pinafore. Hannah peeked out from behind Florence.

"Let me see you, poppet." Rose held out her hand and Hannah skipped over. "Don't you look like a big girl today." She straightened the white satin rose pinned into Hannah's hair that had been made by Gracie from the last few scraps of fabric.

"She does," agreed Gracie. "We're all ready? Then let's go."

Holding up their skirts, they picked their way carefully down the hill until they reached Barkerville's main street. Harrison waited there with his wagon and mule team.

Rose giggled at the straw hat perched between Nancy's ears. It sported a white satin ribbon wound around the crown, and the hat gave Nancy a jaunty air. She seemed to like it, for her ears pricked forward pertly. Earlier today the three children had picked fireweed and slipped it into the bridles of all the mules. The wagon also carried a festive air as Florence and Hannah had woven white ribbons through the spokes of the wheels.

And beside the wagon, Harrison. He stood patiently, resplendent in a thigh length, black jacket with velvet lapels, crisp white shirt and maroon silk tie.

"Reverend Sheepshanks is waiting for us," he said. Gracie and the children climbed into the back of the wagon and Harrison handed up Rose onto the bench beside him. His admiring gaze settled the nerves in her stomach and she leaned back to enjoy the ride. Bystanders waved and whistled as the wagon rattled by, and she smiled and waved at them all.

In a few minutes, they reached the plot of land Harrison had bought just beyond Barkerville. He and William had been busy, for already wooden frames marked the house and mule shed, and posts outlined the shape of the corral.

A small crowd waited there, including Mrs. Sheepshanks, who rushed over and hugged Rose when she alit from the wagon. "School's in, so I left the children with a neighbor," she said. "I wouldn't have missed this for anything. I worried about you, you know, off in these gold fields by yourself."

Rose nodded. "It's been an adventure." She peered around the reverend's wife and noticed William and Wa Lee and his wife. Gracie and her two children had joined them and stood chatting with Ming, the cook at the Hotel de France. "But not only did I find myself a husband, I've made some good friends."

Harrison took Rose's hand and squeezed it. Rose squeezed his hand in return. She liked the uneven feel of the calluses rimming his palms. It made him seem more solid, somehow, as if he could conquer their world with his bare hands.

Hand in hand, Harrison and Rose stepped eagerly over to stand in front of the Reverend, and he commenced with the ceremony immediately. The short service proceeded in a blur for Rose and it was all she could do not to stare at Harrison. When he slid a slim gold band set with a row of diamond chips on her finger, she could only gawk at it. So long she'd worn her mother's ring, now here she had her own. A ring not of deceit and a mother's affection but of promise and a husband's love.

Soon enough the familiar words rang through the air. "I now pronounce you man and wife. You may kiss the bride."

She lifted her face and locked her gaze with his. A slight smile curled up his lips, and joy lightened his eyes.

"Gladly," whispered Harrison and he dipped his head to brush his lips against hers. He held her close and her toes curled with pleasure.

Here was a man who stood by those he loved in a place they both loved. Barkerville had given them each what they wanted, the beginning of a new life. A life they would share together.

* * *

A few days later

Crack! The sound of a pistol shot split the air. "They're off!" shouted someone.

Rose gathered Hannah close and, from their vantage point on the balcony of the Hotel de France, the two watched the wave of horses thunder their way down Barkerville's main street. Churning hooves flung clods of mud every which way, and cheers from the spectators lining the course rumbled through the air.

"Look, there's Papa." Rose pointed. She'd spied Harrison in the middle of the lead pack, which consisted of a few horses. A second bunch raced along behind in a jumble, unable to pass because of the narrow width of the street.

He rode Brutus. Somewhere along the way, he'd lost his hat and his hair streamed in the wind. Hanging low over the horse's neck, he didn't see them. As they passed, he slapped Brutus's hind quarters with his glove, and the horse surged forward, taking the lead. A few strides more and Brutus broke the ribbon stretched across the road. A roar went up and Harrison slowed Brutus to a walk.

"Hurrah! Papa won!"

Harrison rode back, looking for them, and pulled up when he spotted them overhead. He held up a small canvas sack. He shook it and it jingled with the clink of coins. "Now we can buy an extra team and wagon."

She pointed to his bare head. "And perhaps a new hat."

Brutus pranced and circled, and Harrison tugged on the reins. "Easy, boy," he soothed, then gazed up at the two on the balcony. "He needs to walk a bit more. I'll be back as soon as I can." He lifted a hand and trotted down the street to the cheers of the remaining spectators sitting on the sidewalks and hanging off the balconies.

How he loved this place, he thought as he trotted past the buildings and businesses lining the street. It seemed almost every other day some new venture came into being, or someone's mine somewhere had been successful. Here a man could earn respect and not be handed it by an accident of birth.

At the edge of town, he found a small knoll and pulled Brutus to a stop. His gaze swept the surrounding mountains and the sparkling blue sky. He sucked in a huge breath of air, mountain fresh and tinged with the rich aroma of moist earth and indomitable human spirit.

His grand visions of striking it rich and returning to England a wealthy man had not come to pass, but he'd found a wealth even greater here in the British Columbia wilds.

With a shout and a grin, he headed back into town.

To Rose.

The End

If you enjoyed this book, please leave a review.

This Author is Counting on You.

Thank you.

Author's Note

Even today, Barkerville, British Columbia is remote, situated in the interior of British Columbia between Kamloops and Prince George, and 87 kilometers east of Quesnel on Highway 26. I can't imagine how isolated it was during the Cariboo Gold Rush, even after the building of the Cariboo Wagon Road in 1865, constructed by the Royal Engineers and considered to be the eighth wonder of the world at that time.

The road still passes Charles Morgan Blessing's lonely grave. The poor fellow was murdered, and he's buried at the place where it happened. His friend, the barber Wellington Delaney Moses, helped solve the case. The murderer, James Barry, was found guilty by Judge Begbie and hung in August, 1867 in front of the Richfield courthouse.

The influx of thousands of people attracted by the Cariboo Gold Rush resulted in the British Parliament putting forth a bill making the area formerly known as New Caledonia a crown colony. It became known as British Columbia, which, in Queen Victoria's opinion, was "the best name". British Columbia became Canada's sixth province on July 20, 1871 on the promise by Canada to absorb their debt and build a transcontinental railway link.

The name Cariboo is a misspelling of caribou. The gold rush started on the Fraser River and eventually spread into the interior river systems and the Barkerville area. The town itself is named after William Barker, the Englishman who struck gold on Williams Creek in 1862 after digging down fifty two feet. (Although some sources say he dug down only forty feet). I wasn't able to discover how the claims were actually staked and registered, although it's thought information was actually written on the claim posts themselves.

I chose to set the story in the summer of 1867 for a couple of reasons. First, 1867 was the year of Confederation and this book is part of Books We Love's Canadian Historical Brides series celebrating Canada's 150th birthday. Second, Barkerville burned to the ground on September 16, 1868. It was 90% rebuilt within six weeks but never really attained its former glory, and I wanted to show the town at its height.

Trying to portray history can be challenging, and there are a few instances where I've taken a few liberties.

Quesnel was known as Quesnellemouth in 1867, but I chose to use the modern term to avoid confusion. I used miles rather than kilometres and ounces instead of grams because the metric system of measurement was not in use in Canada at that time.

Harrison stabled his mules at the Mundorf Stables, but during the summer of 1867, Mr. Mundorf was already in the process of converting the stables to the Crystal Palace Saloon.

Also, no Anglican priests were sent to Barkerville during the summers of 1866 or 1867. I knew Harrison's mother would prefer to see Harrison and Rose married in the Anglican Church so I had to keep her happy! The Reverend John Sheepshanks was actually sent as a missionary during the summer of 1863. Caroline liked the name, so I used it even though he wasn't there when the story takes place. There was indeed an Anglican church in Yale in 1867. Rose traveled with the Sheepshanks family from Victoria to Yale but those characters are all fictitious.

I've added a bit to the actual article on the Dominion of Canada that Harrison read in the *Cariboo Sentinel,* the newspaper in Barkerville at that time.

Mr. Foster, the surly clerk at Oppenheimer's who gave Rose such grief, is a fictional character. One of the actual partners of Oppenheimer's became the second mayor of Vancouver.

As far as the Parlour Saloon, I've seen it spelled both Parlor and Parlour but opted to use the British spelling. Wa Lee Laundry did exist and he did have a wife. Their descendants became merchants in Quesnel. Also, the laundry may have been combined with a store. All other businesses I've mentioned did exist at that time.

I've included as many real people as fit the story: Wa Lee, owner of the laundry and Rose's boss. Wellington Delaney Moses, the barber, because of course Harrison needed a hot shave!

Moses, originally from the West Indies, came to Barkerville by way of San Francisco and then Victoria, and ran a small store along with his barbershop. Madame Fannie Bendixen (so named because she was French) ran several saloons in Barkerville over the course of the years. Also Dr. Wilkinson, who came to Barkerville to mine gold but soon realized he could earn more practicing medicine. Finally, Judge Begbie, a tall, imposing Scot who took seriously his appointment as judge of British Columbia and the representative of Her Majesty Queen Victoria. Although he was known as the hanging judge, he actually only sentenced two Cariboo men to the scaffold. Nonetheless, he was honest and fair and feared for his sentences which ensured relative peace and order in the community.

No one knows how many thousands of Chinese people lived in Chinatown during the Cariboo Gold Rush, although at that time they outnumbered every other nationality. The Chinese generally kept to themselves, although they did mine for gold too. They also raised livestock and had terraced gardens on the hillside behind town where they grew vegetables. A large part of their life revolved around the Chinese Freemasons, and the Chinese Masonic Hall played an important part in their community. They referred to the surrounding mountains as "green dragons and white tigers", which I think is quite a pretty description.

Today Barkerville is a living museum open during the summer months and well worth the visit. For a good, basic overview of Barkerville and the Cariboo Gold Rush, I recommend the website http://cariboogoldrush.com The www.barkerville.com website includes archived newspaper articles from the Cariboo Sentinel containing a lot of information on daily life in the town.

Other BWL titles by A.M.Westerling
The Countess' Lucky Charm
Her Proper Scoundrel
A Knight For Love
A Heart Enslaved

Bibliography

Boissery, Beverley and Short, Bronwyn. *Beyond Hope: An Illustrated History of the Fraser and Cariboo Gold Rush*: Toronto, Canada: Dundurn Press, 2003

Ramsay, Bruce. *Barkerville:* Second Printing: Vancouver, Canada: Mitchell Press, May 1966

Wright, Richard Thomas. *Barkerville and the Cariboo Goldfields:* Heritage House Publishing House Co. Ltd., 2013

http://www.cariboogoldrush.com

https://www.facebook.com/barkervillebc

http://www.heritagebcstops.com

https://royalbcmuseum.bc.ca/exhibits/bc-archives-time-machine

http://www.barkerville.com/nwarch.htm#otherstories (Newspaper excerpt from the www.barkerville.com website: "Cariboo Sentinel", Dominion of Canada, June 10, 1867.)

http://bcgoldrushpress.com/2013/04/food-prices-wages-in-the-cariboo-gold-rush

https://www.hellobc.com/cariboo-chilcotin-coast/culture-history/gold-rush-history.aspx

www.thecanadianencyclopedia.ca/en/article/**british-columbia**-and-**confederation**/

Lyrics from "Beautiful Dreamer" by Stephen Foster

"From Vikings to viscounts, join the adventure, live the romance."

Living by the motto "You don't know unless you try", A.M. Westerling started writing historical romance because she couldn't find the kinds of fun stories she enjoyed. After all, she thought, who doesn't enjoy a tasty helping of dashing heroes and spunky heroines, seasoned with a liberal sprinkle of passion and adventure?

Westerling, a former engineer, is a member of the Romance Writers of America and active in her local chapter. As well as writing, she enjoys cooking, gardening, camping, yoga, and watching pro sports. She lives in Calgary, Canada. Visit her at www.amwesterling.com
www.Facebook.com/A.M.Westerling
Or follow her on Twitter
www.Twitter.com/AMWesterling

bookswelove.com